WILD

Wild

© Copyright 2022 Micalea Smeltzer
Original copyright 2018 title: Wild Collision
All rights reserved. This book or any portion thereof may not be reproduced or used in any manner whatsoever without the express written permission of the publisher.
This is a work of fiction. Names, characters, businesses, places, events and incidents are either the products of the author's imagination or used in a fictitious manner. Any resemblance to actual persons, living or dead, or actual events is purely coincidental.

Developmental edits by: Melanie Yu, Made Me Blush Books
Cover Design: Emily Wittig Designs
Cover Photo: Michelle Lancaster

WILD

Janiece, this book is for you because without what you've done for me it wouldn't be here. You saved my life. You're my hero. Forever and always.

PLAYLIST

MAROON - TAYLOR SWIFT

GLITCH - TAYLOR SWIFT

DANCING WITH OUR HANDS TIED - TAYLOR SWIFT

SINGLE - THE NEIGHBORHOOD

SOMEBODY ELSE - THE 1975

ABOUT YOU - THE 1975

NOBODY'S LOVE - MAROON 5

ELECTRIC TOUCH - A R I Z O N A

YOU! - LANY

LOVE SOMEBODY LIKE YOU - JOAN

WAKE ME - BLEACHERS

HAVE YOU EVER BEEN IN LOVE - THE IVY

TWENTY SOMETHING - NIGHTLY

MY THOUGHTS ON YOU - THE BAND CAMINO

UP ALL NIGHT - MATT DIMANO

PROLOGUE

Hollis

The pounding pulse of the club music vibrates through my entire body.

It doesn't matter what country or city you're in, all these places are the same.

Too loud music, overflowing drinks, and sweaty bodies gyrating together.

The sexy brunette who's latched onto me for the night grinds her ass against my dick.

"Someone's getting laid tonight," Cannon, one of my best friends and the bass player in our band, calls out to me.

I smirk back at him even as he looks on in disapproval.

Last night. Tonight. Tomorrow night.

They're all the same, only different faces—and fuck, most of the time I don't even remember them.

The girl turns, wrapping her arms around my neck and pushing her rock hard fake breasts into my chest. I suppress a groan.

She licks her plump overly filled lips, looking at me through hooded eyes. "My place or yours?" she purrs.

"Neither," a new voice growls.

I turn, stumbling in my drunken state.

"Oh shit," I mutter.

My bandmates exchange similar sentiments.

"I drove all the way to D.C. for your sorry asses. Why am I not surprised you're at a place like this?"

The middle-aged man shakes his head, clearly disappointed with us.

"Hayes, man," I plead, my vision slightly blurred. "It's only some harmless fun."

"Yeah, harmless fun when you're supposed to start recording your first studio album tomorrow. You might've had a few successful singles but don't think for a minute if you fuck up people won't move on to the next band."

I swallow thickly at his threat.

Joshua Hayes is the guitarist for one of the biggest bands in the *world* and we're damn lucky he wants us to be his first producing job.

"I'm sorry."

He looks like my words mean nothing. I guess they

don't—they're some of my favorite and I rarely mean them, so why would now be any different.

"We thought one more night of fun before we buckled down to record our album would be okay," Fox, another friend, and the guitarist, calls out. He's the jokester out of all of us—the rest of us are far too broody and serious, at least according to the media. They have no idea who we *really* are. We've only just started to have a taste of fame and it's already obvious that the media will paint you however they want.

I prefer to think of myself as introspective and a deep thinker.

Unless you put a hot chick in front of me—then all I think about is *ass, ass,* and more *ass*.

Maybe the media isn't too off base on me then.

"Yeah, well it's *not* okay. At least not for me. I want to know you're serious—because if you aren't then I'm not wasting my time. What you're doing here ... *this* does nothing to alleviate my worries."

Harsh.

"How'd you find us anyway?" Cannon asks, having ditched the girl he was dancing with and joined us. He crosses his muscled arms over his chest.

I belatedly realize the girl I was with has left, blending into the crowd and lost from my sight. I pout like a petulant child that's lost a toy. Ugh, I've definitely had too much to drink.

Hayes tosses us a look like a pissed off dad who found his kid sneaking out the bedroom window.

"Rush," is all he says.

The three of us turn and as one we cringe when we spot our drummer on top of the bar, with a bottle of whiskey, live on fucking TikTok.

TikTok, the reason our band went viral in the first place, and has this chance to work with Joshua Hayes.

"Get your asses outside and into my car. It's the Range Rover. I'll get Rush."

He's already pushing through the crowd, away from us toward the bar.

"I thought he was our producer, not a fucking babysitter," I mutter.

"He *is* part of one of the most successful bands ever, maybe we should listen to him." Cannon shoves his hands deep into the pockets of his jeans, his shoulders shrugging up to his ears. I swear I hear a girl moan when she gets a look at his neck tat.

I have a bigger cock.

And isn't that what's most important?

"Fine, whatever." I weave my way through the crowd to the exit, Cannon and Fox on my heels. I might be drunk, but I know better than to refuse Hayes's request to leave the club.

"He's going to be unbearable tomorrow," Cannon sighs, pulling a pack of cigarettes from his pocket. He smacks the new box against his hand and pulls one out, sticking it between his lips but not lighting it.

"Why?" Fox asks with a laugh, though he already knows the answer.

"No pussy for Hollis means he's an insufferable bastard."

I don't even try to defend myself because they're right. It's one of the best parts of being in a band, girls throw themselves at you just to have bragging rights that they fucked a lead singer.

We step outside into the crisp fall air and spot the Range Rover easily.

"Shotgun," I call, and stand by the passenger's side before one of these fuckers gets the bright idea to steal it from me.

We wait outside the car and it's a few minutes before Hayes comes out, supporting a stumbling Rush.

"My boy never can handle his liquor," Cannon chortles, tossing his cigarette on the ground.

Hayes unlocks the Range Rover and I slide into the passenger seat while the other guys tumble in the back. Hayes dumps Rush with them.

Hayes jogs around the front of the car and into the driver's seat.

Glancing in the rearview mirror he warns, "Don't throw up in my fucking car."

"Of course not, sir," Fox replies, flashing a cocky smile. "We would never do that."

Fox is way too fucking jovial. I want whatever he's on—not that he does drugs, that's just him, always so fucking happy.

Hayes stares for a moment longer before pulling out into traffic.

We barely make it to the stoplight before Rush retches up whatever cocktail he's consumed tonight.

"We'll pay for the detailing." Cannon says in a tone that says the three of us better not argue with him.

Hayes pinches the bridge of this nose. "What have I gotten myself into?"

What indeed.

ONE

Mia

I trudge into the house through the garage, my backpack slung over my shoulders.

It looks like I'm doing the walk of shame. I'm definitely not. But my dad is bound to give me a lecture anyway, even though I did call home last night to let my parents know I was staying at my best friend's apartment for the night since we were studying. Crashing on her couch isn't exactly my idea of a good time, but it is better than making the drive home late at night. Sometimes I wonder why I chose to continue living at home while I went to university. Our house is nearly an hour away from campus, and where I work, but I'd hated the thought of leaving my parents and siblings so I chose to commute instead. I know if I'd wanted to stay on campus they would've supported my decision ... well, my mom would have. My dad on the other hand... he takes overprotective to a whole new level even now with me being twenty-two.

The alarm chimes, signaling my arrival.

"Mia? Is that you?" My mom calls out.

"Yeah, it's me," I sigh, dropping my cheery yellow backpack by the stairs.

I'm tired. Kira's apartment is small with only her bed and the couch—which means I sleep on the latter. Kira always offers for me to crash in her bed with her but she's a bed hog, so I choose the couch over being kicked onto the floor in the middle of the night. Yeah, that happened once.

My neck is stiff and my back feels like someone kicked my spine all night long, but this pain can't be blamed on Kira. For all I know there are little gremlins living inside her sofa.

I follow the sound of her voice to the kitchen and find her making breakfast. Eggs and pancakes. My tummy rumbles but I have more pressing matters at hand, like peeing and taking a shower. Oh, and changing my clothes. I slept in my actual clothes and not my pajamas and it shows. It feels like my jeans are glued to my legs.

My two younger siblings sit at the kitchen table waiting for breakfast. Adalyn is so absorbed in her phone she doesn't even look up upon my arrival. Noah gives me a cheeky smile and lifts his feet onto the table. He winks. We both know Mom will blow a gasket when she spots his stinky feet on the table.

Adalyn and I look a lot alike. We both have red hair, but hers is closer to a strawberry color and not my vibrant hue. We even have features that match our mom's, but she got Dad's eyes.

Well, there was no way I'd have gotten Dad's eyes—he's technically my adopted dad, but he's all I've ever known as a father, and therefore in my mind, he *is* my dad.

Noah, on the other hand, is a complete clone of our dad. Same sandy shaggy hair, same shade of blue eyes, and perpetual smirk. It's uncanny at times and like looking at a teenage version of Josh Hayes.

The only difference is where our dad eats, sleeps, and breathes music, Noah prefers building things—ranging anywhere from Legos to legitimate robots which actually *work*. Noah's a borderline genius. Heck, maybe he's an actual genius for all I know. Point is, the kid is *smart*.

"Do you need help?" I ask my mom.

She shakes her head. "No, no, I'm fine," she assures. "I wanted to see you."

"You saw me yesterday morning," I remind her.

"Am I not allowed to miss my daughter?" she jokes, blowing a stray piece of red hair from her eyes.

I stick my tongue out. "I guess."

"Have you eaten yet?"

I shake my head, my shoulders sagging with tiredness. "No, I wanted to get home first. Save me some, please. I want to shower. I feel icky." I pull my day-old shirt away from my body.

She waves me away. "Go shower then. I'll save you a

plate." She glances significantly in Noah's direction because we both know if she doesn't save me a plate the little shark will eat *everything*. She spots his feet on the table and glowers. "Feet. Off. The. Table."

He doesn't move his feet. I'm not sure if it's to purposely defy her or because it seems that boys are born with selective hearing.

"Do I need to get your father in here?" she warns with her hands on her hips.

He drops his feet immediately, mumbling something we can't hear under his breath.

Honestly, our dad is a pushover. He hates scolding any of us, but if Mom is mad enough and calls for him ... yeah, he gets scary if we don't listen to her.

I slip from the kitchen making my way upstairs to my bedroom.

It's my favorite room in the house, mostly because it's *mine*.

I push open my bedroom door and smile. Three of the four walls are solid white, with the main wall where my bed sits painted with horizontal black and white stripes. The four-poster bed is accented by a large canopy hanging from the ceiling by ropes. In the corner is my desk with a wire chair and fluffy pillow. The desk is blue, matching the blue quilt on my bed. Blue and yellow are speckled throughout the room along with more items in black and white. Like my black dresser with a large yellow-framed mirror hanging above it. It's different, but it's my style.

I kick my shoes off and they land on the fluffy white

rug. It was important to me to have a large rug to soften the floors since the whole house is hardwood.

I take off my outer shirt, leaving me in a white tank top and jeans. I press the button on my Bluetooth speaker and music begins to play.

Music is the steady drum that beats my heart. Without it I would die.

I guess that's why I decided to study music production and composition. Growing up so close to the music industry—my dad is a member of one of the most popular bands in the *world*, Willow Creek—it was bound to rub off on me.

When I told my dad I wanted to pursue a career in music, but behind the scenes, he told me he was proud but it was on *me* to make it happen. He wasn't going to give me a leg up in the industry.

I admire him for it. I didn't want it handed to me anyway. I want to make a name for myself and not be known as Joshua Hayes's daughter who only got where she is based on her last name.

He does let me work at the record company he started in our small town to get hands-on experience, but I'm a coffee bitch, more commonly known as an intern.

We all have to start somewhere and I'm not going to complain.

The door to my bathroom swings open, steam billowing out and I whirl around, my body sliding effortlessly into a fighting stance.

My jaw drops.

"Who the hell are you?" I stare at the gorgeous guy in front of me. His brown hair is damp and shaggy, hanging into impossibly golden colored eyes. His chest is bare and while he's on the thinner side it's obvious he works out a lot. He's muscular and ripped. I swallow thickly, my eyes zeroing in on his bare chest and then sliding down to the towel hanging precariously on his hips.

Mia, stop staring at him! He's probably homeless and broke into your house. Do something!

"I know jiu-jitsu," I warn.

His lips tip up into a half-smirk. "Is that so?" His voice is raspy and impossibly sexy.

Snap out of it! You don't even know who this guy is and he just came out of your bathroom.

"Why are you in my bathroom?" I ask, not losing my fighting stance.

"Uh ... I needed a shower ... obviously."

"There are like fifteen bathrooms in this house, why mine?" I ask. Okay, there aren't fifteen. More like five and a half, but whatever.

"Because I was told by Mrs. Hayes, I could use this one since my friends needed to shower too," he says in a *duh* tone, swinging his thumb over his shoulder back toward the bathroom. "Are you going to stay in that position forever?" He flicks his fingers lazily over me.

"*Yes,*" I seethe. "I don't know you. You could've broken in."

He crosses his arms over his chest. "I explained to you I was *told* I could shower in this bathroom. If I was told, why would I be a burglar? Also, if I was breaking in, there are a lot more interesting things I could do. I mean ... looking at this girly room of yours, I'd say searching for your diary would be far more fun." He looks me over and I glare, my eyes on fire.

"I don't have a diary."

"Oh really Curly Sue?"

"My name is Mia," I bite out.

"I know."

"You know? How is it possible you know me, and I don't know *you*."

I hate to admit it, but his face is not one I'd be likely to ever forget.

"You're Hayes's daughter."

"You know my dad too?" I seethe.

Who the hell is this guy?

He chuckles. Clearly amused and not at all bothered his towel has slipped even lower during our conversation.

"He's taken me and my band under his wing. We're recording our first studio album with him."

My lips part and I vaguely remember my dad talking about this band he heard at a music festival when he was in California, how they'd been at it a few years with no luck but were really good and had recently started having some viral success.

I squinted a bit at him. Maybe he did look a tad familiar.

I don't give this cocky asshole the information. It'll go

straight to his head and I can tell his ego is already inflated enough.

"I still don't know your name," I remind him.

"I'm not in the habit of revealing that information to girls who look like they're about to knock me out. Do you really know jiu-jitsu?" he inquires, an almost surprised but curious look on his face.

"Yes," I grind out. "My father insisted my sister and I learn if we ever encountered any assholes in the wild or in our *room* we could take them out."

"Is that supposed to be funny?"

"Um ... no." My brows furrow. "I could knock you out in two seconds flat if I had to. Don't test me."

"That's not what I meant," he chuckles. "The Wild is my band's name."

"Oh. I didn't know."

That's why he looks vaguely familiar.

I recall now seeing some videos of his band on YouTube. In one video in particular I remember his sweat-drenched hair, it shouldn't have been a sexy look, but with the red lights shining on him and the way he practically made love to the microphone I had thought it was hot.

"Now you do." He grins. It's the kind of smile that makes girls everywhere fling their panties off. But not me. Growing up around cocky rock stars my entire life has thankfully made me immune to their charm.

He steps toward me and I'm frozen. I can still punch him if he tries something. I'm not afraid to break pretty boy's nose.

He's taller than me by a lot and I feel impossibly small under his looming height.

He lowers his head, and his lips come dangerously close to my ear. I feel a sweat break out across my brow bone.

"My name's Hollis," he says in a low voice. "Hollis Wilder. It's ... nice to meet you, Mia Hayes." I swallow thickly as he steps away and winks.

I finally move then and it's a bad idea because he's still close enough that our legs get tangled together and we both fall to the ground. Somehow, he cradles me, and I end up on top of his toned chest, my fingers grazing the small smattering of chest hair there.

We stare at each other for a moment and then he breaks the silence with a wicked grin.

"If you wanted to get on top of me, all you had to do is ask."

"Ugh, you *asshole*," I groan, smacking his chest as I disentangle myself and stand. Thank *God* his towel stayed in place.

He smiles cockily from the floor, his body lifted on his forearms and elbows.

"I've been called worse."

"Get out of my room!" I shriek like a banshee, pointing my finger toward the door.

"Whatever you say." He pulls himself up and saunters from my room like he owns the damn place.

Why is he even in our house? My dad didn't mention anything about a band staying with us.

He better not be staying here the entire time he's recording his album, or I'll lose my mind. Cocky jerks like him give me a migraine. I don't have time to deal with someone like him on top of school and helping my dad.

Oh, God. This is the band I'll have to help with.

My dad gave me a folder on the band he'd be working with just last week and because of classes I haven't bothered to look at it. Every time I've told myself I'm finally going to read up on them is usually the moment I finally pass out from exhaustion. He even tried to have an in-person meeting with me about it, but our schedules didn't line up.

I'm really regretting not making it more of a priority to research this band. Then I wouldn't have been so caught off guard and I'd actually be prepared. Stupidly, I thought I had more time, but now they're in our house.

I let out a small scream and slam my door closed, making sure to lock it as well.

"That guy is infuriating," I mutter to myself. "Hollis Wilder," I repeat in a mocking tone. "Ugh, even his name screams self-righteous asshole."

At least he's a hot self-righteous asshole.

"Dear God, I'm in trouble."

I head for my bathroom and shower, but even it can't cool my temper.

It doesn't take me long to shower and dry my hair. I dress in a pair of high waisted shorts since it's hot as balls today, and a cropped gray tank. My stomach rumbles, reminding me it's getting closer to ten o'clock and I haven't eaten yet.

I wander downstairs and find yet another guy I don't know in the kitchen.

His back is to me as he rummages in the refrigerator.

"Can I help you find something?" I ask.

The guy jumps away from the fridge.

"Yeah, sorry." He gives me an apologetic smile. "I'm hungry."

"I gathered that. I'm Mia, by the way."

"Fox," he answers.

He's a little shorter than Hollis with dark spiky hair and stubble on his cheeks. He's thin and lean, but at least he's dressed in a pair of athletic shorts and a t-shirt.

"Let me guess, you can't cook and you're waiting for something to magically appear?"

He gives me a sheepish smile. "Maybe."

I sigh. "How many of you are hungry and useless?"

"Four of us—although, Cannon can cook, he just refuses to cook for all of us and only himself. Bastard made himself an omelet this morning and we all had to smell its deliciousness while he scarfed it down."

I sigh. "I'll make something for the rest of you then." I say it mostly so I won't have to deal with a bunch of hungry guys pestering me. I really shouldn't give into them, obviously my mom didn't since they're grown ass man, but this guy has this sweet puppy dog look about him that has suckered me in.

I flick my hand, ushering him away from the refrigerator and out of my way.

He takes a seat on one of the barstools at the island. So much for me getting to eat *my* breakfast. My mom and siblings have disappeared Lord knows where, now I'm stuck here with not one arrogant asshole, but apparently a total of four. At least this guy seems funny and nice. Maybe the other two I haven't met yet won't be so bad either.

I pull the eggs out, some spinach, and peppers. Since he mentioned an omelet I decide to make those for the other guys. At least it's heartier than scrambled eggs—which had been my first thought to make, but I'm sure a bunch of guys this age would be hungry five minutes later. Noah's way younger than them and eats like a wild beast. I've legitimately seen the kid eat an entire box of cereal in a mixing bowl. Who does that?

I set about making the breakfast. I feel Fox's eyes on me and the silence between us unnerves me.

I clear my throat. "Are you guys going to be living here at the house?"

While I'm stuck with him, perhaps I can get some answers from him.

"Nah, we have a suite near the studio, but your dad picked us up last night and brought us here since it was late, and our room isn't supposed to be ready until this afternoon anyway."

I finish the first omelet and put it on a plate for Fox.

His mention of the studio reminds me even if they're not living here I'm not going to be able to escape these guys.

"Something smells good," a new deep male voice enters the room.

I look over my shoulder and—oh my God what is in the water where these guys came from? The guy is tall with blond hair and built like a football player. Wide shoulders, narrow hips, and abs for *days*. I know because he wears a pair of loose sweatpants hanging low on his hips. *Too* low. His arms and torso are covered with dark tattoos.

"Like what you see?" he asks, making a kissy face at me.

I turn red—which with my red hair makes me look like a damn lobster.

"Shut up," Fox tells him.

I hear a scuffle behind me but I don't dare look.

I finish the next omelet and give it to the new guy who has joined Fox at the bar counter. His eyes linger on me appreciatively—well, they mostly linger on my breasts.

"My eyes are up here, bud."

"You have nice tits."

"Oh my God." I throw my hands in the air.

Fox knocks the guy on the back of the head. "Shut it, Rush. That's Hayes's daughter. You can't look at her like that unless you want to die."

I have to suppress the urge to snort. Unfortunately, he's not wrong. These are exactly the kinds of guys my dad wouldn't want me to end up with. Not necessarily because they're in a band—God knows my dad and his band mates are obsessed with their wives and would never cheat—but because they're cocky and arrogant.

The new guy, *Rush*, grumbles something under his breath sounding a lot like, "I'll look all I want."

I move on to the next omelet for Hollis.

I'm tempted to spit in it but I'm not that mean.

When it's finished, he still hasn't joined us. I place a cover over it and leave it on the counter so Fox or Rush can't eat it if they decide they want seconds.

I heat up my own breakfast and sit down at the table.

"We don't bite," Fox says, chewing his last bite. "I mean, we might be a bit uncivilized at times but we won't bother you."

"I'm fine over here," I reply.

To my dismay Rush grabs his plate and joins me. Fox does the same after cleaning his plate in the sink.

"We might as well get to know each other." Rush winks. "I figure if you're Hayes's daughter we'll be seeing you a lot."

"You have no idea," I mutter.

"Why's that?" Fox asks.

I clear my throat. "I intern at the studio when I'm not at school or working."

"You work? But like ... your family is rich," Rush stutters.

"My mom and dad don't want any of us to use our money as an excuse to be lazy. We're expected to work when we can."

"Don't you get recognized? I mean, your dad's *super* famous." Fox seems just as stunned as Rush over this news.

I shake my head. "Everyone in this town knows who we all are anyway. They're used to it by now. They're not even fazed by Maddox, Mathias, Ezra, or my dad. Perks of a small town I guess," I say with a shrug. "I think that's why all the guys chose to continue living here full time as much as they could. It's ... peaceful," I finally decide. "Whenever we travel for whatever reason chaos ensues."

"Was it weird for you growing up?" Rush asks around a mouthful of food.

"Sometimes," I admit. "But my parents were really good at keeping that part of our lives separate. We knew it was Dad's job."

As if on cue the garage door opens and a second later my dad enters the kitchen his eyes narrowed. "Y'all better not be hitting on my daughter."

I roll my eyes as the two guys across from me give me a horror-stricken look. "Cool it, Dad. We're talking. It's not like my panties are slung halfway across the room."

He slams his hands over his ears. "La, la, la, *la*. You are never to speak that word ever again."

I sigh heavily. "What? Panties?"

"Meh!" He screams at me. "Stop!"

"You do realize I'm twenty-two. I know what a penis looks like."

"Nope, no, no you don't. You're not having sex ever. Nope."

My dad is still in denial that I know what sex is, let alone have had it.

"Who's not having sex?" Hollis asks, finally coming up from the basement Or so I assume. I figure Dad told the guys to hang out down there. There are two guest rooms, a bathroom, and our media room downstairs. There's even a home studio, but it's really small and not practical for an entire band.

"My daughter," my dad growls. "If any of you losers even look at her funny I will pack your shit myself and send you home."

Fox raises his hands in surrender. "Seriously man, we were only getting to know each other."

"It's not you or Cannon I'm worried about." He glares at Rush and then a little longer at Hollis. "These two on the other hand..."

I burn a hole in the side of Hollis's face, daring him to say one word about what happened this morning, because if he does, I'll be in as much trouble as he will be and it's not even my fault he was in my room.

He pats my dad on the shoulder. "Don't worry, Hayes. We'll be perfect angels."

His gaze then falls to me and he winks. His smile tells me he hasn't forgotten this morning, and I very much doubt he's done with me. I feel like a small cornered animal being stared down by the big bad wolf. Too bad this wolf doesn't know who he's messing with.

"Your plate's over there man." Fox points to the omelet I made earlier.

"Ooh, sweet." Hollis sprints in front of my dad and over to the plate.

"You okay?" My dad asks me.

I laugh. "Dad, I'm fine. It's just breakfast. Besides, shouldn't I get to know your new band?"

He shrugs. "Yeah, I guess," he grumbles. He looks around at the three guys with a pointed stare. "No funny business, I mean it. We head to the studio in an hour."

He heads off down the hallway, probably in search of my mom. Even after they've been together all these years they can't keep their hands off each other. It's gross at times, sure, but it's been nice growing up seeing that kind of love and respect. I want it for myself one day.

I startle when Hollis plops down beside me on the built-in bench.

"Is he always like that?" he asks me, piercing his fork into the omelet for a too big bite.

"Overprotective?"

"Yeah," he chuckles.

"Always," I sigh. "He interrogated my prom date to the point the poor guy wouldn't even touch me the whole night, not even to dance. It ended up being the worst prom ever."

"Damn," Rush whistles. "You know, it's kind of unfair how girls are told it's wrong to sleep around and guys are slapped on the back for it with a *job well done, son*. You should be free to do whatever and whoever you want."

"Thanks for such an amazing speech," Hollis chortles.

Rush shrugs. "You know I'm right."

"Who made this?" Hollis asks. "It's fucking delicious."

Fox points at me.

"Really?" Hollis turns surprised eyes to me.

"What? Do I look like I can't cook?" There's a challenge in my tone. At times I might be—okay, definitely am—a little too sensitive to people thinking I can't do certain things. There seems to be this belief that if you're famous —or in my case, by association—that you're incapable of doing things on your own. Oftentimes in school growing up I was bullied by other kids for assumptions they made about me.

"Nah, I just assumed you guys had like a chef or something."

I shake my head. "Is getting famous all about the perks to you? Because trust me, if you haven't learned yet, it's not all it's cracked up to be. I've seen the media spin so many stories on the guys of Willow Creek, on their wives too. I've had to see headlines saying my dad's cheating on my mom. Even when you know it's not true it still hurts. The less people you have nosing around to sell fake stories the better—also, staying as normal and level-headed as you can is the key to success. The minute you think you're all that is the minute you fall." I snap my fingers. "Remember, the climb to the top takes time and is hard as hell, but the minute you fuck up and piss enough people off it all disappears."

The two guys across the table sober, but not Hollis. Oh no, he continues to look at me with a cocky ass smirk. I want to smack it off his face and I've never felt like this before. I only met this guy not even an hour ago and he's already under my skin.

"I'll take my chances."

"Whatever," I say. "You're nothing to me. I don't care what happens to you—but whatever you do," I glare so he knows I'm serious, "don't fuck with my dad. He's a good guy."

With that I give him a push, forcing him off the bench so I can get up and leave. I drop my plate in the sink with a clang, not even bothering to rinse it like usual, and stride from the room.

Hollis Wilder has no clue the fire he's playing with.

TWO

Hollis

I watch the beautiful redhead leave the kitchen, my eyes following the sway of her hips and pert ass. I know she's the last woman I should be looking at because she could get me in loads of trouble, but I can't help it.

Something hard hits me in the head. "Ow." I rub the bump. "What the fuck was that for?"

"Don't even fucking think about it," Rush warns me.

Rush of all fucking people. Rush who's the reason we got hauled out of the damn club last night like a bunch of prepubescent boys sneaking into a strip club.

"What?" I ask, playing dumb.

"You can have any pussy you want, but not that one."

I narrow my eyes. "Who said I want that one?"

"The drool pooling out of your mouth says otherwise," he snaps. "We need Hayes, man. This is the big break we've been waiting for, and we don't need it fucked up because you can't keep your dick in your pants and fuck the boss's goddamn *daughter*."

I've never seen Rush get so worked up over something.

He continues, "We've worked our asses off for years to have a chance like this and if you fuck it up for us..." He trails off.

"You'll what? Kick me out of *my* band?"

"No," he says. "But I know I'd never forgive you."

The deadly calm voice he says it in tells me he's not bluffing.

"Don't worry about it," I assure him. "I'll be on my best behavior."

I try to put as much meaning into my words as I can, and I must succeed because he nods, but in my gut I know it's a lie. There's something about Mia that intrigues me. She's fiery, and not only because of her hair. I've never met a girl who seemed to dislike me so much and ... well, I guess I want to change her mind.

After all, I'm fucking amazing.

I finish my omelet and I have to admit Mia is one hell of a cook. If she can make an omelet this damn good what else can she do?

Fox clears his throat and says, "Seriously, bro, this is our time. We *need* this. We don't need anything fucking it up."

"Why do you guys assume *I'll* be the one to fuck it up?" I defend. I didn't tell them about what happened in her room this morning so I don't know why they've zeroed in on me as the problem child of the group.

Fox says softly. "We saw how you looked at her."

Him and Rush exchange a glance and I snort. "How did I look at her?"

Rush tilts his head. "The same look you always get when you like a challenge."

"We don't need anything fucking this up," Fox repeats quietly. "This might be our last chance."

I grow quiet. I know he's right. We've had moderate success, some singles that have done really well, but no actual album under our belt. Hell, I'm only twenty-five but time is ticking by on how long I, and the guys, can keep this up before we have to face reality and get 'real' jobs. Everyone tells you to follow your dreams, but dreams don't always pay the bills.

I refuse to imagine a life where I fail. Where *we* fail. We've fought too hard for this, and yes I can be a cocky bastard at times, but I've never, not once, believed we couldn't do this. Hayes taking us under his wing, signing us to his record label, and being willing to produce our first record is *huge* for The Wild.

It pisses me off they think I would do anything to jeopardize how hard we've worked to get to this point. Yeah, Mia intrigues me. And yes, under normal circumstances I'd have her under me in five seconds flat, but I'm not stupid. I know I can't fuck this up.

They don't say anything else, knowing they've pissed me off and shouldn't push their luck. I don't look up as they get up and leave, Rush surprisingly cleaning his plate and the one Mia left behind before he leaves.

I sigh, finishing my omelet even if I can hardly taste it now.

Nothing but sourness clings to my tongue.

AN HOUR LATER THE FOUR OF US ARE PILED INTO HAYES'S SUV headed for the studio. I sit up front and no one argues, they know I'm in a mood and it's best to give me space. I'm also nervous. I'll never admit it out loud, but I am. We've been in a recording studio before, sure, but never when it meant what it does today. The first step to a full-length album. There's a lot riding on this. Our pride, our dreams, our futures. If we fail there is no fucking safety net to catch us. It'll be a free fall straight down to the damn concrete.

I look broodingly out the passenger window at the passing mountains and farmland. It's so different from the hustle and bustle of L.A. The guys and I all grew up in Tennessee, but we've been in California for so long now that the rolling hills of the Appalachian Mountains seem foreign. However, I'll admit the quiet of the country is almost welcome.

The hour or so drive goes by in silence. I think after

last night the guys are all scared to rock the boat with Hayes. I don't blame them. He was *pissed*.

Hayes parks his SUV behind a building and then we follow him around the front where *Mist Records & Studio* is frosted on the window. Hayes unlocks the door and ushers us inside.

"I need a smoke first," Cannon grumbles.

"Don't be too long," Hayes warns, and Cannon nods in response, already sticking a cigarette between his lips.

Cannon sends me a look, trying to gauge where my head is at. I give a subtle nod to let him know I'm okay.

The three of us follow Hayes inside the studio. From the outside it looked impossibly small, but inside it's spacious. It opens up to a main room with original hardwood floors, tin ceilings, and brick walls painted white. Several mismatched sofas are strewn about, and one wall boasts pictures of the members of Willow Creek at different venues over the years. Looking at the photos I can see the bond they share, similar to the one I have with my friends. We're friends before bandmates, and I think it makes all the difference.

Hayes starts down a hallway and we trail behind like good little soldiers. There are several recording spaces, and a common area with chairs and a small kitchen.

"Nice vibe," Fox comments.

"Thanks," says Hayes. "I'll admit, Arden," he refers to his wife, "and my friends' wives helped decorate. Fuck knows I can't decorate worth a shit."

"Why Mist Records and Studio?" Rush asks as Hayes

opens the door to one of the recording rooms. There's a couch against the wall and a chair in front of all the studio equipment.

Hayes cracks a grin. "Inside joke," is all he says.

The three of us take a seat on the couch and Hayes straddles the chair facing us with his arms draped over the back.

"We've already discussed the songs you all want on the album and I've approved them. It's up to you to decide which one we start with. I want to get a single out there in the next couple of months, hopefully by the first of the year. Build hype for your first full-length album."

The three of us exchange glances. We've already discussed this extensively as a group. We know Hayes gets the final say, but the fact he wants our input means a lot.

"We were thinking *Midnight Eyes*," I answer.

Hayes grins. "My choice as well."

Cannon saunters into the room then, the stench from his cigarette clinging to his skin.

"You need a shower man," I joke.

He gives me the finger.

Cannon is a man of few words.

He plops on the opposite end of the couch beside Fox.

"All right guys, let's get to it."

Hayes claps his hands and we get to work.

Hours later we're all tired, but really fucking pleased. Everything we did today was magic. It was more than any of us ever hoped to dream of.

Hayes takes us out for dinner—we worked right through lunch—before dropping us off at the hotel and making sure we're checked in.

Handing us our keys he says, "If I find out you're out clubbing again and getting into trouble I will shred your contract before you can utter a pathetic *I'm sorry*. Don't mess with me." His tone screams he's not kidding. "You're here to record an album. Don't fuck it up. The vehicles you requested will be here tomorrow. Think of them as a gift, but one toe out of line and they're gone."

We all nod.

"Yes, sir," Fox mumbles, head bowed like a child that's been scolded.

"Ass kisser," I cough.

Hayes glares at me and I wince.

"Trust me, if you leave this hotel I will know." He makes eye contact with each of us. "You did good today," he praises. "I see great things in your future if you stay on the right path. Night."

Before we can respond he's heading for the revolving glass doors.

The four of us pile into the elevator and I press the button for the top floor. Even if we wanted to go out, we're tired. There's something about being in the studio, that while exhilarating, is entirely draining.

The elevator doors open and we don't have to walk far

to the suite door. I swipe my key to unlock it and it swings open. I'm pretty sure I'm not the only one staring in shock.

I mean, I expected a decent place to crash but not *this* and not in this small ass town.

"We're definitely not in Kansas anymore," Rush whistles lowly, then takes a running start and jumps on the blue velvet couch.

The place is decorated to the nines. It looks like something you'd find in a Las Vegas resort, not a tiny college town seventy-five miles west of Washington D.C. and in the middle of nowhere. I find myself beginning to sweat as I think about how much this room, the cars, *everything* must be costing Hayes. It shows how much faith he has in us and if we screw up ... if *I* screw up the consequences will be dire.

Our bags sit in the foyer of the suite. I have no clue how they got here, but Hayes is bound to have an assistant.

The guys and I explore the rest of the suite and then fight over who gets which room. It's ridiculous since they're all basically the same size with their own ensuite bathroom.

I crash onto my bed and stretch my arms and legs out, laying claim.

I can't help but think back to my ten-year-old self first learning I had a voice, music bleeding into my soul, and dreaming of the day when all this could be mine.

I wish I could go back in time and tell him, *"You'll do it. Never stop believing in the power of you."*

THREE

Mia

"Shit, shit, shit, *fuck*."

I dash around my room, yanking on jeans and nearly falling over. My alarm chose *not* to go off this morning and now I'm going to be late for my first class. I won't have time for breakfast either, and I turn into a hangry bitch when I don't eat.

I yank on a tank top, since the September weather has been unseasonably warm, but grab a jacket since some of the classrooms are as cold as the Arctic.

I struggle into a pair of Vans and grab my yellow backpack off the floor.

There was no time for makeup and I barely managed to brush my hair or teeth, so I'm looking like a hot mess.

I take the stairs two at a time, call out a "Bye Mom," and I'm gone.

Outside I climb into my red Audi TTS Coupe. If there's anything my dad will splurge on, it's cars.

The engine purrs to life and hums as I gun it down the long driveway and onto the windy private road.

I reach the gate a mile away and push the garage button that opens the huge wrought iron monstrosity.

My dad takes safety very seriously after I was kidnapped by my 'real' dad when I was three. I don't even remember the guy and never think of him as my father—only my sperm donor. Joshua Hayes is *my* dad. He chose me and I chose him.

If I've learned anything in my short twenty-two years it's the people you choose to love are as important as the blood relations. I love my immediate family and I love the 'cousins' I have in the kids of my dad's bandmates. I look at all of those guys as my uncles and their wives my aunts.

I turn onto route seven heading toward my university. I keep eyeing the time and cringing. Being late is my biggest pet peeve. I know when I arrive to the lecture hall all eyes will turn in my direction. At least most of my classes don't have many students ... but maybe that makes it worse, because then there's no being discreet. Ugh.

I drive as fast as I safely can and as I approach Winchester my chest grows even tighter. Class starts in five minutes and I know there's no chance I'll ever make it, but maybe I'll only be a few minutes late.

Luck is not on my side however as traffic grows heavier as I reach the town. In fact, it crawls at a damn snail's pace.

My fingers tighten around the steering wheel.

Finally, I resolve myself to my fate and some of the tension leaves.

As I reach the university, I gun it into the parking lot.

It's full.

I drive around and around before I finally find a place to park—at least a mile from my lecture hall. Silently cursing my stupid alarm, I grab my backpack and begin the trek across campus.

My stomach rumbles and my lips pout with grumpiness. I need food and I need coffee. Neither of which are attainable at the moment.

I speed walk through campus and finally make it to the classroom. I can hear Professor Jameson droning on and on.

I'm a good student, an excellent student, but he doesn't like me for some reason. If I had to be late for class, why did it have to be this one?

I pause outside the door, taking a deep steadying breath before I reluctantly grip the handle on the door and pull it open.

Eight sets of eyes, including those of the professor, turn to me.

I don't say a word as I find my seat and sit down.

Silence.

Professor Jameson clears his throat. "Tardiness is unacceptable, Miss Hayes. I don't care who your father is I will have to deduct marks for today."

My teeth grind together. His issues with me become clear. My father is successful and famous, and someone like Jameson is envious of it, so he takes it out on me. Never mind this man had no hopes of ever making it big, ending up a professor instead.

I smile despite my irritation. The picture of ease and he bristles. "Understood, Professor. It won't be happening again."

If I have to set my alarm for five in the morning so I'm never late to this class again, I will.

Clearing his throat yet again he returns to his lecture and I pull out my notebook and pen to take notes. Everyone else clacks on the keyboards of their computers but I've always preferred pen and paper. I swear it helps me to remember what I've learned better. As if somehow by writing the words down myself, in my handwriting, I commit them to memory.

Professor Jameson continues to glower at me throughout his lesson. I pretend not to notice, even if his angry gaze makes me uncomfortable. If I was a bolder person, I'd shout at him about how jealousy looks ugly on everyone, especially a washed-up wannabe like him.

But I keep my lips zipped tight. I need this class in order to graduate next year and he's the only one who teaches it. If he bans me from class, I'm screwed.

When the lecture ends, I gather my stuff up in a hurry

and dash out of the room before he can stop me. I don't want to be left in a room alone with him.

My next class doesn't start for thirty minutes so I stop by the dining hall and grab a breakfast bar and banana. It's not much, but I know it'll do the trick and keep me from dying of starvation in the middle of class.

"There you are," Kira chimes, looping her arm through mine as I find a table in the corner to sit at. "You didn't answer any of my texts this weekend."

"Sorry, I was busy," I lie. Well, it's not a total lie, I did work on more assignments I have due in the coming weeks, but mostly I couldn't stop thinking about Hollis and our encounter. Replaying it over and over in my mind, thinking of what I could've done or said differently. I don't know why it matters to me, hot or not, I don't even *like* the guy.

Why can't you stop thinking about him then?

I nearly groan out loud in frustration but manage to stifle the sound before Kira can ask too many questions.

A year younger than me, but both juniors since I waited a year before starting, Kira and I have been friends since high school when she moved here. I didn't have many friends before Kira. Not for lack of trying. I quickly learned most people only wanted to get close to me in the hopes of seeing my dad and his bandmates. Even with all the guys being the age of their parents, the girls in school still talked about how hot they were, asking me if I could get them an autograph or handing me tour shirts to take home to have signed. At times it was humiliating, at others it was damn frustrating. When I told my parents what was going on they spoke with the principal who shut the harassment down ... well, mostly. After, all I received were glares and muttered words of *bitch* and *snitch*.

But Kira? She's never cared who my dad was or about the band. She likes me for *me* and it's a breath of fresh air.

"Let me guess, your nose was stuck in a book?" Her lips tilt up at the corners, her rich dark brown hair slipping over her shoulder. The dimple in her chin crinkles as she fights laughter.

"Homework," I supply.

"Ugh," she groans, "you need to get out more, girl. You're going to shrivel up and die if all you do is study, read, and do homework. Get out and live a little. Ride some dick and then ride some more."

I shake my head, laughing. "You're crazy."

"Crazy right." She winks, shooting finger guns at me and pretending to blow them out. Sobering she says, "But in all seriousness Mia Lee, you need to do something fun for once. You come to school, you go to work, you study, you write papers, you practice the guitar *sometimes*, and that's about it. I don't want the spark inside you to dim because you refuse to let it rage. We can't be perfect all the time. Rules are meant to be broken."

"I can do things after I graduate," I reason.

She rolls her eyes. "Um, no, because you'll go straight into working for your dad's studio and then you *really* won't have a life. Your dad will also have you right where he wants you, under his thumb so you can't ever get laid. You need some dick."

I snort. "No, I definitely don't."

My last relationship, if you could even call it that, hadn't ended well. While I was over him and he wasn't worth my time, it still stung badly enough that I didn't want to bother going down the same path again.

"A boyfriend then," she continues.

"No," I say steadily. "Can you let me eat in peace?" I plead, finally tearing open the foil on my breakfast bar. I haven't even touched my banana yet.

"Oh, you're hangry," she surmises. "It all makes sense now."

I roll my eyes and bite sloppily into the bar, pieces raining down on the laminate tabletop.

Standing, with her hands flat on the table, she says, "I still say if you got laid it'd loosen you right up. You're too uptight."

"Thanks for the advice I didn't ask for."

"Any time." She sticks her tongue out at me. "See you for lunch?"

"Starbucks?" I ask. "I *need* coffee."

"Sure," she agrees. "I gotta go. Love ya." She blows me a kiss as she leaves and then cackles when I pretend to bat it away.

I finish my cereal bar and the banana before hurrying to my next class.

Hurry here, hurry there, hurry, hurry, hurry everywhere and still I get nowhere.

Kira and I sit down at one of the vacant tables in the Starbucks down the road from the University. It's close enough we could walk if we desired, but we never do.

I take a bite of my sandwich. The food I grabbed from the dining hall had done little to tide me over.

Kira gives me an amused glance.

I don't care if I look ridiculous as I savor my food.

"Are you working today?" Kira asks. Both of us work at the Sub Club. A local sub shop. It's all about normalcy in the Hayes household.

"No." I shake my head. "Jess," I refer to one of the girls we work with, "asked to trade shifts so I'll be at the studio today instead."

The studio. I gulp. Somehow, for a moment at least, I forgot Hollis and the guys will be there. I still haven't met the one member. Considering I'm basically a glorified gopher ... there's no telling what they'll ask me to do. I can picture Hollis getting a kick out of making me run around like a chicken with its head cut off. If he tries anything I might punch him. I always try to avoid violence, but even after only two encounters with Hollis I want nothing more than to wipe that smug smile off his face.

"Earth to Mia." Kira waves a hand in front of my face.

"Sorry." I give an apologetic smile.

"It's going to suck working without you. It's always more fun when we work the same shift," she pouts, resting her elbow on the table and her head on her hand.

"Ditto," I agree.

The time always passes by faster with Kira and I both behind the counter. Even if I have to keep an eye on her and her sharp tongue. If a customer takes too long or even looks at her funny, she gets mouthy. It's one of the things I love about her, but in a work situation it can be a severe hindrance.

We finish up our lunch and head back to campus for our last few classes of the day.

I'm unable to focus, because all I can think about is what I'm going to have to deal with later.

I PARK MY CAR IN THE BACK LOT BESIDE MY DAD'S ROVER. Taking a moment, I gather my thoughts and take a deep, steadying breath. I can't lose my temper, because if I do it'll be bad for me *and* the band. As much as Hollis might've riled me up, I don't want to jeopardize this for him and his friends. I need to remain professional. Surely, I can do that?

There is no back entrance to the studio, so I walk around to the front and enter into the lounge area. I can hear the clanging of drums and the beat instantly finds its way inside my veins. I head down the hallway in search of my dad, my head on a swivel, when—

"What the fuck?"

"Oh my God, I'm so sorry," I exclaim, rubbing my forehead where I *think* I smacked into someone's chin.

I look up and my eyes connect with amber ones.

"Oh, it's you," I grumble, nose wrinkling like I smell something bad. Not that he smells gross, whatever cologne he's wearing is nice, not too strong.

"Why are you grumpy? I'm supposed to be here, remember," he says, rubbing his chin.

I sigh. Something about this guy brings out the worst in me and I seem to be helpless to stop it.

"Besides, we were only in your house one night. Shouldn't you be thrilled?"

"I am. Jumping for joy," I say sarcastically and give a pathetic little hop.

I swear he almost smiles. A *real* smile. Not one of those cocky smirks he's worn so far.

"I need to find my dad," I mutter, scooting around him.

I can't believe I wasn't paying attention and literally ran into him.

"He's this way." He tilts his head and I have no choice but to follow him to one of the recording rooms. Inside I see Rush laying down beats on the drums. Earphones cover his ears, his eyes closed. He's so into the music nothing else exists.

My dad is smiling from ear to ear. Whatever they've been doing today ... he's thrilled. I like seeing him so into this. Representing new bands has been a dream of his. The Wild is his first whack at it. Since he opened the studio a few months ago Willow Creek has been the only band to record here, since it's *his* band, it hasn't had the same effect. I love he's found something else he's as passionate about.

Hollis slips by me and onto the couch beside Fox and the other guy whose name I don't know.

I swallow thickly as I take the new guy in. He's big, impossibly wide shoulders and a more muscular build than the others, almost like a bodybuilder but not quite. He has neck tats, and tattoos all over his arms, and I'd bet his chest too if I could see beneath his shirt. Idly, I wonder how far they go and a blush stains my cheeks for even thinking it. His ears boast a smaller set of gauges, and even his nose and lip are pierced. His dark hair is thicker on top and slicked over to one side, the sides shaved. A toothpick sticks out between his full lips. He chews on it idly, like he doesn't even know he's doing it.

When I tear my gaze away my eyes collide with Hollis's and I swear he looks pissed. I look away quickly from him too. I can feel my skin flushing red with embarrassment.

"Dad?" I inquire and he swivels his chair toward me, still grinning from ear to ear. His smile is infectious and I find my lips lifting in response. "What do you need me to do?"

"Right now," he begins, his eyes flicking back to Rush in the booth. "Observe."

I nod, moving to the corner.

Hollis makes a noise of protest. "Sit," he orders.

"I'm fine here."

He rolls his too pretty eyes at me. Everything about him is too pretty, from his amber eyes to his perfect lips.

He stands up. "You sit, I'll stand. I'm next anyway."

We stare at each other, a war of personalities vying to see who will win.

I've never been outmatched by anyone before, but suddenly I find myself taking a seat while Hollis wears a triumphant smirk.

I cross my arms over my chest, irritated at having given in, but soon the beat of the drums takes over my senses and I forget why I'm pissed. Even Hollis's self-satisfied smile does nothing to me.

I'm so wrapped up in the music I don't even notice when Rush finishes and Hollis grabs a bottle of water from the mini-fridge before heading in.

"Scoot over, Red," Rush commands and I make room for him on the couch. With the four of us we're squished together, but at least I don't react to any of these three like I do Hollis who makes my very blood boil.

"Red?" I ask him. "Because of my hair?"

He grins, stretching his fingers. "That and your fiery personality. I can already tell you're a force to be reckoned with."

"I'm glad you've noticed," I joke.

"Shh," my dad hushes us.

Inside the booth Hollis takes a seat on the stool, sliding the headphones over his ears and angling the microphone toward his mouth.

He waits for the thumbs up from my dad and then the background music begins to play. The beat wraps around Hollis's voice and I'm lost. Drowning in it. I feel the song in my soul. It pierces right through me.

Hollis closes his eyes as he sings.
"They say she's bad news, no good for me.
They say to stay away but I say no.
Those midnight eyes will drown you, they say.
They say, they say, they say.
They don't know those midnight eyes hold a promise.
A promise of something more.
Where they see darkness I see light.
Her midnight eyes are my salvation.
My promise.
My promise of something more."

My heart jumps as he sings. His voice is not at all what I expected. The song softer and more a ballad than the rock I expected. With his raspy melancholy tone, it's perfect. Chills snake up my spine and I shiver. Beside me Rush gives me a small smile as if he knows what the song is doing to me.

But he can't know.

He can't know how it breathes life into me.

How I feel every word reverberate through my body.

"Be afraid, they tell me.
Those midnight eyes will swallow you wide.
She'll swallow you whole.
Lies, they're all lies, lies spoken from fear.
She uses her beauty as a weapon, those midnight eyes piercing the soul, but I see her.
I see her, the real her, the true her.
They can say what they want to say, but I know, ohhh I know, those midnight eyes will never hurt me."

I feel a tear fall onto my cheek and I wipe it away in the hope no one sees.

I dash from the room before Hollis is done singing. I need to collect myself.

My feet carry me to the break room and I search for anything I can busy myself with but there's nothing. Not even the counters need cleaning. I never expected to be affected by a song in such a way. Music has always spoken to my soul, sure, but never like that. In the studio, magic is being woven. I'm sure of it. It's easy to see what my dad saw in them, why he wanted to snatch them up before anyone else could.

"Did you not like the song?"

At the sound of Hollis's voice, I whirl around and face him.

I swallow thickly. I want to tell him I hated it, that I thought it was ridiculous, but I can't lie. It was too perfect, too beautiful, for me to lie.

"No," I say, my voice no more than a whisper. "It was the most beautiful song I've ever heard. It wasn't what I was expecting."

Hollis smiles. It's a genuine smile and it makes him look younger, more boyish. The light shines on his hair, showing honey and chestnut tones interspersed with the brown. It's unique.

"I'm glad you liked it."

"It was truly amazing," I admit. "You should be proud. I see why my dad wanted to sign you guys." Giving him a compliment is ... difficult. I still don't like him. It's easy to see he's a cocky womanizer, but talent is talent.

He turns and walks away, back to the studio, and I stand there for a moment longer replaying the song in my head, the lyrics, his voice, letting it seep into me where it will stay forever.

FOUR

Hollis

It shouldn't fill me with so much joy that she liked our song, but it does. I have the feeling Mia Hayes is a hard person to win over and she *loved* our song. She thinks no one saw, but even from the booth, I saw the single tear she wiped away.

For me, I've always hoped to move someone with my music. Yeah, I've enjoyed the perks of women throwing themselves at me, the parties, the booze—but at the end of the day, in my heart, the music is all that matters. It comes first, always.

I step back into the studio listening as Hayes replays what we've recorded today and goes over what needs to be redone tomorrow. All in all, I can tell he's pleased.

"I think this single will be ready sooner than I anticipated," he admits. "If you guys are as on as you were today this album might be ready for a release next year."

I try not to show my shock. It's September. If it released next year ... well, it's more than we ever hoped for. I can't seem to wrap my brain around it. We've worked *years* to get here, to sign with someone we admire and trust, to put out a real and true album and now the dream we've been working toward might be realized in a matter of months.

It's almost too much.

"Fuck yeah," Rush cries, high-fiving all of us.

Mia slips back into the room, I don't even see her, but I feel her. It irks me the way my body reacts to her, how I sense her. I don't know her, and most of our few encounters have been far from pleasant, and yet I seek her out. I saw her leave the room and I had to go after her. I had to know what she thought of the song even if I already knew. I wanted to see if she'd be honest or lie. But she couldn't lie, and I know why, because music is as much a part of her as it is me, and when you eat, sleep, and breathe music you can't deny when it's good.

We work for a few more hours, starting the base track for another song while we're on a roll, with plans to fine tune both tomorrow. Mia stays in the room as much as possible, only leaving when she needs to get someone coffee or something to eat.

By the time we all head out and Hayes is locking up, it's dark.

The guys and I walked here this morning since the

studio is only a block from our hotel, but as they head on—Cannon shooting me a warning look as he goes—I linger in the darkened shadows, hoping Hayes leaves before Mia. When I see the Range Rover pull out of the lot I head for the back and nearly get run over by a little red car.

The window rolls down and Mia screams, "Are you crazy?"

"Possibly," I admit.

I move to her open window and cross my arms as I bend to lean inside.

"What do you want?" she asks. She doesn't sound irritated, only tired.

"We got off on the wrong foot. I thought maybe we could start over. I'm Hollis." I stick my hand out to her with a grin.

She narrows her eyes on my hand as if it has some kind of flesh-eating disease.

"I'm not sleeping with you if that's what you think," she blurts.

I throw my head back and laugh. "Did I ask you to sleep with me, or did I conveniently forget that part?"

Her cheeks burn. "I know your type," is all she says.

"We're going to be spending a lot of time together," I say by way of explanation. "I figured I should clear the air of any hostility. I can't promise not to hit on you, I'm a natural flirt," I joke with a hint of a smile, "and I can't promise to not be an asshole sometimes or to mess with you, but—"

"This is the most pathetic starting over speech I've ever heard."

"Have you heard many?"

"Only this one," she admits, fighting a smile. "But it doesn't take a genius to see how pitiful it is. I expected more groveling."

"You already saw me naked."

"Practically naked," she shrieks, turning redder.

My lips twitch. Messing with her is way too easy.

"Look, I'm trying here," I say in a placating tone.

"Fine," she grumbles. "I'm Mia. Nice to meet you douche nozzle."

"Ouch." I place a hand over my heart. "That hurt."

"Good. Can I go now?"

"No goodbye kiss?" I jest.

She narrows her eyes. "Nice try."

I crack a grin. "Goodnight, Mia."

She rolls up her window without another word and pulls away. I head back out on the sidewalk, watching until her taillights disappear around the corner.

I can't help but feel like I won something pretty important tonight.

"Where have you been?" Cannon asks from the back of the couch, chewing on a toothpick. He always gets antsy when he's stuck inside and can't smoke.

I shrug, my hands shoved deep into the pockets of my

jeans. "I walked around for a bit. I wanted to clear my head," I explain.

He stares at me, brow raised, like he's assessing my truthfulness. After a moment he turns back to the flat screen TV. That's his silent code that he's calling bullshit but doesn't feel like getting into it with me right now. I'm sure he's already figured out I stayed behind to speak with Mia. Nothing gets by Cannon.

Rush watches me from the chair. His lips fighting a smile. I want to punch the smirk off his face.

Is that how Mia feels about me?

"If you were scouting for chicks, you could've told me," he says.

"Like I said, I was only walking around."

"Mhmm," he hums, not believing me, but I'm actually telling the truth.

With a sigh I stalk past the two guys and into my room, closing the door behind me a little sharper than I intended. The clang of the door reverberates in the room.

I start stripping out of my clothes as I head into the bathroom. Turning on the shower I wait a moment before stepping under the steaming spray. I tilt my head back, letting it pour over my face.

All my mind should be on is music, and the magic we created in the studio today with Hayes—fuck, he was so pleased he wanted to start on a *second* song—but instead, all I can think about is Mia.

His *daughter*.

It's wrong of me, for more reasons than one, but mostly

because I can't put my—*our*—career in jeopardy. Being a part of a band is about working together toward the same common goal. If one person steps out of line it throws the entire balance off and it can be hard to recover. Bands break up all the time. Ones you've seen splashed across magazines and those still playing in garages. I can't risk losing my guys because of a girl. One whom I met a few days ago, one I don't even know. I'm not the boyfriend type and I know from looking at Mia she's not a fling type of girl. One-night stands are all I know anymore. If I have no intention of being her boyfriend then I need to stay away, for my sake, hers, and the guys.

And yet, when I close my eyes all I see is her face.

Her eyes.

Her lips.

Fuck, I'm screwed.

And not in the way I want to be.

FIVE

Mia

Exhaustion seeps into my bones, but I keep working. The Sub Club has had an almost non-stop line ever since I got to work. Kira works beside me, swiftly wrapping the subs I make. We're a great team, and work together quickly. It's the main reason why we're always scheduled on the same shift. I think otherwise, because of our friendship, we wouldn't share the same shifts most of the time.

Closing time is soon, and I can't wait to sit down and have a sub of my own before I go home.

At least I'm caught up on homework. Once I'm out of here I can head home, shower, and dive into my bed. It sounds like heaven.

Kira checks the customer out and finally, blessedly, there is silence.

For a moment at least.

The chime over the door rings and Kira and I exchange a frustrated glance. We haven't even had a chance to catch our breath.

"Well, well, well, look who we have here. Mia Hayes working in a *sub shop*. Color me shocked." I look up to find Hollis on the other side of the glass, a hand pressed mockingly over his chest. Beside him is Rush, pretending to look around the place but really his eyes stray to Kira every two seconds.

"My parents insist on normalcy—therefore I work. Money isn't handed to me on a silver platter despite what people may think or the media might portray."

His lips twitch with amusement.

Plastering on a fake smile I say, "What can I get you?"

I know in my green work shirt and hat, with sweat dampening my brow, and my hair in a sloppy ponytail I look a mess. I don't care. I'm not ashamed of working. It's not beneath me. If you want to have things in life, you have to work damn hard to have them. My parents might gift me with some nice things, like my car, but things like my clothes, my shoes, anything I *want* I pay for. Don't get me wrong, they clothed me as a child, but now I'm an adult and it's on me.

"If you don't stop leering at me I'm going to punch you in your smug ass pretty girl face," Kira tells Rush.

Hollis and I both stifle our laughter.

Rush looks taken aback, as if a girl has never spoken to him in such a way.

Honestly, they probably haven't.

"Well, aren't you the sweetest thing," he retorts.

"You haven't seen anything yet," she warns. Turning to me she asks, "You know these losers?"

I sigh. "Meet Hollis and Rush." I point to each guy and they nod. "They're in the band my dad signed," I explain.

"Oh. In that case, give me your autograph so I can sell it on eBay," she tells Rush and his brows raise. "I was *joking.*"

"Are you guys done recording for the day?" I ask, trying to be nice since Hollis and I have some sort of truce going on right now. Who knows how long it'll last.

He nods. "Yeah, Midnight Eyes is pretty much wrapped up. Everything is going smoothly. There's still some minor tweaking to be done on the producing end, and we might have to re-record some things, but for the most part, it's done."

"Cool," I say, and realize once the word leaves my mouth how pathetic I sound. "Um ...what can I get you guys?" I ask again.

Hollis rattles off his order as well as two more for Fox and Cannon who didn't come. Then I do Rush's order and Kira wraps everything up, checking them out.

Rush heads out first followed by Hollis who stops with his hand on the door and looks back right at me.

"See you," he says with a tiny little smile.

I'm baffled by it, by the shyness in it, almost like he's not used to being genuine.

"Bye," I say back and he ducks out the door, heading down the street to his hotel. I have no idea where they're staying but it must be within walking distance to here and the studio. I saw no other cars parked in the lot yesterday, and I know my dad was providing them with vehicles. They wanted it to be a part of their contract to have transportation for themselves, and my dad being my dad bought them each a car. He's a softy.

Kira turns to me. "Why didn't you tell me about this?"

"Um..." I hesitate, confused. "Because it wasn't important."

"You didn't think it was important to tell your *best* friend one of the hot guys in your dad's new band *likes* you?"

I snort. "Hollis? He doesn't like me—not like that. I definitely don't like him either."

She gives me a look. "Are you stupid? He has the hots for you."

I give her an incredulous look. "Nope, he doesn't, I promise you. He's ... he's the kind of guy who prefers a different girl warming his bed every night and I'm *not* that girl."

She rolls her eyes at me. "I'm right and I know I'm right." She places her hands on her hips.

"Kira, even if you are, I'm not interested."

"Mhmm," she hums. "Keep telling yourself that."

I balk. "I'm serious. He's arrogant, cocky, an asshole—"

"A hot, arrogant, cocky, asshole," she interrupts.

"You're impossible," I groan, throwing my arms in the air.

"Impossibly right." She sticks her tongue out at me.

With a sigh, I shake my head as another customer comes in and we get back to work.

I LIE IN BED, MY DAMP HAIR SPREAD AROUND ME, STARING AT the ceiling.

For some reason I can't get Kira's words out of my head about Hollis liking me. It doesn't seem plausible. He can't possibly like me. A guy like him looks for easy, for girls who throw themselves at him, and I'm not one of those girls. There's nothing wrong with being that way, but it's not me.

It makes no sense for him to like me, and if she's right and he *does*, my dad would kill him for it, I'm certain. He's never taken kindly to anyone I've dated in the past—not that I want to date Hollis—and I know he'd hate it if one of the guys from The Wild dated me. He's always warned me away from guys in bands—and when I asked him why, considering *he's* a musician and the best dad ever, he said he hadn't always been the greatest person, he'd done many things he was ashamed of, but meeting my mom and me changed things for him.

I doubt he'd think Hollis was capable of change, and frankly, I'd agree with him.

I don't even know the guy; a few encounters doesn't make us best friends. We don't know each other's favorite color or finish each other's sentences. Even if we were friends—which is laughable—I can't imagine us as a couple.

Mia, why are you even thinking about this? Guys like him ultimately don't give girls like you the time of day. Besides, you don't even like him.

I don't like him.

Not a little bit.

Nope.

I don't.

I really don't.

Why don't I believe myself then?

SIX

Hollis

I nod along to the music, a smile on my face. The guitar notes for Midnight Eyes linger in the air as Fox redoes some of his part.

Magic, it's what we're creating here with Hayes. Our music is flowing and sounds like it never has before.

It's better, somehow more powerful.

It's a risk to release our ballad first, especially when pop is so huge, but this song encompasses who we are as a band. What we want to sound like, who we want to be, and Hayes agreeing with us means the world because he knows the music industry inside and out. If he didn't think releasing this song first was wise, he'd strike us down and pick the single himself. He has the right to do it too.

In front of the booth Hayes grins from ear to ear, bopping his head along.

The door opens and Mia pops in with a cup holder full of coffees and in her other hand a bag of burgers from a local diner. Hayes asked her to run out since we were all starving and in no place to leave.

She doles out everyone's coffee and food. We have regular drinks in the fridge and I grab a water since I have no desire to drink coffee with my burger.

Mia sits down in the chair we moved into the room for her since after the first day she refuses to sit on the couch and let me stand. In fact, she avoids me at all costs and it's beginning to boil my blood. It's not like I have some life-threatening disease she'll catch by breathing the same air as me.

Even if I'm irritated by her behavior, I can't help but watch her every time she's near.

I try not to, especially with Hayes so close, but she's like a siren and I'm caught in her dangerous melody. The way she moves, the way her hair falls over her shoulders, the way her eyes flicker taking in everything around her, it all draws me in. I've never been like this before. Not ever. I don't know what it is about her that's different. I haven't even thought about going out and picking up a chick since I first encountered Mia. It's ... weird.

Then again, with as hard as we've been working it's not like there's been the time. Plus, Hayes banned us from partying, so going out hasn't been on the agenda at all.

I try my best to force thoughts of the redhead from my

mind, but even as I eat, my eyes keep straying in her direction. Thank God Hayes is so into what's happening in the booth he doesn't notice me glancing at his daughter every two seconds.

I only wish I could understand why I'm so drawn to her. Yes, she's fucking gorgeous, but millions of women are. It has to be more than her looks and those staggering curves, something only Mia possesses that no one else has.

Cannon nudges his leg against mine and I know he's caught my wandering eye.

A silent reminder of everything I could fuck up if I pursue this ... *thing* I feel.

I know, I know. As much as I want to see where these feelings could lead, I'm forbidden from it.

I can't risk this for the guys, and I can't risk it for me either, not over a woman.

I give her one last lingering stare as she curls her legs under her, eating her burger without a care in the world. A lot of women would've gotten a salad, not wanting to look like a pig in front of us guys—guys who are *definitely* pigs in more ways than one. But Mia doesn't care. She's not looking to impress anyone, especially not us, and it's refreshing if I'm honest with myself.

Even with our moderate success, women still shove themselves at us. We're nothing to them as much as they're nothing to us. They use our fame and we use their bodies. It's mutual, but someone like Mia ... she looks down at us. Fuck, if it doesn't make *me* look down at myself for everything I've done in the past. Everyone I've used for one brief moment of pleasure. She doesn't know the long list of mistakes I've made. She barely talks to me, avoids me, all she judges my character by is her assumptions. If she knew ... well, everything she already thinks and her reasons for avoidance would indeed be valid.

I swallow past the lump in my throat, not used to the shame clinging to me like a second skin.

What's happening to me?

Why the fuck do I care what she thinks?

She's nothing.

We're nothing.

Not even friends.

Definitely not lovers.

I stare down at the food in my lap, making myself eat, but not actually tasting it.

When I finish it's my turn to re-record some of the vocals on the bridge.

I head into the booth and when I sit down, slipping the headphones on, I look out and she's gone.

ONCE AGAIN, I FIND MYSELF LINGERING AS THE GUYS GO BACK to the hotel and Hayes leaves.

I made it seem like I was leaving since Mia had to stay behind to clean up, restock the refrigerator and do other odd things around the studio. I'm trying hard not get on Hayes's bad side. I guess not hard enough or I wouldn't be staying back at all.

Now, I slip back inside. Already, she has music playing. I can't place the song, it's not one I recognize but it's hypnotic. The female's voice alluring, the words poetry.

I stalk through the studio and find her in the kitchen area, standing on her tiptoes to place a box of cereal on a top shelf.

"Let me get it," I say, reaching out for the box.

She startles, and jumps, falling into my chest. Her body is soft and warm against mine, her curves pressing into me.

"Don't sneak up on me like that," she seethes, slapping my chest. It leaves a sting, but I know I deserve it. I didn't mean to scare her, but I should've known I would.

I put the cereal away and face her.

"I thought you left," she accuses. "Why are you still here?"

"You left," I blurt.

Her brows furrow. "Uh ... no. I'm pretty sure I've been here the whole time."

I shake my head. "No, the recording room. You left when I went in."

"Oh." She looks away, nibbling her plump bottom lip.

My eyes zero in on her lips and I'm helpless to look away.

"Why?" I ask.

It shouldn't matter.

It *doesn't* matter.

Lies.

It does matter.

She shrugs, wrapping her arms around herself. "It's too much," she finally responds after a moment of pause.

"What is?" I ask, and somehow I've moved closer to her without doing it consciously.

She swallows thickly. Her impossibly blue eyes, so striking with her red hair and creamy skin, look helplessly up at me.

"Feeling." Her answer is no more than a whisper. Barely a breath.

"Shouldn't feeling be a good thing?"

She shakes her head, taking a step away from me. "Not this kind."

"Why?" I approach her. I'm afraid if I let her get too far she'll flee. I wouldn't stop her, but I don't want her to go. I guess it makes me a selfish bastard, but I already knew I was one.

"I don't want *you* to make me feel anything."

A stab to my heart. I've never had words pierce me before. Not like hers do.

"Why are you afraid of me?" I ask, my voice low, my head angled toward her.

"I'm not afraid," she says vehemently. "But I won't have my heart broken—not when I know better. I know your type. You use, you use, and you use again and *again* with no care for who you hurt, even yourself. I won't be a part of it. I'm too smart to fall for it."

"You think this is an act?" Anger laces my words.

She nods.

"I wouldn't *pretend* to get in your pants if that's what

you're thinking. I'm as confused by this as you are, but you can't deny it either can you?"

"Deny what?" Her eyes shift away.

She already knows.

"The chemistry, this thing between us. You felt it the first time we met too. I know you did."

"Stop it," she growls out, throwing up her hands. "Leave me alone, *please*."

"I wish I could," I admit. "It'd be easier. I risk everything with every second I'm near you."

"Why?"

"You know why."

"My dad," she whispers on a sigh.

"I still want to know you," I admit.

"Know me?" she repeats.

I can't help smiling. "Yeah, I want to know you. Maybe be your friend."

"Hollis Wilder, I think you're incapable of being any female's *friend*."

"I'm willing to find out if you are."

Her eyes dart away. "Even if nothing happens between us my dad will assume if he catches us."

I give her a toothy smile, like a shark, a predator. "Then we'll make sure he doesn't find out."

SEVEN

Mia

I sit across from Hollis at the pub a block from the studio.

How on Earth did I end up here?

How did I allow myself to get suckered into this?

I'm lying to myself. I know why.

Because Hollis is right. I can deny it all I want, but ever since the first time I met him there's been something drawing us together. A tug. A bond. It makes no sense. I hated him on sight, his cocky smirk and every word that left his stupid smart-ass mouth.

We ordered our food, and I got a drink, a strong one, in order to get through this without spontaneously combusting on the spot. I have to limit myself to only one since I have to drive home and it doesn't sit well with me. A drunken stupor would be helpful at a time like this. Then I could pretend this whole encounter was a dream.

The Wild has barely been in Virginia a week, and here I am. Out with Hollis as *friends* when we both know the simmering heat between us does not lead to friendship.

More like friction between the sheets.

But I refuse to go down that path. I've been burned in the past before and *not* by someone in a band who is known to be the worst for loving and leaving. I refuse to be another tally in whatever book he keeps of his conquests.

Hollis takes a swig of beer, his throat bobbing with the motion.

Even his throat is sexy. It's entirely unfair.

"Why are we here?" I ask, spreading my arms wide.

We're sitting on the outdoor deck. It's packed enough I have to raise my voice to be heard. Above us fans whirl quickly, trying to keep patrons cool from the humid evening air.

"Getting to know each other." He lays his corded muscled arms on the table.

"So far, we haven't done much of that," I remind him.

He smiles. "Ask me something then."

I press my lips together. "What's your family like?"

"Dad left when I was barely two years old. Haven't seen the bastard since. My mom worked her ass off to support us. She's amazing. Her side of the family is all I know and they're pretty cool too. All I want is to be able to take care of her so she doesn't have to."

I'd be lying if I said my heart doesn't stir at his confession.

"Where'd you grow up?"

"Tennessee—that's two questions so now I get two," he warns, waving his fingers in front of my face.

"Fine," I grumble.

"What's your biggest desire?"

I narrow my eyes and he groans.

"Not what I meant. I mean, what do you wish for most? What do you hope for? Get it now?"

I sigh, thinking seriously about how I want to answer.

"I want to be successful on my own merit. I don't want people to whisper I'm only where I am because of my dad or my last name. I want people to value my opinion because it's *good* and *important* to them. I want to be my own person, Mia, not Joshua Hayes's daughter."

"I respect that. One more question." He thinks for a moment. "If your life was a song, which would it be?"

"Beauty in Madness," I say, referring to one of Willow Creek's songs. "When you have a famous parent, there's a lot of beauty to it, lots of amazing opportunities, but there's the madness and chaos too. It can be a beautiful exhausting mess. My turn?"

He nods.

"Why am I different to you?"

I don't know what makes me ask the question. Why it's so important to hear his answer.

He swallows, picking up his bottle of beer and swirling it around. He shakes his head. "I don't know. You just are." He takes a sip of the beer looking contemplative.

I'm not mad at his answer, because it's sort of how I feel about him, so I understand.

He leans forward a bit, a smirk tilting his lips on one corner. "Easy one—what's your favorite color?"

"Yellow," I answer with a small laugh. "Yours?"

"Navy blue."

"Interesting," I muse.

"Why?"

"I expected you to say black."

"Why?" he laughs.

"Isn't it the color of debauchery?"

He shrugs. "I wouldn't know."

My lips twitch as I try not to laugh. "Funny, I thought you were King of the club."

"They kicked me out," he parries easily. "Apparently I'm not as much of a badass as they thought."

"Really?"

"Yeah—apparently the motorcycle wasn't enough."

"You have a motorcycle?" My eyebrows rise in surprise. "I'm intrigued."

His eyes glint with mischief, that strange amber color flashing. "I'll take you for a ride some time."

"Sounds fun."

This, right now, is too easy. I don't want to like him. I want to hate him. It would be better for both of us. Despite myself, despite him, I don't. There's something about him, about us, that clicks.

As the sky darkens from sunset into the dark blue color of night, the lights around the deck twinkle. Below the deck is another seating area and a stage where local artists sometimes play. I can't help but wonder what the gathered crowd of college students would think of the song The Wild has been working on. It's a ballad. Slow, sad, but uplifting in a strange way. A reminder we're never alone, even when we think we are, someone is thinking of us. Someone is in our corner. Someone *sees* us for who we truly are even when no one else does. I'm surprised they're releasing it as their first single, it's a risk, but it's a beautiful song and my dad seems confident.

My dad.

If he knew I was here, with Hollis, he'd be mad at me but he'd skin Hollis alive. I know I'm an adult. I can hang out with whomever I want. I'm not afraid of my dad, not in the least, but I hate disappointing him and it's what I'd do if he knew what I was up to. Who I'm spending my time with.

But having dinner with Hollis doesn't mean I'm going to jump into bed with him.

My dad might not trust Hollis, but what about *me?* Can he not trust me to make my own judgment call? Does he have so little faith in me?

He's your dad, Mia. He can't stand the thought of you with anyone. Get used to it.

It's true. I could be eighty years old and he'd come back from the grave to tell me I couldn't date. Sometimes I think he's even more protective of me than Adalyn when it comes to the male sex, and I'm sure it stems from what happened with my sperm donor—the fear he felt at the thought of losing me. What he fails to understand is one day when I meet the right guy, fall in love, and get married he's not losing me, he's gaining something entirely new.

"What's wrong?" he asks and my thoughts evaporate like smoke.

"Nothing—I was thinking."

"About what?" He leans back in the barstool, completely at ease.

"My dad," I admit. "I wish he could understand I'm not a little girl anymore. I'm going to leave the nest one day."

"I was wondering ... why do you still live at home? It seems like your life is here and a nearly hour drive each way every day sounds exhausting."

"Some days I want to get an apartment here and stay," I confess out loud for the first time ever, and to Hollis of all people. "But ... I love my mom, dad, my sister and brother ... leaving them feels permanent somehow. Like I know once I move out, a part of my life is over."

"It's all a part of growing up," he agrees. "It's not easy being an adult."

"It's not. Some days I wish I was a little kid again. I miss the naivety of childhood."

"Don't we all." He smiles easily.

Our waiter finally appears with our food and my stomach grumbles. I love food. I can't help it—food is life.

My phone vibrates beside me. It's a text message from my dad.

Dad: Have you left yet? Drive safe.

I bite my lip, pondering my response. I hate lying, but what choice do I have?

Me: Not yet, grabbing a bite to eat with Kira.

Dad: Okay. Let me know when you start home.

My dad is the biggest worrywart on the planet, but I appreciate that he cares. A lot of people don't have parents who do.

Across from me, Hollis arches a brow. "Was that Daddy Dearest?"

I turn my phone over. Sliding it away. "Yes."

"Is he always like this or is having us in town making him extra anxious?"

"Mm," I hum. "Pretty much always."

Hollis smirks. "So, what you're really saying is that we're nothing special?"

I laugh, tucking my hair behind my ears. "That's exactly it."

As we eat Hollis asks, "Did you go to regular school or were you homeschooled because of travel?"

"I actually went to a regular public school most of the time. But whenever the band toured all of us kids went along and we had a tutor."

"Are you all close?"

"Nuh-uh. It's my turn to ask a question," I sing-song, wagging a finger at him in warning. I hate to admit it, but talking to him is easy. When he's not being an overt flirt he's kind of nice to talk to.

He sighs. "My bad. Go on."

I take a bite of my pasta and think. "What makes guys like you make a sport of bedding as many girls as you can?" I challenge.

He twists his lips in thought and counters, "What makes you think I'm one of those guys?"

I tilt my head and give him *the look*. "I've seen pictures. Don't act like you're a saint."

"Googling me?"

I shake my head. "No, you're plastered all over my Instagram feed because every girl in a hundred mile radius is jumping at the chance to be the next to land in your bed."

He winces. "It makes me sound ... conceited."

I snort. "You *are* conceited."

He chuckles. "I guess it's true. Now answer my question."

"Yes, all of us kids are close. Like cousins. My dad's bandmates are my uncles and their wives my aunts."

"Having a big family sounds nice. At least I have some family, but..." He trails off shrugging.

"Talking to you is easier than I thought it would be," I admit quietly.

His eyes twinkle. "Why—did you think it would be difficult to talk to someone so devastatingly handsome?" He rubs his chiseled jaw.

I roll my eyes at him. "You wish. The way you came off at first was so full of yourself, but..." I pause, searching for the right way to phrase it. "I see now it was an act. A shield. To protect yourself."

His lips part and I realize I've stunned him. I have a feeling Hollis Wilder is rarely ever surprised.

"If no one knows the real you, then it doesn't hurt when they leave or try to sell you out," he confesses.

"Why let your guard down now?" I can't help but ask.

"I guess I sense a kindred spirit in many ways."

He stares at me with those strangely golden eyes and it feels as if he can see all the way down to my soul.

We're toeing a dangerous line, but I stay seated. I don't leave—I don't want to.

EIGHT

Hollis

The weekend arrives and with it a strange feeling. One I've never felt before and don't even know how to describe, but I know it stems from the fact I won't see Mia for the next two days. Maybe longer, depending on her work schedule.

We have an understanding now, maybe even a friendship, though I still can't help but rile her up at times. It's too fun.

I don't think the guys know yet how much time I'm spending with her. At least, I pray they don't and I'm not the praying type. They'll skin me alive and hang me by my toes if they learn I'm hanging out with Mia, even if nothing is going on.

Which nothing is, but they won't believe me.

I'd be lying too if I didn't admit I think about her as *more* than a friend at times. For the first time in my life, it's not only about her looks. It's *her*. It's how she makes me feel, her very essence. She's intelligent, funny, independent, sassy, strong—

I'm losing my fucking mind over a chick—a chick I'm pretty sure doesn't think the same way about me. Don't get me wrong, I can tell she thinks I'm attractive, but ... I can also see she's not interested. It irks me I'm so tangled up in these strange new feelings and she's completely unbothered. Maybe this is some sort of punishment. I finally like a girl for who she is and she doesn't like me back. The world is cruel like that.

I remind myself I've only known her a week.

One fucking week and I need to stop feeling sorry for myself. By next week someone else will have caught my eye. Most likely.

It's a lie I tell myself easily, but one I don't believe.

This feeling is too new, too different, too fucking unique to be a fluke and gone in the blink of an eye.

Maybe she's my muse.

I'm so fucked.

There's a knock on my bedroom door and I mutter, "Yeah?"

Fox opens the door and pokes his head in. His dark hair sticks up in every damn direction.

"We thought we'd go out exploring today. You in?"

"Yeah, why not," I agree quickly, because sitting around

in an empty hotel suite pining over my boss's daughter doesn't sound like my idea of a good time.

"Cannon wants to leave in an hour," Fox warns.

If Cannon says an hour, it means sixty minutes and nothing over. He has the look of your stereotypical brooding bad boy, but he's basically the dad of our group, ordering us around and sticking to his goddamn schedules he imposes on the rest of us. It's annoying, sure, but without him, our band would've tanked from the start. He keeps us in line, even if he is a man of limited words.

I hop out of bed and shower, wishing I could wash away thoughts of Mia and have them slide down the drain, but it isn't going to happen.

I scrub my fingers roughly over my scalp as if I can forcefully rid myself of my treacherous feelings for the redhead who haunts me when I'm awake and when I'm dreaming.

There's no escaping her.

It makes me angry we have to hide the fact we're friends. I curse myself for my reputation, and I curse her father for warning her away even if he has a point. I'm not good enough for Mia, not even to be her friend. Hayes knows that more than anyone. He's a musician, he had a wild side in his early years, so of course he doesn't want his daughter around us. Around *me*.

It's *me* I'm angry at. Not him. I know my past actions scream I'm not a good guy. I've had more girls than I care to admit, but they willingly threw themselves at me, at all of us. It's not like they were forced into anything.

But it paints a picture of a guy who only sleeps around.

And ... well, I loved it. I loved the attention, the women fawning over me. But already in one week I feel disgusted at myself for thinking my fame should mean women dropping at my feet, mine for the taking.

Something about being stuck in this small town, in a studio with Hayes, and around Mia is changing who I am. I'm seeing things in a whole different way now—by not being in L.A. I see how the city corrupted me, all of us except maybe Cannon. How I lost sight of what truly *matters*.

The music.

The way it speaks to me.

The way it lifts my heart.

The way one song, one note, can entirely change my mood, my perspective, my thoughts.

I think back to our first night in D.C. It feels so far away now, but it was only last week. I remember how comfortable I was to be in a club, drinking myself senseless with a nameless woman in my lap.

I can see Mia's disapproving look now, and it angers me because I was content until she came along. Everything was fine, and now ... I don't know whether I'm rediscovering my old self or changing, but it's jarring.

Rinsing the shampoo out of my hair I shut off the shower and get out, drying my hair and skin roughly. I throw on a pair of shorts and a t-shirt, and head out of my room to grab something to eat before we go.

Knowing Cannon, wherever he's taking us, he won't be stopping for food or pee breaks.

AN HOUR LATER THE THREE OF US FIND OURSELVES HIKING through the goddamn woods behind Cannon.

"I thought we were going sight-seeing," I gripe. "All I fucking see is trees, trees, and more fucking trees." I sneeze loudly. Stupid allergies.

Cannon whips around and his pale green eyes flash with irritation. "All I fucking hear is you complaining, complaining, and more fucking complaining."

"It's hot as balls out here," I mumble, wiping sweat from my brow with the back of my hand. "Why wouldn't I complain?"

Cannon only picks up his pace.

Asshole.

We trek behind him, mile after mile. I'm in shape, it's not like I don't work out, but I'm used to busting my ass in the gym. Not outside, in the roaring late summer heat, with all kinds of sounds that could be any freaking animal.

It isn't long before the trail grows wider, the trees clearing, and we see why Cannon wanted to come here.

"Holy fuck," Rush gasps out and I have to agree with him.

The four of us stand side by side, staring at the mountains, a river rushing below. The view stretches for miles. None of us seems to have any more words. I don't know how long we stand there staring, but I know it must be a while.

Sweat stings my eyes and I rub at them.

"I brought food," Cannon announces and finds a spot to sit in the shade, removing his backpack.

The three of us follow him as he doles out the food—peanut butter and jelly sandwiches and chips. He then tosses each of us a bottle of water. I gulp mine down greedily.

Even after we've finished eating, we linger, unable to leave such a stunning view behind. It's inspiring, the beauty of it. The way the green of the trees seems too vibrant to be real, the sunlight sparkling on the water below, even the mountains seem larger than life even if I know larger ones exist elsewhere.

We start back down the trail in better spirits than when we came up.

Laughing, joking, and occasionally breaking into song.

"Do you hear something?" Fox stops suddenly.

We grow quiet.

"I don't hear anything," Rush says.

"Shh," Cannon hushes, holding up a hand.

Then we hear it. Shuffling, sniffing, and a growl.

"Oh, shit," I curse, crouching down. "It sounds big."

"What do we do?" Fox squeaks, his voice high.

All our eyes swing to Cannon.

"What do we do, Dad?" I joke, trying to lighten the mood but I only get glares from my friends in return.

All their faces pale as they continue to look at me.

My smile falters. "What?" I whisper.

"Don't. Move." Cannon hisses. "I mean it."

My heart begins to beat rapidly.

There's a snuffling sound behind me and I turn my head the slightest bit, spotting a mama black bear with two cubs right behind me. They seem oblivious to the four of us, focused on wherever they're going, but they're so fucking close. If I took two steps backwards and reached out I could touch the mama bear's thick charcoal fur.

Nothing much has ever scared me, but in this moment I have to admit I'm absolutely terrified. Especially when I look down, seeing the mama's claws. They could rip me to shreds in a heartbeat.

"We're so dead," I mutter under my breath.

At least, if we're going to die, this is one hell of a way to go.

NINE

Mia

"What do you mean you're in the hospital?" My dad shrieks into the phone. I look up in worried surprise at his words. More conversation is exchanged, my dad's lips parting in surprise. "I'll be there as soon as I can. Don't leave."

He hangs up the phone pinching the bridge of his nose. "What is it, Dad? It's not Grandma is it?"

He shakes his head. "No, it's Hollis. Apparently, he was attacked by a bear."

My jaw drops. "What?" I gasp. Worry zips through my veins, suffocating me. "Wait, a *bear*?"

This sounds like a joke.

"Yeah," he says, searching his pockets for his keys.

"Dad, calm down," I say seeing he's becoming flustered. "Do you want me to come with you?" I offer partly out of selfish reasons, wanting to see Hollis with my own two eyes, but it's also clear that this news has shaken my dad and he's in no state to be driving.

"Yes, please," he breathes a sigh of relief.

Once we locate his keys we pile in the car and head for the hospital. It's over an hour drive, but with my speeding, we make it in forty-five minutes. I can tell my dad is flustered or he would tell me to slow down.

We head into the emergency room. At first they won't let us back, saying there are too many people in the room, but for once my dad pulls the, "Do you know who I am?" card and we're let back immediately.

It's a card he doesn't like to use, but I think in this case it's worth it.

As we stroll through the halls searching for his room number I know when we're getting close because I hear him complaining.

"It's a *scratch*, this is ridiculous. Let me go already."

We round the corner and find Cannon, Rush, Fox, and a doctor huddled around Hollis sitting on a stretcher with a blood pressure cuff strapped to his arm. They've made him put on one of those ridiculous gowns. It's quite comical seeing the normally put-together guy have to wear one of those silly things. Nobody looks good in a hospital gown, but Hollis somehow manages to carry it off.

"You could have rabies," Fox hisses. "Don't people die from that?" He looks around for confirmation.

"Seriously, it was a cub and it was only playing."

"You're lucky the mom didn't attack you," Cannon growls. "You fucking idiot."

"It's not like I *asked* the cub to play with me, it just did. Stop getting your granny panties in a twist."

Cannon huffs and crosses his muscular arms over his chest. Out of all the guys, he's the biggest. Massive, like some impenetrable wall.

"What's going on here?" My dad voices. "Someone start explaining. *Now*." He pinches the bridge of his nose like he's beginning to get a headache.

The guys launch into a story about how they went on a hike to see the mountain views and on their way back a mama bear and two cubs happened to walk up. One of the cubs ran up to Hollis and nipped at his ankle, leaving behind several small punctures, not one of them deep enough for stitches.

"It's not a big deal," Hollis says. "I didn't even want to come here, but Dad insisted on it." He points an accusing finger at Cannon.

Cannon raises his hands in surrender. "Excuse *me* for being worried about my friend. A fucking bear bit you."

"Yeah, a *baby* bear. And I swear to God if I find out they put that cub down I will lose my fucking mind. It wasn't trying to wound me. It didn't even hurt."

I feel silly for how relieved I am he's not seriously injured. Now, hearing the story, it's actually quite comical.

Hollis stands up and does a twirl. "See, I can stand. I can walk. I can dance." He does a little jig to prove his point. Thank God he's still got his boxer-briefs on or we could've all gotten a show we didn't sign up for. I can tell my dad is troubled by the whole situation because he doesn't say a thing about it. "I'm a-okay and ready to *go*." He glares at the doctor.

"We still have to give you a shot to prevent potential infection since this is a bite from a wild animal and there's lots of bacteria in their mouths."

"Then give me the shot doc so I can leave." He swirls his finger in the air in a hurry up gesture.

"Only one person can stay with you," the doctor says in response.

My dad glances at me. "You stay with him, I want a more detailed explanation of what happened from these three." He tosses his thumb over his shoulder at the standing guys and their shoulders sag, fearing trouble.

I wait for them to leave, not wanting to look eager to get close to Hollis.

The doctor leaves, probably in search of a nurse to take care of getting the shot and discharge paperwork ready.

I sit on the edge of the bed by Hollis. We're close enough the heat of his arm brushes mine. I glance down at his leg, surveying the size of the bite, and he's right. It's barely anything. But it *was* a wild animal so I see the cause for alarm.

"Nice battle wound," I joke.

He groans, leaning his head back. "I'm never going to live this one down. *Hollis Wilder gets attacked by a baby bear.* I can see the headlines now. Not to mention once the guys are no longer worried, I'll never hear the end of it. The little guy only wanted me to play with him." He shrugs like it's no big deal. "The mama didn't like it and hauled him away, though. We could've had fun." He gives me a grin.

I bump his shoulder with mine. "I thought my dad was going to lose his mind when he got that phone call."

He's quiet. "And what about you?" he finally voices.

I bite my lip. "It worried me too," I admit.

"You? Worried about me?" He places a hand against his bare chest. "I'm flattered, Mia."

I shouldn't like the way my name rolls off his lips.

I'm pathetic.

He brushes a piece of hair behind my ear that's fallen loose from my ponytail, his fingers lingering against my skin. He's so close to me I can count every eyelash if I want to.

"I like knowing you were worried about me," he breathes on a whisper and I swallow thickly.

What's happening between us scares me. It's happening so fast, like a free fall, and I don't know yet if a net is going to catch me or if I'm going to slam straight into the ground. I don't want to find out, but I'm helpless to walk away. I've never had anything to *feel* like this before. None of my past boyfriends ever made me feel remotely like Hollis can with one glance and we're not even close to dating. We're barely friends.

His forehead brushes mine, and I think he's going to kiss me, but the nurse chooses that moment to enter the room and we both jump apart like we've been electrocuted. I suddenly feel cold all over from the loss of his body heat.

I sit quietly while she gives him a shot and then goes over things to watch for as far as possible infections.

"I'll get your discharge papers," she announces, leaving.

The room is charged with energy, but neither of us moves closer to the other.

We're playing a dangerous game, and we both seem helpless to stop it.

I could lose my dad's trust. Having him disappointed in me seems like the worst kind of punishment even if I am an adult now and can technically do as I please. But more importantly, Hollis's career is on the line. I don't want to be responsible for my dad dropping him and The Wild because of something happening between us. I would never get over the guilt.

We don't exchange another word as the nurse returns with papers for him to sign. I turn my back to let him change, his amused laughter echoing behind me.

"You can look, Mia, and we both know you want to touch too." I squeak, slapping a hand over my mouth. Damn him. "I'm decent," he says a moment later.

We spot my dad standing with the three guys outside. They haven't seen us yet and Hollis's hand grasps my arm, pulling me into a darkened corner where if they do look inside they won't see us.

"I don't know what's happening here," he confesses, his Adam's apple bobbing. "It barely makes sense and confuses the hell out of me, but I don't dislike this feeling either. You're making me rethink how I've acted in the past, fuck even last week, and it's not like you've even said anything about it. I've used plenty of girls in the past, for sex, publicity, whatever. I didn't care. You make me care. I'm trying my best to be content with being your friend and I think I can be that, you deserve it, and we've basically only met anyway, but I want you to know if one day this does go further than this ... it'd only be you. I might've been a douchebag in the past, but you ... you make me want to be better."

I stare up into those mesmerizing eyes, the color of whiskey and amber, at a loss for words.

I can't deny I'm attracted to him. But I also can't deny who he is, where he's going, and it scares me. My parents might've been able to make it work, but I don't know if I could. If this goes somewhere, if it'd become serious, how would I feel when he's gone months on end? My life's here ... his isn't.

"We can't do this," I say, and my voice cracks.

My body screams at my words, my desire for him crying out, begging me to give in even if only for one night. But I have to be strong. I can't give in to this, it'll only end in disaster.

His jaw clenches. "I understand."

"I'm okay with being friends. But beyond ... it can't happen."

I swear I feel my heart shatter into a million pieces in a way it never has before, and I don't understand it. Why now? Why this guy? There are a million other nice, normal, sweet guys out there. Why is it my heart yearns for Hollis Wilder?

"Friends hang out right?" he questions.

"Y-Yes," I hesitate.

"What time do you have lunch on Monday?" he asks and I tell him. 'Meet me in the parking lot. We're going somewhere."

"We're playing with fire," I tell him.

He leans down, his lips finding my ear. "I don't care."

I close my eyes, breathing in his scent. Pine, wood, and something entirely Hollis.

I don't care either, and it's what terrifies me most.

TEN

Hollis

We're playing with fire.

Mia's words echo through my skull as I wait in her school's parking lot for her class to finish. She texted me the building name and I parked as close as I could get. On the damn sidewalk so she can't chicken out on me.

I know she's right with what she said, and I should walk away, not even try to be her friend. But when someone awakens something in you, something so magical that's never been there before, walking away seems like the most impossible thing in the world.

It figures when I finally feel something *real* it'd have to be with my boss and mentor's *daughter*.

My teeth snap together as I think over my shitty behavior in the past, how Hayes found us in the club in D.C., me with some woman draped over me. I didn't even know her name. I hadn't cared.

Of course, he'd want someone like me to stay far away from his daughter. Mia is perfect and she deserves a perfect guy. I've done nothing to prove I'm that person for her. Everything points to the self-righteous asshole type. I enjoyed being that way. I won't lie and say I didn't have fun, didn't enjoy it, because I did.

But from the moment I walked out of her bathroom, Mia's gotten under my skin in a way no one has before. I can't explain it. It's not love at first sight, that shit's crazy, but it's a connection of some sort. Something pushing me to her saying this person is meant to be in my life in some way.

The doors to her building open and students begin strolling out.

I search for vibrant red hair. It isn't long until I spot her. She smiles at someone and I read her lips as she says goodbye and heads toward me.

Her smile grows blinding as her eyes meet mine and fuck if her smile doesn't feel like an arrow straight to my heart.

What is happening to me?

I smile back and she stares appreciatively at me. No, not at me, at my motorcycle.

"Nice ride," she says as she approaches. "I also like the color."

She takes in the cherry red Yamaha motorcycle. "For the record, I picked this color before I ever met you."

"Maybe it was a subconscious decision."

Then this chick has the nerve to look at me and wink. *Wink!* My dick twitches in response and I struggle to find words.

I hold out a matching helmet to her and say, "Climb on."

Now all I can see is her climbing on my dick, her red hair spilling over creamy skin.

I start counting backwards from one-hundred before things head in a dangerous direction.

She fits the helmet over her vibrant hair and climbs on behind me.

"Did you really have to park on the sidewalk?"

I shrug before putting my own helmet on. "I thought I might have to chase you down."

She laughs and the sound makes me smile.

"Where are we going?"

"No idea," I answer honestly. "You're the one who lives here, not me."

She laughs again. "You invite me out and don't even know where we're going?"

"I like to live dangerously," I tell her, kick-starting the bike.

I race off the sidewalk and speed through the lot—not too fast, but enough I feel her arms wrap tightly around my torso. Her breasts push into my back and as fun as I thought this would be, I kind of wish now I'd borrowed a car from one of the guys.

I know I can't drive far, since she has to be back for class, but heading downtown is dangerous too in case we run into her father. This isn't a date, far from it, but he won't know and will jump to conclusions.

Driving the bike in the opposite direction I search for a place for us to grab lunch. I should've thought this out more, but as per usual, I didn't.

Mia squeezes tight, not in fear, but excitement and selfishly I hope because she wants to be closer to me.

I spot a sign for a farmer's market and turn onto the road. It isn't long until we come to the small market, surrounded by an apple orchard.

The bike bumps into the lot, and I park. Mia eases off the bike, removes the helmet and shakes out her long hair. I'm glad she can't see me through the dark screen of the helmet because I'm fucking mesmerized by her. I swallow thickly before pulling off my helmet and attaching it to the bike. I do the same with hers before we fall into step side by side and into the market. We walk around the small store, finding they have a café. We both order a hotdog with chips and wait for our order. Once we have our food in hand, we skip the tables and head outside to eat under the shade of one of the gnarled trees.

"For not having a plan, you did pretty well," she admits, crossing her legs.

"I find things always work out in the end if given enough time." I shrug.

"Is that so, Yoda?" Her eyes shine with barely contained laughter.

"Yeah, it is." I playfully pinch her side and she swats my hand away.

I've never experienced this ease with a woman before.

I open the container holding my hotdog. Mia's already biting into hers. She doesn't hesitate.

"This is so good. I was starving."

"Academia makes me hungry too. I spent all of high school starving to death."

She laughs, covering her mouth. "I'm pretty sure all teenage boys are starving twenty-four-seven. My brother eats enough for five people. It's gross."

"True," I agree, tipping my head in her direction.

"Are we ever going to do anything except eat together?" she asks with a raised brow. "This is beginning to feel like you're secretly tricking me into going on dates with you."

I nearly choke on the food I'm about to swallow.

"What?" She mocks with a grin. "Allergic to the word *date*?"

When she lets her guard down, joking with me, it makes me feel like I've won something. This side of her is something I feel few people ever have the pleasure to witness.

"No," I say forcefully, "but I'm offended you think I'd have to trick you into dating me." Lowering my voice and getting dangerously closer to her so her scent invades me, I say, "One day soon you'll be begging me for a date. Trust me, there will be no doubt about what we're actually doing."

She swallows thickly, her pulse visibly jumping and I can't help the smile spreading over my face at having rattled her carefully constructed walls.

They might only be rattling now, but soon they're going to come crumbling down.

I return to my previous position, completely changing the subject, like I'm not at all affected by being near her, I begin, "It really is cool here. The mountains and farms. The rivers too."

Mia shakes her head as if fighting a fog. "Y-Yeah," she stutters, and I can't hide my grin. "I wouldn't want to live anywhere else."

"Really? Even having traveled the world you'd rather stay here?"

Mia's seen more of the world than most people ever experience, countries I probably don't even know the names of, and as nice as it is here it still surprises me she'd choose to stay.

She nods, tucking a piece of hair behind her ear. It's futile as the wind immediately blows it into her face. "Don't get me wrong, I love traveling and I've seen so many amazing places, but this is home. I always end up back here. I think I'm suited to the vibe of a small town."

I finish a bite of my food, thinking over my words. "Growing up I couldn't wait to get out of Tennessee. I thought everything I wanted, needed, was in L.A. I never thought I'd end up back in a small town, but here I am.

Everything seems to be aligning as it was meant to," I confess. "I think what I was running from is what I needed all along."

I stare at her significantly.

I never wanted to attach myself to anything that meant growing roots. Now, here I am desperately seeking the thing I fled from. It's not only Mia, though she's a big part even if she doesn't know it, it's this place. It's Hayes and how I feel our music flourishing under his guidance, becoming bigger and better than I ever thought it could be.

I think being forced to get serious, no clubbing, no girls, or booze, is clearing my mind of the fog I've been in since I stepped foot in L.A. Something about the city puts you under a spell, twisting and molding you into a whole new being. Some probably become a better version of themselves, but most, like me, turn into a stranger. There's something about chasing fame that has the ability to turn you into some vapid version of yourself.

Glancing beside me at Mia I feel a rush of something I can't explain. She's not looking at me. Instead, she has her face tilted toward the sky, her eyes closed as she soaks in the heat and breeze caressing her skin. The gnarled trees paint shadows on her face and before I can second-guess myself I hold up my phone and take a picture. She doesn't even notice. Glancing down at the photo on my screen I feel a stirring inside me. One of pride and appreciation. Sure, she looks beautiful in the photo, but what strikes me the most is how peaceful and comfortable she is. When's the last time I was at peace like her?

She turns toward me and I stuff my phone in my pocket before she can ask what I'm looking at.

"Have you ever felt at home anywhere before? Like I do here?" she asks softly, the sun a halo behind her.

I start to say no, I want to say no, but those aren't the words leaving my mouth. "I do now."

Belonging and existing are two completely different things. All this time I've merely been existing until I came here, and now I feel like I belong. Even the guys are different here, as if we've all been searching for this place, these people, this whole time.

Mia's eyes shimmer with an emotion I can't decipher and then she completely changes the subject. "How's the recording going?" she asks.

"Slow," I reply. "But good. Your dad is being more particular, but it's what we need. We can't get better without critique."

She nods. "You guys are fantastic—and it should mean a lot to you coming from me, because I'm super picky about music," she laughs, the sound like tinkling bells. She bumps her shoulder playfully into mine.

Friends, I remind myself.

Just friends. It's all she wants from me.

I know she's attracted to me, that much is obvious, but … if she feels anywhere near what I feel she's damn good at hiding it. Unfortunately, I think she's content being friends and fuck if I don't feel hurt by it.

It shouldn't bother me, I wish it didn't, but it does.

The universe finally gives me a girl I'm genuinely attracted to for more than sex and I can't act on my feelings for several reasons. Even if her dad wasn't an issue and my career wasn't on the line, I'd never try to pressure her into anything she didn't want to do. I might be an asshole at times, but I'm not a total douchebag.

Realizing I've been quiet too long I say, "It does ... mean a lot."

Mia Hayes has grown up around music all her life, it's what she wants to do in the future too, and I know she has an ear for sound. Therefore, her approval does mean the world to me. I can tell it's not something she gives out lightly.

She smiles at me, a rare, entirely genuine smile. It's one she doesn't usually give me, but maybe she's growing to like me more. Why is it I selfishly hope she is? The fact of the matter is I don't deserve someone as pure hearted as Mia in my life let alone as a friend or lover.

"We better head back," I warn her.

She looks at the time on her phone, cursing under her breath. "You're right."

We throw the trash away and hurry back to the bike. I haul ass back to her campus, thankfully it's not far, and she squeezes me tight the whole time.

I'd be lying if I said I wasn't soaking in the feel of her body wrapped around mine, afraid this might be the only time I ever have her this close.

ELEVEN

Mia

Only a few hours have passed since my lunch with Hollis when I walk into the studio, Dean Wentworth hot on my heels. He's my age, and the boyfriend of my cousin Willow. Technically, Willow and I are not cousins by blood, but since she's Maddox's—the drummer in my dad's band—daughter it totally counts.

"Come on," Dean whines behind me, on my heels like a dog. "It's one song. I want to record it for Willow and give it to her for Christmas."

"We're not running a charity here," I grumble, turning to look at him over my shoulder. His Pokémon shirt is pulled taut over his lean body. He's the definition of the word adorkable and it makes perfect sense why he clicks so well with free-spirited Willow.

"Please," he begs.

"No," I snap. I actually like Dean, but he's all too fun to mess with.

"Uncle Hayes will let me." He narrows his green eyes on me.

Dean and I are *actually* related by blood. His dad and mine are cousins. But I've always grown up closer to my dad's bandmates' kids than him and his siblings. On the road, we only had each other. It made sense to stick together.

Dean follows me into the back and straight into the recording room The Wild has been occupying.

"Jesus, I can't shake you," I grumble. Looking up my eyes connect with Hollis's and he looks livid eyeing Dean behind me.

Someone's jealous.

"Dean," my dad crows. "What a nice surprise."

I toss my thumb over my shoulder. "In Dean's words, he'd like to *commandeer* one of the booths to record a song for Willow to give her for Christmas." I pretend to gag. "Love makes me choke," I joke. I actually *like* being in love. The problem is the guys I fall for end up being jerks and I end up hurt. It's why I know I have to keep Hollis at arm's length. It'd be all too easy to fall into the abyss that is him and he's one man I'm not sure I could recover from. I can't help but glance in his direction and watch as his eyes settle from a blazing gold to a soft amber as he realizes I'm not interested in Dean nor is he interested in me.

I practically vomit at the thought.

"Not a problem," my dad says. "Let me know when you need a booth and I can help you out. Or Mia can. She knows what to do." I glare at my dad but he's oblivious.

Dean gives me a triumphant smile and I stick out my tongue. I can't help but dissolve into laughter. Pretending to be irritated with Dean never lasts long. He's too big of a goof to *actually* be mad at.

"I gotta get back to work," he says, shoving his shaggy hair out of his eyes. "See you guys later."

"Tell Willow we need to hang out," I call after him.

"Will do." He gives me a mock salute.

"Why do you insist on giving him a hard time?" My dad asks and I glance toward the booth, seeing Fox paused in his recording, his guitar hanging in front of him as he watches us through the glass.

"Um … because it's fun. He's practically like a brother. It's all too easy to mess with him."

My dad simply shakes his head and pushes a button to speak to Fox.

"Is anybody hungry? Coffee?" I ask.

"Pizza!" Rush cries loudly.

"Yeah, pizza sounds great," Cannon says in a deep voice. He barely ever talks, at least to me or in front of me, so I'm startled to hear a complete sentence out of him.

Hollis nods in agreement.

"I'll order pizza then." I duck from the room and head

for the kitchen. I pull my phone from my pocket to order pizza from a place downtown that makes the best wood-fired pizzas.

I finish ordering and turn around to find Hollis leaning against the wall, his arms crossed over his chest. His shirt rides up a bit, exposing a tiny sliver of tanned smooth stomach. I swallow past the lump in my throat.

Those wicked eyes stare me down. He doesn't say a word. He doesn't have to.

He stalks toward me, and I back away like a cornered animal, ending up right where he wants me with my butt pressing into the counter with no means of escaping.

He lowers his head to the crook of my neck and my breath stutters, thinking he's going to kiss me there. Instead, he whispers a confession against the heat of my skin. "I'm trying so fucking hard to be your friend, Mia—to not be the guy you think I am, that I was—but it's killing me. I've never been the jealous type, but I wanted to rip that guy's head off for being close to you."

I don't know what to say. I can barely breathe.

I've always been the cautious type but ever since Hollis stepped out of my bathroom, I've felt like I've jumped feet first into a pool of water and my feet never found the bottom. Now I'm desperate for air but the surface is too far to reach.

If I could stay away from him, if I hadn't proposed this whole friends thing, maybe eventually I'd be able to wade through the waters I've tumbled into, but it's impossible.

There's no avoiding Hollis Wilder—and even if I tried to ignore him, I know he'd find me.

"You need to step back," I say. "If my dad—"

He growls, cursing under his breath but does step away. He shoves his fingers roughly through his brown curls.

We stare at each other, so little distance between us when in reality we're miles apart.

I can't deny the way my heart beats around him. I can't deny some of the thoughts I've had. I may not be able to deny them, but I can't act on them either. This attraction between us is only that—an attraction—and I'm not the kind of girl who does one-night stands. I don't judge someone who does, but it's not for me, and I know Hollis will eventually grow bored of me. Then what? Besides, he's working on an amazing album I feel certain will do extremely well and then they'll end up going on tour. Touring means temptation at every turn. Heck, I can recall being small and even with the wives and kids traveling with them half-clothed women still threw themselves at my dad and the other members of Willow Creek.

"We can't be more than friends," I tell him. "It has to be this way. I'm sorry."

His jaw works back and forth. "I want to be that guy for you—a good guy. The one who doesn't push you for more, who's there for you, but I'm not so sure I can be your friend. I'm trying. I really am, but I can't stop feeling the way I do either and it's killing me. It's *killing* me, Mia."

Gone is the cocky guy who strutted out of my bathroom and in his place is a stranger. Someone who's a mere shadow of the other guy. The vulnerability he displays nearly knocks me unbalanced. I wish the other version of him would come back, disliking him was easier. Hating this new Hollis is impossible.

But if he can't be strong enough to resist this, then I'll have to do it for the both of us.

I SPEND THE NEXT TWO WEEKS AVOIDING HOLLIS AS MUCH AS I can. I still see him at the studio, but I avoid his glances and questioning gazes. I also make sure he can never corner me alone.

In the short time we spent together I really grew to like him, and now with not spending time with him I actually miss him. But I know staying away is for the best. I need to focus on school, he needs to focus on his music, and anything between us would be way too complicated.

I'm sure it's only a matter of time before he figures out how to get me alone, I can see his irritation growing stronger every day, but eventually he'll realize I'm protecting the both of us.

Besides, he might think he has *real* feelings for me, but there's no way. It's too fast and with the life he's lived the last few years ... there's no freaking way wanting a different woman in his bed every night just goes away. I'm sure once his album is complete and he can leave here, he will. He can return to his clubbing, drinking, man-whoring ways.

At least, that's what I tell myself so I can feel better about avoiding him.

The hurt in his eyes, though? It's real. I can't deny it.

I walk into the studio, precariously balancing the coffee I picked up as well as the subs I brought along from the Sub Club. I don't normally work there and then come to the studio, but my dad said they'd be working late and he wanted the extra help.

"Whoa, careful there." Cannon who's lounging in the front room hops up from the couch he was sprawled on, setting his book aside, to help me carry the load in.

He takes the cup holder from me and his big hands nearly dwarf it.

"Thanks." I flash him a smile.

Cannon, covered in tattoos and the epitome of bad boy, happens to be the most levelheaded of the guys—the mother hen, if you will. Looking at him you'd assume he'd be the worst of the bunch, but it's proof of how you should never judge a book by its cover. He's a genuinely nice guy from what I've seen. It's hard to get to know him when he barely ever speaks.

The two of us head to the back and he hands out the coffee while I pass around the subs. I purposely hand Fox his and Hollis's so I don't have to risk eye contact or even the chance of our fingers brushing.

Hollis glares at me. I can feel his eyes searing into the side of my face, and I know it didn't escape his notice as to what I did.

The air simmers between us, like some visible mighty

thing, so I quickly duck out of the room with an excuse of needing a soda.

Grabbing a Mountain Dew from the refrigerator in the common area I crack it open and take a sip, trying to calm my racing heart.

Pissing off Hollis was never my intention, but it was kind of inevitable.

He can be mad all he wants—but I'm standing my ground on this.

When I feel calm enough, I return to the room and take a seat to eat my food. No one's in the booth right now, instead we all eat. The guys discuss with my dad the progress of the day, things they want to tweak, and what they want to record next.

Hollis steadfastly ignores my presence now.

It's what I wanted, but suddenly I feel chilled and it's not from the temperature of the room.

After we eat, I clean up the trash while they get back to work.

Once I have the trash disposed of my dad has me pull up a stool beside him and allows me to be a part of the recording. I love this part, bringing life to a song, breathing magic into it. I can't help the smile permanently glued to my lips as I work beside him.

When I glance up, in the reflection of the glass I find Hollis watching me closely. His legs are crossed, his thumb and forefinger resting over his full bottom lip as if he's deep in thought. I look away quickly, hoping he didn't notice me looking back at him.

I hear a small chuckle and I curse myself because he totally caught me.

Hours pass and it's nearing midnight before my dad calls it a day. My body feels heavy and tired. I have no idea how I'm going to drive the hour home. I'm tempted to see if I can crash at Kira's but since I hadn't planned for this, I don't have any of my stuff. Not that it wouldn't be the first time I've slept in my clothes on her couch.

As everyone else leaves I stay behind to tidy up yet again and make sure everything is in order. It doesn't take long before I'm locking the front door behind me and heading for my car.

I don't feel too comfortable being downtown by myself this late so I shuffle to the back lot as quickly as I can.

The headlights on my car flash, illuminating a humanoid shadow.

Before I can scream the shadow turns and Hollis stands in front of me.

I shove him. "Don't scare me like that," I seethe as my heart threatens to break free from my chest.

He glowers down at me. "It's the only way I can get you to talk to me," he spits out. He's angry, rightfully so.

"I don't know what you want from me," I finally say.

He pushes his long fingers roughly through his curly hair. "Fuck, I don't know, but I expect more than the silent treatment."

"I'm trying to protect us," I explain, sidestepping him but he immediately blocks my path. "Hollis," I complain, pleading with my eyes for him to drop this and let me pass.

He pushes closer to me, spreading his arms and closing in around me so my back is pressed against the brick of the studio. He angles his head, looking at me as he thinks through what he wants to say.

I square my shoulders, refusing to be intimidated. He works his bottom lip into his mouth and dammit if it isn't the sexiest thing I've ever seen.

"You don't want anything to do with me then?" he asks softly, a challenge sparkling in his eyes.

"I ... it's too dangerous to even be friends."

He presses one hand to the column of my neck, angling my head up.

"You mean to tell me, if I leave here right now, find a willing chick, take her back to the hotel, and fuck her until her pussy is raw you'll be okay with it?"

I struggle to breathe at the visual he's painted. I want to rip out the imaginary girl's eyes with my fingers.

I know what he's trying to do to me, and it's working.

Damn him.

"Y-Yes," I stutter, the words barely a whisper. "I-I'd be okay."

Lie. Such a fucking lie.

His lips tilt into a crooked grin. He knows I'm lying and he's gotten exactly what he wanted.

He steps away from me, shoving his hands in his pockets. "Okay. Goodnight, Mia."

He turns, walking through the alley and disappearing onto the street.

The whole way home, all I can think about is him

making good on his threat. If he does ... I'll be more than happy to punch the arrogant smile off his face for proving me right—but my gut says he won't do it. No, he merely wanted to see how I'd react, and I gave him exactly what he expected.

THE WEEKEND PASSES UNEVENTFUL, UNLESS YOU COUNT THE fact that I ran into Hollis at the gym since I have a membership to one near my campus, which I don't because it totally didn't affect me at all.

I also might be lying to myself.

I wish I could kick myself for letting him crawl his way under my skin to the point of falling asleep thinking about his sinful lips. The guy is too attractive for his own good and he knows it.

I walk across campus with determined strides, heading to my second class of the day. Thoughts of Hollis need to be shoved from my mind so I can focus on school. But no matter what I do I can't shake him. He's either in my thoughts or appearing in front of me. It's really quite frustrating.

Entering the building I head for the classroom and take a seat in the back.

As the lecture begins, I do my best to listen and pay attention, even taking notes, but my mind is elsewhere—with someone else.

This whole avoiding Hollis thing is quickly blowing up

in my face, because if I'm not mistaken the heat between us has reached scorching levels in the past few weeks of me avoiding him. It's like by not letting some steam out of the pot we've reached a boiling point there's no coming back from.

I might've completely fucked everything up by trying to protect us.

It'd be my luck all of this would blow up in my face.

I chew on the end of my pen, trying desperately to pay attention.

When class finally ends, I can't recall a single word the professor said the entire lecture and my notes barely make any sense. Frustration runs rampant in my veins.

I'm thankful when lunch comes, Kira and I slipping away to a local café.

Kira stares across the table at me pointedly.

"You might've gotten away with ignoring me about the whole Hollis thing on Saturday, but not today missy," she warns, referring to running into the gym. Since she was with me she knows about the whole debacle.

I frown. "I don't even know what to say."

"Why don't we start with you explaining the whole lingering stare thing and the heat simmering between you two. I swear I saw sparks flying. Hop on that dick girl and get *laid* already. It'll loosen you up."

"Not with him," I mutter.

"Why? Because last I checked he was super into you, I mean there's no missing it even if you're blind, and he's hot too which is a bonus. Also—thanks to those tight ass shorts Rush was wearing when I spotted him ... I'm totally reexamining my decision to avoid him." She holds out her hands showing me a measurement and mouths, *"Huge."*

"It's not that simple, Kira," I whine in frustration. "He's ... he's a musician, one who's already had moderate success and I'm certain after their full-length album release, and with my dad's backing, it's going to explode. That kind of attention and scrutiny ... a relationship can't make it with that."

She stares at me blankly. "Um ... what about your parents? Maddox and Emma? Ezra and Sadie? Mathias and Remy? I think you have plenty of proof it *can* work—besides, I didn't say anything about a relationship. I think a little harmless fun would be good for you."

"I don't think I can do that," I admit with a shake of my head.

She rolls her eyes at me and huffs a breath.

"Look," I begin before she can start a rant. *"Anything* between Hollis and me is a bad idea. It'll only lead to disaster. I refuse to jeopardize his career if my dad found out—which he would, he always does."

I rest my elbows on the table and my head in my hands. I stare down at my food for a moment, suddenly not hungry anymore.

She blinks at me, looking at me like I've lost my mind. "Who gives a flying fuck what your dad thinks?"

"Kira," I scold, as we get a dirty look from the older couple sitting nearby at one of the round tables.

"Whatever." She gives them a dirty look right back.

"Anyway, back to our conversation, it shouldn't matter what your dad thinks. You're a grown woman—you're allowed to be with whomever you want and he has no say."

"It's about respect," I mutter.

She sighs. "I understand how much you love your parents, especially your dad, and not wanting to piss him off, but this is *your* life, Mia. Not his. What if you miss out on something great because you fear his reaction? I'm not only talking about Hollis, either."

I bite my lip, because unfortunately, she has a point.

I was only three when he came into my life. I don't remember a life without him in it. We've always been close, he's my dad in all the ways that count, I just want him to be proud of me.

"I don't know," I answer honestly.

"Think about it," she pleads.

I nod. "I will."

It'll be all I can think about, because it's all that's been consuming me anyway.

ENTERING THE STUDIO IN THE AFTERNOON I STROLL TO THE kitchen area, dropping my backpack on the counter. I grab something to drink before poking my head into the recording room.

My dad claps his hands, grinning from ear to ear, and says, "One more time," to whoever is in the booth. I glance to the glass and find Hollis. Instantly, my throat closes up. What his voice does to me...

"Do you guys need anything?" I ask the three guys sitting on the couch.

They all shake their heads no.

"I have homework I'm going to start. If you need me, I'll be out there." I point over my shoulder like they don't already know where I'll be.

I slip from the room before Hollis can start singing again. The last thing I need is to get ensnared by his mesmerizing voice.

Grabbing my backpack from where I left it, I head to the front of the studio and sit on one of the couches, spreading my work around me.

I keep looking up from my work, expecting Hollis to pop into the room, but he doesn't. I silently curse myself for being disappointed. I want him to stay away, it's for the best, but when he does then I get like this. It's pathetic.

I get halfway through my work before everyone's complaining about how hungry they are. I place an order at a restaurant a few blocks away.

"The food should be ready any minute," I tell them, poking my head into the recording room. "I'm going to walk over now."

Hollis clears his throat. "I'll go with you. You shouldn't walk alone."

I open my mouth to protest but my dad speaks before I can.

"That's nice of you, Hollis." For someone who's so overprotective he's really quite oblivious.

Hollis gives me a triumphant grin. I wish I could smack it off his too handsome face.

He doesn't say anything as we head out onto the street. We're a block away before he speaks.

"We're really not good at this whole friends thing."

I sigh heavily, crossing my arms over my chest. His eyes go straight to my boobs and I glare at him before dropping my arms. "Eyes up here, bud," I scold, giving him a look. He merely grins from ear to ear at me, not at all bothered. "And no, we're not," I add with a sigh.

"What is it about me that bothers you so much?" he inquires. He tries not to look bothered by the question, but I can tell he's worried about my answer.

We reach the end of the street and I push the button so we can wait for the signal to cross.

"It's not you per se," I hedge, looking out to the street beyond so I don't have to meet that amber eyed gaze. "It's ... it's what you stand for."

"What I stand for?" He practically snorts. "What the ever-loving fuck does that mean?"

I force myself to turn to him, having to tilt my head up to look at his face. "I refuse to be some casual fling—it's not me. I'm not saying I need promises and declarations of love and marriage, but I won't be yet another girl who falls in your bed once never to be seen or heard from again. Because despite everything I actually *like* you, Hollis, and I won't lose a friendship or whatever this is because of sex."

"You're not even talking to me right now," he growls as we stalk across the street finally. "I don't see how you can call me your friend when you won't speak to me or barely even deem me worthy to look at."

His shadow nearly blocks out the sun as he towers over me, his body curled so close to mine as we walk I'm surprised I'm not being sucked into his vortex.

"Are you sure you're protecting yourself from *me* or *you?*" He continues and I nearly trip from his close proximity.

"If we made a pro-con list of all the reasons why something between us is a good idea or bad idea—bad would win."

His eyes flash. "Forget a fucking chart, Mia. What does your heart say?"

Right now, my heart says I want to push my body into him and press my lips against the angry hard line of his and kiss him until I forget my name, forget everything. But I don't tell him that.

"My heart says I can't do this right now," I snarl back, picking up my pace. Even with my long legs I get ahead for all of two seconds before he's right there beside me.

"You're lying," he bites out the words, his anger making them short and clipped.

I feel tears begin to prick my eyes but I hold them back.

"You're scared," he says, his voice softer than before but still with an edge.

"No, I'm not," I lie.

"It's okay to be scared," he says, his tone softer. "Fear isn't something to ever be ashamed of."

"And tell me, Hollis, what are *you* afraid of?" I challenge, hands on my hips. We're stopped in the middle of the sidewalk, but thankfully there aren't many people on the street.

He swallows, his Adam's apple bobbing. His golden eyes stare into mine and he presses his lips together before admitting, "Never being good enough."

Something about his words is like a kick to the stomach. He looks utterly vulnerable and I want to slap myself. Hollis is a lot of things, but at his core he's like everyone else, looking for someone to understand him completely.

For some odd reason he thinks *I'm* that person.

He reaches out a gentle hand, cupping my chin between his fingers. My heart beats a mighty rhythm in time with my breaths.

"I know I'm not the kind of guy you think is worth taking a chance on, but I'm willing to prove you wrong. I *will* prove you wrong." He ducks his head, his lips sweeping against my cheek before they find my ear. "I'll be waiting when you're ready."

He turns from me then, walking ahead, and I can do nothing but follow along.

TWELVE

Hollis

My hand flies across the page, the words pouring out of me. I spill them across the page, the dark ink a stark contrast to the white hotel notepad. Normally, Cannon writes our songs—we all help sure, but he's the one with the talent for songwriting.

But tonight, as I think on what I said to Mia this afternoon, the truth of my words, I can't stop the words I ache to get out, to make them into song. A promise, my truth, a shout into the void for her to hear my sincerity.

That's how I know what I feel is real, and song, lyrics, music is the only way I know how to prove it.

The first time I saw her I thought she was hot and I

would've loved to have fucked her right then and there in that blue and yellow room. Now I know her, I *feel* for her, and I know once with Mia would never be enough. It's almost like she's inside me now, her soul a beat mine recognizes and responds to.

I *ache* for her in a way I didn't know was possible and I've had more cold showers in the past few weeks than I did in my entire teen years.

Under my breath I sing the lyrics as my hand flies across the page.

Each word bares my soul a little more.

I've never been so personal in any lyrics I've written before. I've always tried to keep a bit of myself, because as your fame grows so does the group of people who think you belong to them. You have to keep something to yourself to remind you of who *you* are and not what everyone else wants you to be.

I lost sight of that for a long time, turning into someone I don't recognize when I look back. It makes me sick to speculate about what my mom must think of the person I've been. The excessive drinking, partying, fucking. All of us let the small bit of fame we got from going viral change us—well maybe not Cannon, but for the rest of us ... we let it consume us. We let it go to our heads, making us into even bigger cocky assholes than we were before.

Honestly, it's a miracle Mia didn't punch me in the face when I came out of her bathroom, all swagger and smart-ass words. I would've deserved it too.

Being here, on Hayes's tight leash, has sobered us all in more ways than one.

At first, I was livid, especially when he showed up at the club in D.C. treating us like a bunch of unruly teens who snuck out of the house on a school night.

Now, I'm grateful for it.

It's funny how quickly perspective can change. It doesn't take much to change as a person—only the ability to *want* to change.

This change has nothing to do with Mia. It would've happened with or without her once I came here, I'm sure of it, but she's definitely pushed things along. With her, I see what's at stake if I fuck up. My past keeps her from giving in, my future too, though she won't admit it. I can't blame her, growing up like she did she probably wants nothing more than *normal*, and fuck ... I definitely can't give her normal. Music is in my blood, in my veins, without it I'd shrivel up and die.

I don't know why, when I finally feel something so deep, so real, for a woman, the whole situation has to be completely fucked up.

I suppose it's the consequences of my own actions, coming back to bite me in the ass. There was no regret at the time for what I did, sex isn't something I want to be ashamed of, but what does bother me is how it looks to other people. Like Mia's dad.

How would I ever be able to convince him that I'm different now when I highly doubt he'd ever give me the chance to prove myself?

THIRTEEN

Mia

The four guys stroll into the Sub Club and I instantly stiffen at their commanding presence. There's a table of three girls I'm sure go to the University and they instantly spot the guys, eyeing them up and down. One juts her chest out, like it's a spider web that can ensnare men. I roll my eyes at the ridiculousness of her behavior.

"Hey, hot stuff," Hollis croons stepping up to the counter.

"Hey, douchetard," I counter.

He grins from ear to ear. "That's my girl."

"I'm not your girl."

His smile falters a little, the other three watching us with shrewd eyes. Cannon in particular seems the most suspicious.

"Sure you are," he croons. "But keep telling yourself you're not."

"Where's the chick with the nice ass and big boobs?" Rush asks, trying to peer behind me as if Kira is hiding there.

"I heard that!" Kira calls out from the back. She rounds the corner, drying her hands. "Ugh, it's you." She mock gags, but she's now looking at Rush the same as he is her—like he's a piece of chocolate she wants to devour. Slowly. Letting it melt in her mouth.

I leave Kira to start the orders, while Hollis continues to stand across from me.

"Are you coming by the studio when you're done here?"

"Don't I usually?" Normally, if I'm working here, I don't go to the studio, but lately my dad's been requesting my appearance every day.

He bites his lip, and damn him it's sexy. He glances to his right, making sure the guys are occupied giving their orders and then lowers his voice.

"Tonight, stay late—I want to show you something."

"What?" I ask hesitantly. Hollis and me alone in a room together doesn't sound like the brightest idea.

"It's a surprise." He smiles, and it's a genuine, almost shy and nervous smile.

It's the smile that does me in and I nod. "Okay, I'll stay."

"Thank you," he mouths the words before joining the other guys to order.

I might regret what I've agreed to, but his sincerity has me believing I won't.

Kira slides a finished sub my way and I wrap it up before tabbing it into the register. I do it three more times before Cannon hands me a card and I swipe it. I can feel the brooding tattooed man watching me. Cannon makes me nervous, not like he frightens me, but I get the impression he's good at reading people.

"See you guys later," I say with a smile, because despite myself I've actually come to like all of them.

Rush winks at Kira. "See *you* later."

As they file out, I wait for the door to close before turning on Kira with a raised brow and one hand poised on my hip. "Later?"

"Oh, don't give me that look. After I saw what he was packing at the gym I decided I would be an absolute idiot to miss out on that peen while I had the chance."

I shake my head. "You are crazy."

"I am," she agrees. "I'm also going to have crazy, hair-pulling, screaming orgasm sex tonight. You should try it sometime. Maybe you wouldn't be so uptight." She winks at me and I stick out my tongue.

The girls at the table in the corner glare at us. It's only then I realize the guys only paid *us* attention and didn't glance in their direction at all.

When my shift ends at six o' clock I say goodbye to Kira who has to stay until close and hop in my car, heading to the studio. Between school, work, and the studio I'm rarely home anymore—basically only to shower and sleep. Luckily, I have fewer classes next semester and will hopefully have a chance to breathe—I just have to survive that long.

Inside the studio the front lights are dimmed to attract less attention from the outside. You wouldn't believe the number of people who have wandered in here thinking the studio is an art gallery or museum. I'm losing my faith in humanity and their ability to read basic English.

I stroll into the room and barely say hello to the guys before my dad has me sitting beside him helping with the controls. He's taught me a lot in a short time, more than I've learned in school. I'm happy he's actually letting me participate. Any time he's been in here recording with his band I haven't been allowed to touch the controls—mostly because Uncle Mathias is a control freak, so I've only made sure they have food, coffee, and whatever else they might need.

But now I'm getting to do what I really want, what makes me happy, why I know my future is in music. I don't want to be on the front lines, but behind the scenes is where I belong, making the magic happen.

I smile the entire time I work, my body moving with the song. I feel it. I live it.

This song has a faster beat, almost a pop edge to it compared to the first one they recorded. I love it just as much, but in a different way.

It doesn't take a genius to see The Wild has what it takes for longevity in this business. They have the same thing Willow Creek has and it's something rare. My dad was able to recognize it in them when other studios didn't—but once they realized my dad wanted to sign them to his new company *then* they started to take more notice. But The Wild? They put their faith in my dad, and I'm glad they did. The smile he wears is contagious, like these guys have become his other children and I can see how proud he is of them and we're only in the recording stage.

We're all so in the zone we don't realize how much time has passed and that it's another late night. Reluctantly my dad calls it a day and everyone begins packing up to head out. Hollis goes through the motions, giving me a warning look telling me I'm not to leave. I give him a smile in return.

"I'm going to stay and clean up," I tell my dad. "So, don't worry if I don't get home until late. I might see if I can crash with Kira," I add, because if whatever Hollis wants to show me takes a while I might have to.

He nods and gives me a hug. "If you do come home, drive safe," he warns. "The deer on the mountain are a nightmare right now."

Don't I know it. When I was seventeen, I hit one and it was traumatizing. I cried, not for the ruined front end of the car, but for the poor deer who lost her life. When I called Dad sobbing, he thought I killed an actual person. It probably didn't help that I named the deer and was crying that I killed Petunia.

"I will," I say in reply, and he smiles, saying goodbye to

the guys before heading out. Cannon, Fox, and Rush head out too, waving goodbye.

Cannon pauses outside the door, giving Hollis an inquisitive look but Hollis waves him on. Cannon's eyes seem to narrow in warning and Hollis ignores him.

With a shake of his head, Cannon disappears with the others.

I have a feeling a confrontational talk might be in Hollis's near future.

"I really do have to clean up," I tell Hollis.

He has his hands shoved into his pockets, his shoulders drawn forward. "I'll help then."

Between the two of us we make quick work of picking up the trash and then I wipe everything down with a disinfectant, getting rid of any traces of stickiness.

While I'm wiping down the counters Hollis excuses himself to prepare for whatever it is he's going to show me. When I finish, I wash my hands before entering the room.

I find Hollis in the booth at the upright piano and he waves me into the room.

"You play?" I ask as the door closes behind me.

He grins. "Shocked, are you?"

"A little," I admit.

"I learned piano before I realized I could sing. I kept having lessons, though."

"Your mom was encouraging then?"

He smiles fondly. "Oh yeah. She knew from the time I was a baby music was in my soul. She went without so I could have lessons. She's always been proud of me, even when I feel like I don't deserve it. Now sit."

He scoots over, making room for me on the bench.

"I wrote a song the other day—normally Cannon writes our music or it's a group effort, but ... I was inspired."

He wets his lips and those golden eyes focus on the keys beneath his long strong fingers. There's something sensual about his hands. The veins running through them, the quiet strength they possess.

He begins to play, the sound of the piano bleeding into me. His fingers move across the keys quickly, creating a melody unlike anything I've ever heard before. I can't help but think even my Aunt Emma, an incredible piano player, would be envious of his raw talent. I'll have to ask him why he doesn't play piano on any of their songs.

Then, he opens his mouth and begins to sing and I know immediately the words, the passion, pain, and hope woven into them are about *me*.

"*I don't know how to prove this to you,*

so I put pen to paper, my heart on my sleeve,

bleeding out for you. Here I stand, just a man telling you this is real.

This spark isn't a flickering ember, it's every star in the sky.

I'll give you the world.

I'll give you me,

if you just see this is real.

I'm here to stay, to make you mine."

He turns then, his eyes connecting with mine. I wipe away the tears falling freely.

"I want to give you the world,
whatever you ask it's never too much.
Anything it takes to make you mine.
Please believe me when I say,
this is real.
Oh baby, this is real."

The whole time he sings I can barely contain my emotions. Everything I've put into avoiding him, to keeping him at arm's length, is ripped away.

It's only me, him, and the sound of his voice wrapping around us in this tiny room. There's no denying this anymore.

As his voice fades and the last notes of the piano linger in the air, we look at each other, there's so little distance between us.

My eyes flick down to his lips, and his breath catches. He presses a warm hand to my cheek, fingers tangling in my hair.

Neither of us moves, only a breath between us waiting for the other to make the first move.

I know I'll have to be the one to close the distance. Getting to know him, only to avoid him. It's funny how I think of him as being not a good guy, but really I'm the one who's been cold and distant.

His fingers flex against my face as if he's fighting to not pull me closer.

I close my eyes and before I can second-guess myself, I press my lips to his.

He doesn't move at first. I think maybe I've shocked him—I think I've shocked myself too.

I start to pull away in embarrassment, but then his left hand joins the right in cupping my face and he angles his mouth over mine. He deepens the kiss, taking and giving, breathing life into me. I've never had a kiss feel like this one before. Simultaneously igniting a fire within me and turning me into ice. I'm hot all over, but somehow frozen in place.

I make myself move, pressing closer to him, seeking, searching, needing.

He grabs my leg, hooking it over his hip until I'm sitting fully in his lap. Normally I would be embarrassed. I've been with guys, but my experience is limited and I'm not the boldest person.

He tilts my head back, trailing a scorching row of kisses down my neck before he reclaims my lips once more.

I've never understood why some people use the word *devour* when describing a kiss, but now I get it, because it's exactly what he's doing to me.

Completely and utterly devouring me.

His kiss reaches into the deepest part of my soul, awakening something I didn't even know slumbered there. It roars at finally being unleashed and I roll my hips against his, my whole body aching. I tremble with need.

If I thought this heat simmering between us was strong before our lips touched, it's now enough to decimate the world around us. I kiss him back like my life depends on it, without him I'll cease to exist.

I slide my hands under his shirt, his skin heated beneath my palms. He lets out a throaty growl and it stirs something inside me.

I push his shirt up higher and he lifts his arms so I can remove it completely. His skin is hot beneath my palms, almost scalding. I trace my hands down his stomach, smiling against his mouth when I feel him shiver.

His hands move down to my hips, his fingers digging in with a bruising pressure.

There's a part of me that knows I should stop this but I'm tired of holding back and always denying myself what I want.

And I want Hollis Wilder more than I want anything else in this world.

I lean back and my elbows land on the piano keys with a clang. Neither of us pauses at the sound. He continues to kiss me, like we have all the time in the world and no time at all.

My fingers delve into his silky hair, pulling him closer. I've never been kissed like this before, so thoroughly devoured. Before it's always seemed as if the guy I was with felt like it was an obligation, not a necessity. Not Hollis, though. He kisses with the same passion he sings with, like he's making love to my mouth.

We're a tangle of limbs, tongues, and feelings we cannot voice.

It's overwhelming.

Consuming.

He picks me up then, my legs tightening around his waist and my arms wrapping around his strong solid shoulders. He carries me out of the booth and into the room. He lays me down on the couch, the leather cool beneath me . His warm body is over mine in an instant, covering me like a second skin.

He spreads my legs and I gasp helplessly against his lips when his thick hardness presses into my core, straining against the zipper of his jeans.

My fingers go for the button on his jeans and he freezes, his hand covering mine, halting my movements. My heart stutters in my chest.

Surprised golden hued eyes meet mine, his lips parted slightly.

"We don't have to," he pants, slightly out of breath. "That's not what I…" He shakes his head, looking conflicted.

I look up at him, lust clouding my vision but surety strong in my heart. "I want this. I want you."

"Are you sure?"

I nod, rubbing my hands over his smooth chest, and the light smattering of chest hair between his pectoral muscles. More trails below his naval growing darker in color.

"I need to hear you say it," he growls.

"I'm sure."

In a heartbeat, less even, his lips are on mine once more.

I kiss him back with fervor. I can't get close enough to him. I need more. I need him.

I push at his shoulders and he sits up. I climb into his lap, taking his face between my hands as I kiss him deeper. The stubble on his cheeks rasps against my palms.

His hands dig into my waist as my hips move against him. My body shakes with need.

It's like we're trying to melt into one another.

It feels twenty degrees hotter in the room than it was before and sweat already dampens both of our skin. I release his lips and he looks at me with hooded eyes as I sit back and peel my shirt over my head. It falls somewhere on the floor behind us.

His eyes flick down to my breasts straining against my bra. He swallows before he slowly raises his intense gaze to mine.

"We're so fucked," he whispers, his voice gruff, raw, and utterly delicious.

I tilt my head, my hair falling forward to tickle his chest as my mouth finds his ear. "I thought that's what we were doing." I take his earlobe between my teeth and give it a small bite before claiming his lips once more.

Sex has never been like this for me before—and we haven't even gotten to the actual sex part. This is intense, the stuff you read about but don't think actually exists. But here it is happening to me, with Hollis of all people. But the way he looks at me, the way he kisses me, it makes me feel worshiped.

We take our time undressing one another.

It's not hurried or frantic, even though desperation surges through my veins.

I find my bare body pressed into the cool leather and goosebumps speckle my skin.

His lips leave mine, and he kisses his way down my body.

My fingers tug on his hair and he growls low in his throat.

He looks up, his eyes shimmering with a need for approval.

I nod once, my lips parted but I can't find the words to speak.

I have to give him credit. I know he'd stop if I wanted to—it doesn't matter we're both buck ass naked. But I don't want to stop. I've been fighting my attraction to him for weeks, trying to do the right thing, but I can't deny this any longer. I don't want to. Whatever this is between us, we're both smart enough to know it's rare. I don't have any expectations of it going anywhere, not with someone with his reputation, and if this is all I get I'll take it gladly.

My heart threatens to burst out of my chest.

My back arches off the couch as his tongue latches onto my center.

"Oh my God," I moan, my fingers clawing at the couch, at anything that I can hold onto.

He does magical, wicked things with his tongue. Things I didn't even know were possible.

I find myself panting his name and he smiles against me. With a gasp and then a cry I fall apart, my legs shaking. I've never orgasmed so hard in my life and he wasn't even inside me.

Something tells me he's going to kill me—at least it'll be a pleasant death.

I run my hands along the planes of his chest, down his abs, lower—he grabs my hand and growls, "Not yet."

Before I can blink he has both my hands pinned above my head in one of his, his grip strong. I know I could break it if I wanted, but I don't. I know I'm not in any danger.

"Fuck, look at you." His voice is low. Raspy. "I want to tie you up. Handcuff you to a bed and fuck you raw."

With my hands trapped, he takes his time peppering kisses all over my body. When he swirls his tongue around one of my nipples and then the other I make an embarrassing squeaking noise and he smirks. My hips move of their own volition, desperately seeking some sort of friction.

I try to get my hands loose then—if only to wipe the smirk off his face, but he shakes his head and I give in, stilling once more.

He nips at my shoulder, leaving a stinging bite he then soothes with a swipe of his tongue.

Minutes pass as he explores my body, taking his time, memorizing every curve and dip in my body. I won't be surprised if he can draw a detailed map of it later.

He still refuses to let me touch him, growling every time I try to get my hands free. I succeed once and he then clasps each of my hands in one of his. It presses his hard body closer to mine, so really I think I'm winning here.

When he finally lets me go, he reaches over, picking his jeans up from the floor. He grabs a condom from his wallet and rips open the foil, rolling the condom down his considerable length.

I watch everything he does, every movement, every breath. I want to be here in this moment completely with Hollis—where everything will change. I know it, and from the look in his, eyes he knows it too.

There's no coming back from this.

Once we do this it changes everything.

He stares down at me beneath him, his eyes reverent like I'm some mighty goddess spread before him, not plain old Mia.

He grabs the base of his cock, aligning himself to my center and slowly pushes inside. I gasp at the intrusion, my body tightening. It's been a while, and despite myself, I'm nervous.

He lowers his body over mine, his hair brushing my forehead. "Relax," he murmurs. "It's only me."

I want to tell him that's the problem.

Inhaling a breath, I do my best to relax and he slips inside a little more.

I don't know why I expected him to slam into me, to not be gentle. But he's taking his time, making sure I'm comfortable.

I've only had sex with two other guys, only once with one and a handful of times with the other. God, the other. I refuse to even think his name. We dated for a short time before I realized what a jerk he was, that he was only using me. If I *ever* see him again, I'm punching him in the face if only to see the look of utter surprise he'll sport.

"Are you with me?" Hollis asks, his voice hoarse from restraint as he brings me back to the present.

Hollis. I'm here with Hollis. Not *him*.

This is okay. This is right.

I nod, gripping his arms. Probably a little too tight, but he doesn't complain. "I'm with you."

"Breathe," he coaxes, gently brushing his lips over mine.

I listen and as I do, he slides all the way in.

I moan, my fingers clawing at his chest. He lets me, not at all bothered by the damage I'm leaving behind.

He kisses me, effectively distracting me. I kiss him back deeply, with everything I have, and he moans into my mouth. I take that sound and swallow it, savoring it. Seeing him like this is beyond anything I ever expected.

He cups my breasts, testing their fullness in his hands before he glides them down to settle at my hips. He lifts them as he slowly retreats the tiniest bit before pushing back in.

Now, it's my turn to moan.

"Fuck, yes, baby," he pants. "I love your little sounds. I love hearing how I make you feel."

It feels good, too good, amazing even. It's never been like this before, and I don't know whether the difference is Hollis making sure I'm comfortable and enjoying myself or our chemistry, but I'm thinking it's a mix of the two.

He can feel my body relaxing, responding to his touch.

I feel like liquid and the only thing keeping me from slipping away is him.

He slides out further this time and back in.

"More," I beg brokenly. "I'm ready."

He stares at me, unsure.

"Please."

It's the only word he needs to hear.

FOURTEEN

Hollis

Some time later I blink open my eyes, my surroundings coming into focus. I smile at the sight of Mia's naked body curled against mine. Her fist is pressed beneath her chin in sleep, her breaths light and airy, with lashes fanning against her cheeks. She looks peaceful, completely at ease, and I can't help but hope she still feels that way when she wakes up. If she regrets it ... fuck, it'd make me feel guilty, miserable, absolutely pathetic.

I reach over her body for my phone on the floor where it fell out of my pocket, doing my best not to disturb her. She makes a squeak of protest but doesn't rouse. I manage to get my fingers onto the phone and scoot it closer until I can fully grab it.

I lift it up, squinting at the time.

That can't be right.

I stare at it longer, my eyes widening in horror. There are less than fifteen minutes until nine—nine when I know Hayes arrives to get settled before we come in around ten.

We have to get dressed and out of here *now*.

"Mia," I whisper, pushing her long red hair off her face.

"Mmm?" she hums, not opening her eyes.

"Mia, baby, you've got to get up."

Baby. I've never ever called a woman baby before, and while the word feels foreign on my lips it feels right for her.

"Duntwunttu," she slurs, sounding drunk on sleep.

"Mia," I say firmer. "Your dad is going to be here any minute. We have to *go*."

Those words snap her awake. She sits straight up, her eyes threatening to pop out.

"Shit," she curses, and looks like she's about to cry from panic.

She climbs off the couch and I follow suit. We scurry around, hurrying to dress in our discarded clothes.

She spies the trashcan in the corner and hisses to me. "The condom."

"What about it?" I ask stupidly.

She glares at me. "What do you think my dad is going

to think if he sees a condom in the fucking trashcan?" She looks like she's about to crawl out of her skin.

"Jesus Christ," I hiss, because she's right. "I'll deal with it—you make sure everything is in order." It should be, but I can tell from the way she's panicking giving her something to do will ease her mind a bit.

She hurries out of the room, her vibrant hair swishing over her slender shoulders.

I take care of the condom and meet her at the front. She locks up behind us and I follow her to her car. She doesn't fight me as I climb in the passenger seat.

She looks over at me and I brace myself for the regret I know will be splashed across her face. I'm pleasantly surprised to not see *'we shouldn't have done this'*, just worry over our current predicament.

Luckily, we make it out of the lot and away from the street before her father arrives.

"I'm starving," I say.

"Me too," she admits, nibbling on her bottom lip. I wonder if she's thinking about the ways we burned all those calories last night. I know I am.

"Let's get breakfast then," I suggest. Selfishly, I want to spend more time with her—I need to see she's not going to suddenly panic on me and lose her mind over what we did.

"Waffle House?" she asks.

"I fucking love Waffle House," I admit. "It's my favorite of all the favorites."

She laughs, it's not a loose free sound like it should be. It's still tight with worry and stress, but at least she's laughing.

In this town there's practically a Waffle House on every block so it doesn't take us long to pull into the parking lot of one. Undoing my seatbelt I say to Mia, "I could live here forever. Want to know how I know that?"

"How?" she asks, the tightness around her eyes and mouth lessening a bit.

"Waffle House is everywhere. I could have it every day if I wanted."

She cracks a small smile. I'm happy to see her easing up a bit.

We head inside and to an empty booth for two by the windows. There are a few other patrons, but it's mostly empty at this hour.

We haven't been seated long when a waitress arrives for our drink order—both of us asking for orange juice.

Mia glances at the menu for a moment and sets it aside.

"What are you getting?" I ask.

"Omelet," she answers, looking out the window.

I want her to look at me, I need to know she's truly okay with what happened last night. I pray she's only worried about her dad finding out.

I know it should be a concern of mine too, but I can't bring myself to care. If I can't care for myself then I should at least care because of how it affects the guys. This is what we've all worked so hard for, and if I fuck things up with Hayes it ruins everything for them too.

But last night ... it was something I've never experienced before, and for that reason alone I can't regret it at all.

She slowly swings her gaze my way, a small smile tugging at her lips as if she knows what I'm thinking. She opens her mouth to speak, but before she can say anything the waitress is back. I silently curse at the intrusion, but give my order with a charming smile anyway. The poor waitress doesn't know what's transpired between us.

Once she's gone, Mia and I sit in silence, looking at one another and waiting for the other to speak first.

I clear my throat and she winces. Lowering my voice I say, "Last night, please tell me you don't regret it."

I don't know what I'll do, or how I'll feel, if she does.

She hesitates and then shakes her head. "No, I don't."

I breathe a sigh of relief, my whole body sagging with the release of tension.

"D-Do you?" she asks, her eyes downcast as she idly traces random shapes on the table, feigning she's unbothered by her own question and my possible answer.

"Not at all," I answer with surety. "It was..." I pause, unable to find the words to adequately describe what it was. Amazing, spectacular, out of the world, mind-blowing ... they all sound ridiculous in my head so I refuse to voice them.

"Yeah, I know," she says, putting me out of my misery.

She gives me a hesitant smile and I smile back. She squares her shoulders then, sitting up straight as if she's shaking off any lingering embarrassment.

"So," I begin and hesitate, "we've decided neither one of us regrets it, but where do we go from here?"

I know what I want, but I also know she might not be as sure as I am.

She shrugs her small shoulders. "I don't know." I start to deflate. "I guess we take it one day at a time and see where it goes."

I perk up at her last words. "I'm okay with that."

"Good." She gives me a small smile.

"Here you go guys," the waitress sets down our plates—three for me, one for Mia.

As the waitress walks away Mia stares in disbelief at all my food. "Are you seriously going to eat all of that?"

I start peppering my food. "Uh ... yeah. I ordered it all for a reason."

She shakes her head muttering, "Too much food," under her breath.

"It takes a lot of food to look this good," I joke, rubbing my flat stomach.

She takes the pepper from me, sprinkling some across her omelet. "Whatever you say."

I dig into my meal, eating faster than I should, but I feel as if I haven't eaten in days, maybe even weeks. I ordered eggs, bacon, sausage, hash browns, biscuits and gravy—basically an entire smorgasbord.

It's all delicious and Mia can barely lift her fork to her

mouth as she watches me with ... horror? Or is she impressed? I mean, she has a little brother, she should be used to how much a man can eat.

"Eat your food," I command her around a mouthful. The last thing I need is her leaving hungry. I'll feel super guilty and think about it all day instead of focusing on what's happening in the studio like I should.

"What time is your first class?" I ask.

"Not until ten today," she supplies. "I wish I could change my clothes, though."

"Can you borrow something from your friend?"

"She lives near here and I know she'd let me, but then I'd have to explain *this*." She wags her fork between me and her. "She'll never let me live it down."

I shrug. "She'll probably find out anyway."

"Why?" she narrows her eyes angrily like *I'm* the one who will spill the juicy details.

I tilt my head to the side. "Because you're best friends and best friends have the annoying habit of figuring everything out before you even open your mouth."

She lets loose a small laugh. "You're right about that. Plus, Kira is tenacious. If she wants to know something she won't let go until I tell her every detail."

We talk a little while longer before we finish and stand to leave. I insist on paying for both our meals even though Mia balks the entire time. She might think she's not my girl, but she is, and I'm taking care of her.

I have her drop me off close to the hotel, but not close

enough for us to get caught together by her dad or my friends. The consequences would be dire either way.

I give her a kiss before I duck out of her car and she blinks at me in surprise.

I grin from ear to ear and watch her drive away.

FIFTEEN

Mia

*H*oly shit.

I had sex with Hollis Wilder.

I'm pulled into the Starbucks parking lot to have my freakout. I cannot believe last night happened, but I don't have any regrets either. Surprising, since I had so many reservations about him in the first place.

But it's safe to say that it was my best sexual experience.

Hollis made me feel comfortable, cared for, and he knew what he was doing. Maybe I should be upset at the experience he's had to gain that knowledge, but since I was reaping the rewards of it, I choose not to dwell.

Covering my face with my hands, I realize I'm smiling.

I can still feel the way he held me, his body heat cocooning me. He was attentive, seeming to know exactly what I was thinking and feeling. But he didn't treat me like delicate china either.

Composing myself, I send Kira a text asking if I can borrow something to wear, but she doesn't respond. I decide to swing by her apartment anyway.

Parking on the street, I feed a coin into the meter before jogging up the stairs to her second-floor apartment. I knock on the door, more loudly than I usually would, in desperation. If she's already left for class ... I'm screwed.

I hit my hand against the door again and finally, blessedly, hear footsteps on the other side.

The door swings open and my jaw drops.

Rush smirks, leaning against the doorframe. "What brings you here Little Red Riding Hood?"

I stare at him in complete shock and despite myself I can't help but take in his half-naked appearance. A pair of jeans hang super low on his hips, unbuttoned and barely zipped revealing very obviously he's not wearing anything underneath.

And I'm staring. Kill me now.

Something tells me Hollis would have some choice words about me ogling his bandmate after he thoroughly fucked me into oblivion last night, but I'm only human and Rush is nice to look at.

"I need to see Kira," I say, forcing my eyes up, up, up until I'm looking into his dark blue eyes.

He turns his head and for the first time I notice his right ear is pierced.

"Kira," he calls. "Mia is here."

A moment later Kira appears around the corner from her room with a robe wrapped around her.

"What's wrong?" she asks—despite the fact I've caught her at the most awkward moment ever I can tell she's genuinely worried. It's not like I normally show up at her place at this hour of the day. In fact, I've never done this.

"Nothing's wrong. I just..." I glance at Rush, afraid to reveal too much but I don't have another option. "I need to borrow some clothes."

Kira looks me over and her mouth parts in surprise when she notes I'm wearing yesterday's clothes. "My girl got *laid*." She does a shimmy dance.

"Shut up," I plead, embarrassment reddening my face.

She rolls her eyes and stops her dancing. "I got laid too, chillax."

Rush chuckles, clearly amused by us.

"Don't you need to be at the studio?" I ask him.

"Fuck," he curses, rushing back to the bedroom. He returns a moment later with his shirt on and his feet shoved into a pair of boots.

"We're doing this again," he growls lowly and nips Kira's ear. "Bye, Mia." He inclines his head in my direction before departing.

"Clothes?" I plead with Kira.

"This way," she says, crooking a finger for me to follow her to her room.

I'm lucky we're practically the same size.

She opens her closet door and taps a finger against her chin.

"I need something that looks like *me*," I explain. "I have to go to the studio after class." Thankfully I'm not working at Sub Club today. "I don't need my dad acting suspicious. I told him I might crash here since we were in the studio late and if I show up in yesterday's clothes, he'll know I didn't come here."

Then again, he is a man and they can be oblivious so he might not even notice.

She looks me over, waiting for something. When I don't give her what she wants—which I don't know what it is anyway, she asks, "Hollis?"

I press my lips together, feeling heat rise to my cheeks. I nod slowly. "Yeah."

"You dirty girl." She smirks, hands on her narrow hips. "I'm impressed. How was it? Did he have a monster cock? Let me tell you, Rush is *hung*. I barely knew what to do with all of it and *that* is saying something. Luckily, I'm *very* creative."

I search for the right words. "It was ... unbelievable," I finally settle on. I don't remark on her Rush comments, it'll only encourage her to go into details I don't want, or need.

"That good?" She raises a brow.

"So good," I supply. My toes want to curl from the memories alone.

"Wait..." She narrows her eyes. "Where'd you do it? His hotel?"

I'm tight-lipped, eyes shifting.

"No," she gasps, hand flying to her mouth. "The studio?"

I nod.

"Oh my God, I'm so proud of you."

"Kira," I hiss.

"What? There's nothing wrong with being uninhibited every now and then. It's about time you lived a little."

"Yeah," I begin, "but it's Hollis of all people."

"So? He seems pretty nice to me, cocky sure but lots of guys are. Rush is too. It doesn't mean they're bad guys. Besides, you've dated far worse than Hollis, and not nearly as hot either."

She's right, but I still find myself being hesitant. I've been burned in the past, it never really hurt because I was never invested in the guy, not in the way I should have been. But Hollis? I actually like him despite trying not to, and I know if he breaks my heart it'll hurt unlike anything I've experienced before.

"I guess we'll have to wait and see how it goes." I shrug, because I don't have anything else to say.

She pulls out a dress and holds it up. "How about this?"

"Are you crazy?" I shriek, looking at the tiny scrap of fabric.

She cackles. "I wanted to see your reaction." She stuffs it back into the closet and instead hands me a pair of jeans and...

"A Willow Creek tour shirt? Really, Kira?"

She points at it. "Hey, that's from their first major tour. It's practically vintage."

I look down at the dark blue t-shirt with Willow Creek's logo of a glowing willow tree and tire swing. "And you don't think we have plenty of these at home?"

She snatches the shirt back from me. "You're no fun. I thought your dad's reaction would be funny if you showed up in it."

She pulls out another shirt, a simple baseball tee. "That's better," I say, heading for her bathroom. I lock the door behind me and freshen up. Breakfast didn't take too long, but class is starting soon leaving no time to dawdle. I wash my face free of lingering traces of makeup and brush my hair, pulling it back into a ponytail. I change into Kira's clothes and gather mine in my arms to toss in my car.

When I open the door, Kira is already dressed in a pair of high waisted shorts with a body suit underneath. She ties a plaid shirt around her waist and fluffs her hair. Somehow in the time I was in the bathroom she's managed to apply makeup. The girl has makeup lying around everywhere so it isn't like she'd need to be in the bathroom to put it on, unlike me who has the bare minimum and definitely no spares.

We head out together and she locks the door to her apartment.

"I still say you should think about moving into your own place," she says the words lightly but with a slight edge. "You're barely home anyway. It seems like if you had your own place, you'd have more time to relax."

As we reach the street, I look at her and shrug. "It's something I've actually been considering these last few weeks," I admit. "With school starting back up and working *and* helping at the studio ... it's a lot. I wanted to go here to be able to stay home, but even this is too much of a commute."

"It is," she agrees, slipping on her sunglasses. "I've been wondering how you're able to keep up. You're superwoman. I know of some apartments available if you decide you want to look."

"I don't know," I hedge. Getting my own place is a scary decision. I'd be on my own, with no help from my parents. While there'd be plenty of perks to being on my own there would be negatives too.

"Looking isn't deciding," she tells me. "At least it would give you an idea of what's available."

"True," I agree with a sigh. "We better get going."

She waves goodbye and we make plans to meet at the cafeteria later.

I pull out of the spot and onto the street. On my way to school, I pass the studio and I can't help but slow down as I do, peering through the front windows like I can see all the way inside to the recording booth in the back.

I say a silent prayer no one knows what we did last night on that couch.

SIXTEEN

Hollis

I made it back to the hotel, managing to avoid my friends, or else they'd already left. I didn't bother to stop to check when I got there. I took the quickest shower of my life, washing Mia's scent off my body. I hated for it to go, but I knew it was necessary. Then changed my clothes before quickly heading out.

Now, my steps are hurried as I walk down the street. I'm late, and I have no doubt the guys know I didn't return to the hotel last night. I only hope they keep their big fat mouths fucking *shut*.

I open the studio door, heading straight for the recording room.

Hayes swivels in his chair at the sound, his eyes narrowed. "You're late."

"Sorry," I say, trying to sound as truly apologetic as possible. "I overslept."

"Mhmm," he hums.

From the couch Cannon glares at me, shaking his head.

Fox is already in the booth and Rush...

"Where's Rush?" I ask.

"We were hoping you knew," Cannon drawls. "You headed off with him last night and neither one of you returned."

I swallow thickly. He's covering for me, he knows I stayed behind with Mia and what most likely happened. He knows, and he's pissed, ready to go at blows with me but never in front of Hayes.

"R-Right," I stutter. "We got separated, though. I went back to the hotel late," I glare, daring him to contradict me, "but I don't know what happened to Rush after."

Cannon sighs, his lip curling in disgust. "You two need to grow the fuck up."

"Amen," Hayes adds.

I sneer. "Don't act so high and mighty," I tell Cannon. "I've caught you with your tongue down a few random throats."

"Keyword there," he sits up straight, "you said *few*."

I sigh and sink on the couch, shutting my mouth. I can't afford to piss off Cannon. Even if he's angry with me I don't think he'd rat me out to Hayes. We'd all be punished then, so I don't risk it. I'm more worried about how it would bother Mia. She loves and respects her dad, his approval is everything, and ... I swallow past the lump in my throat as I realize he'll never approve of me.

Normally, I wouldn't give a shit about some daddy's approval, but this isn't *some dad*. This is Joshua Hayes, badass guitar player, member of one of the biggest bands in the world, and *Mia's* dad.

I want him to like me. I want to be good enough. It's dejecting to know that no matter what I do Hayes will more than likely never like me.

Fuck, I'm screwed.

I can feel Cannon glowering at me but I refuse to look at him.

There's nothing I can do or say here in front of Hayes to not incriminate myself. Cannon's disapproval rolls off him in waves, and I feel like screaming at him *I know I fucked up* ... but I'd be lying. Last night with Mia, I wouldn't take it back for anything.

A half-hour later Rush stumbles in, his hair damp, with a fresh set of clothes.

I try not to laugh, but it's clear we ended up in the exact same situation.

"What'd I miss?" he asks, trying to play off his lateness with humor.

Once more Hayes swivels in the chair, having already told Fox to pause for the moment. Hayes flicks his eyes from Rush in the doorway to me on the couch and back again.

"I want to make something very clear to the two of you—if this happens again, if *any* of you step a fucking *toe* out of line, you won't like the consequences. I'm an easy-going guy for the most part, but you don't want to piss me off, I promise you that." He makes eye contact with each of us then, even Fox in the booth. "I won't lie and say I didn't screw up and screw around too. I goofed off, sure." He shrugs. "But believe me when I say, those are the things you look back and regret. Yeah, it makes for interesting stories, but it's stories to other people and *your* memories. You have to live with the shit you do, no one else. Think before you act."

"Yes, sir," we all mutter.

"Now, can we get back to work?" he asks with a raised brow.

He phrases it as a question, but we all know it's not.

We nod and he swivels back to face the glass, motioning for Fox to start again.

Cannon mutters under his breath, "I'm going to kill you two."

I eye him, and I'll never voice it out loud but with those huge bodybuilder muscles, he could probably crush us both with his pinky finger in a single second.

An hour later Fox is done. He clasps his electric guitar and bends, picking something up from the floor before he exits.

He opens the door, squinting at the wrinkled paper in his hands.

I stare at it, the blood draining from my face.

My song!

"This is fucking good," Fox remarks.

"What is it?" Hayes asks and Fox, fucking Fox, hands it over to him before I can protest.

Hayes reads over the lyrics, and I can't interpret his expression in the reflection of the glass to gauge whether he thinks it's good or terrible.

"Huh," he says, after he's read it through twice, "you write this? It's ... really good."

He's not looking at me, but Cannon, who writes most of our songs. Cannon holds his hand out for it and reads it quickly.

"Not mine, but..." He pauses, looking at me, having recognized my handwriting.

"It's mine," I confess, raising my hand slowly like a kid in school.

All their eyes turn to me and I want to shrivel into a ball and roll away, but fuck if I'm doing that.

Hayes gives me a nod of acknowledgement, surprise in his eyes. "This just might be your song."

We all know he doesn't mean *my* song, but *our* song, the song that everyone will know is The Wild. The song that will live and thrive even when we're all dead and gone.

"Wow," I breathe.

Cannon pats his hand down on my shoulder, the only praise I'll get from him.

"Do you feel comfortable putting this on the album?" Hayes asks me, his gaze steady. He knows from the lyrics, the words I poured my heart and soul into, how personal it is. He knows I might not want it out there for everyone to hear. I appreciate him giving me the choice to say no. My words for myself, my vows to Mia, do I want everyone to hear them? They won't know who it's about, but I will, she will.

"Can I think on it and get back to you?"

He nods. "Sure."

The guys look at me, Cannon's green eyes seeing too much. He knows who those words are for, why I'm hesitating to say yes.

Before his questioning gaze can probe too far, Hayes calls for him to enter the booth. He pushes off the couch and heads inside, grabbing his bass guitar off the wall.

Relief floods through me at not having Cannon breathing down my neck.

Rush plops unceremoniously into the spot vacated by Cannon.

He smirks at me, tilting his head in…

Fuck.

"Kira?" I ask softly, the word only a hush under my breath.

"Yep." He nods, still smirking—and I know the smirk has nothing to do with getting laid.

"Did you see…?" I trail off, letting him fill in the blanks.

"Yep." He nods again, and I want nothing more than to punch the smile off his face. "Enjoy your night?"

"I'm not talking about this," I growl. It has nothing to do with Hayes being in the room—though it is a deterrent. I refuse to talk about Mia with Rush, with *anyone*.

"Really?" He raises a brow and I know then he's baited me on purpose. "Since when?"

"Since now."

―――

Hours later Mia strolls into the studio in a tight pair of jeans hugging her hips and a white shirt with red on the sleeves.

"Coffee," she says, passing the drinks around.

I give her a thankful smile and nod my head.

Act indifferent. Don't show how much you care. You can't get caught.

After the drinks are passed around, she kisses her dad on the cheek and he swings the chair in her direction. "How was your night?"

I stiffen with worry, but Mia doesn't miss a beat.

"It was good. Kira and I watched some Netflix before crashing."

Rush snorts but covers it with a cough.

"You know..." she begins, then hesitates. "I'm starting to think it would be easier to get a place here."

I startle in surprise and then act like I dropped something to cover my reaction.

"Really?" Hayes asks in disbelief. "You haven't said anything to us."

She shrugs. "Kira brought it up this morning and it has me thinking. I go to school here, work here, the studio is here..." She trails off and he nods.

"You know we don't want you to go, but we'll support you either way. If you find a place, I'll pay for it."

Her eyes widen in shock.

"Thanks, Dad, but ... I'd rather pay for it on my own. If I do find a place. If I even want to move out," she adds.

He shrugs. "The offer still stands."

"Why?" she ventures to ask. "You and Mom have always pushed us to be independent, to not rely on your money to solve everything."

"Because," he answers, "you'll always be my baby girl and I want you to be safe. A nicer place downtown can be pricey. I'd rather cover the cost, knowing you're in a good area, than make you pay and be in a shitty rundown, cockroach infested apartment so I'm up all night worrying."

She laughs at that. "Okay, your argument makes sense. I'll consider your offer then."

He tips his head.

She smiles at each of us and leaves the room.

The urge to follow her is strong, strong enough I nearly fall off the couch fighting it.

But I know looking like a desperate puppy in front of her father isn't for the best.

Luckily, my turn to head into the booth comes next, and for the first time I can't help but notice Hayes always times it so I'm in the booth while Mia is here—at least most of the time.

Sneaky bastard.

AFTER A LONG DAY IN THE STUDIO, WE HEAD TO THE HOTEL for the evening. I didn't get much of a chance to talk to Mia in the studio, but since she flashed me a few smiles I think we're okay and she hasn't completely freaked out about last night.

The last thing I want is for her to regret it.

In the suite, we all head to our separate rooms. It's not late yet, so I figure we'll end up watching a movie or playing some video games.

Tearing my shirt over my head, I whirl around when my door opens.

"We need to talk." Cannon eases the door shut behind him, purposely blocking it with his body so I can't try to weasel out and run away from him.

I drop the t-shirt on the bed. "What do you mean?"

"I'm not stupid. I have eyes. So does everyone else. What the fuck are you doing sneaking around with Mia? Are you that determined to throw away everything we've worked for? Do you not care at all? Did you fuck her? Have you *been* fucking her?"

"Don't." I hold a finger up between us, teeth gnashed together. "Don't you fucking talk about her like that."

His eyes widen in surprise. "You like her."

Hands on my hips, I shake my head in defeat. "Yeah, I do."

Cannon crosses his arms over his chest. "Being with her is a huge risk, not just for you, but us too."

"I know," I admit. The last thing I've wanted to do is put my friends, my band, into this predicament.

"Hayes is protective of her, but also pretty blind too because he doesn't think any of us are stupid enough to try anything with her."

I crack a smile, easing up now that I realize he's not as pissed off as he initially was. "So, I'm the stupid one then?"

"Yeah, you are," he says seriously. At least he's not sugar coating it. "You said you like her ... do you mean, you like her for fun? For now?"

"Aw, Dad, are you asking me what my intentions are?" I joke, trying to lighten the mood.

"Just answer the fucking question, Wilder."

"I've never liked a girl the way I like Mia. Does that answer your question?"

He nods once. "Yes. But sneaking around is only going to lead to trouble. For you. For her. For *us*," he emphasizes.

"I know."

He nods again, reaching for the doorknob. "Shower, you smell like shit." No, I don't. He's just being mean. "It's movie night and it's Fox's choice."

"What'd he choose?"

He looks back at me with a smirk. "*Ratatouille.*"

SEVENTEEN

Mia

"I heard you're moving," Noah announces at the dinner table.

The piece of chicken on my fork dangles halfway to my mouth. "Where'd you hear that?"

"I heard Mom and Dad talking about it."

"You're moving?" Adalyn chimes in, eyes wide with excitement. "Can I have your room?"

"No, Addie," I seethe, "you can't have my room. What's wrong with yours?"

"Nothing." She shrugs, fighting a smile. "But I've always wanted to say that."

I shake my head. Siblings are the worst.

"Were you eavesdropping?" Mom turns her deadly gaze to Noah.

He shrugs. "Maybe," he drawls. "My sources say not to confirm."

"Your sources, huh?" I laugh.

"I have spies everywhere," he stage whispers.

"Ah, I see. I'm *thinking* about moving. I haven't even looked at places yet," I tell my siblings. "Don't go getting too excited I might be gone for good."

"Can I move with you?" Noah asks.

"Noah," Mom scolds, her face taut with exasperation. "You are treading on my last nerve."

"What? Living with Mia sounds fun." He blinks innocently.

As the baby of the family, he's always known how to play his cards.

"Sorry, bud." I ruffle his sandy hair and he leans away. "I don't think they allow you to bring cockroaches in."

"Cockroach?" He seethes jokingly. "I'm a damn unicorn."

"Noah!" This time it's Dad scolding him, his voice raised to a yell. "Do not curse in this house—or anywhere," he adds when Mom gives him a look.

"Unicorns probably aren't allowed either. You know, horns and all."

He shakes his head, giving me a small grin.

If I get my own place, I'll miss out on these family moments and my heart strings pull with the thought. I remind myself I can come home any time I want, having my own place won't stop me from making the drive or having my own key.

A few weeks ago, I would've vehemently said I wasn't leaving, but then my dumb ass had to go and sign up for too many classes. Next semester I have less, but it'll still be a lot with work and my time at the studio. I feel like I've barely had a moment to breathe in the last month and I desperately need a break.

"If Mia moves, neither of you are getting her room or moving with her," my mom says. "She was here first."

"Yeah, you two are basically just interlopers," Dad jokes, pushing the broccoli around on his plate. "Why are you even here?"

"Hey," Addie mocks being offended.

"Does this mean Mia is your favorite?" Noah asks jokingly.

I smile at him and pretend to make a halo above my head. "Of course, I'm an angel."

"More like a she-devil," he mutters and I can't help but laugh, thinking Hollis would probably agree with him.

Our parents shake their heads back and forth in unison, exchanging words with a single glance. I swear they have a freakish ability to read each other's minds.

Talk of me moving settles down and after dinner I help my mom clear the table and load the dishwasher.

"What do you think about me possibly moving?"

She closes the dishwasher and pushes the button to start it before leaning her hip against the counter.

"I think it's a good idea, honestly. I've seen how tired you've become, and ... it's not you, sweetie. You're running yourself ragged and you'll end up burning yourself out. It's not healthy. Besides, it's not like you're moving far away. You'll be an hour away and we're in the area a lot anyway, so we'll still see you all the time. You won't even be able to miss us." She smiles, pulling me into a hug. Whispering into my ear she adds, "It's time for you to spread those wings and fly, baby girl."

She's right, I know she is, but it doesn't mean I'm not still scared.

I LAY IN MY BED, SLEEP DESPERATELY NEEDED BUT ELUSIVE.

I pull out my phone, scrolling through my contacts. I hesitate for a single breath before I hit the call button.

"Hey," the smooth voice answers all too quickly before I can chicken out and hang up.

"You weren't sleeping, were you?" I ask, knowing I should've thought of that *before* I rang.

He chuckles warmly. "No. What do you need? Are you okay?" Hollis asks.

"I'm fine," I sigh. "Can't sleep."

"Ah," he breathes. "Same. Is something bothering you? It's not..."

"No, not that," I rush to assure him. "It's thinking about moving, getting my own place—can you tell I hate change? It's my biggest fear, I think."

The sheets ruffle as I roll over onto my side, my phone against my ear and the pillow.

"I think it's natural to fear change."

"You don't," I counter. "If you did you wouldn't be here right now, recording an album."

"It doesn't mean I wasn't afraid to try, or afraid of failure, but I was more afraid of regretting not taking the chance."

"I have to push past this, don't I?"

"Only if you *want* to," his voice is a lovely croon in my ear. "If this is what you truly want, to take this next step in your life, then do it. The fear won't go away, but you have to be stronger than it."

His words steel me. I can do this—and if I look at places and find nothing suitable, I won't move, but if I do? Then, this is happening.

"Thank you," I whisper.

"I didn't do anything."

"Yes, you did. Goodnight, Hollis."

"Night, Mia."

I hang up, setting my phone on the night table, and when I roll back over I'm asleep before I've barely closed my eyes.

AN ENTIRE WEEK PASSES BEFORE I CAN START LOOKING AT places. I don't tell my dad I'm starting to look because I know he'll come along and my mom as well—I want their approval on wherever I decide on, *if* I decide, but this is something I need to do myself.

Although, I invited Hollis along.

I tell myself it's because I want his unbiased opinion. Truthfully, I want to spend time with him not at the studio or sneaking around town. We haven't had a night like the first since, but we have made out a few times.

I can tell the guys either know or suspect something, but they're not talking and don't seem to be judging me. Instead, I find myself becoming closer to all of them— laughing and joking like old friends. Much to Hollis's chagrin they invited me to come out with them tomorrow night for dinner and something else they won't tell me. I warned Hollis if they had a prank up their sleeves, I was punching *him* in the face for it. But even Hollis swears he doesn't know. At least Kira is coming along too, with Rush. I know she'll protect me if there's trouble.

Kira swears there's nothing more between them other than really amazing sex, her words not mine.

Hollis and I walk side by side down the street and to the first rental property.

We meet the landlord outside and he leads us inside and up a rickety set of stairs to a second-floor apartment. We take one step inside the first place and Hollis shakes his head adamantly.

"No. Absolutely not."

I have to agree. It's small, so small the bathroom is practically in the kitchen. I don't even see room for a bed, let alone anything else.

We turn around, saying an apologetic goodbye, before heading to the next one on my list.

After seeing three more places I'm beginning to give up hope.

"This is pointless," I whine to Hollis, exiting yet another building that smelled moldy and I'm certain I saw a mouse tail disappearing around a corner. "If I'm going to live on my own in a decent place, I'm going to have to let my dad help me," I groan.

"Is that such a bad thing?" he inquires.

"No," I frown. "It's not but..." *I wanted to do this on my own*, I finish in my head.

He stops walking and presses a finger to my lips, forcing me to stop too.

"Stop right there," he says. "You're thinking too much. Do you want to move into your own place?"

I nod. "I do," I admit.

"Okay," he lets his finger drop, "then we keep looking. The right place is out there."

His words reassure me and I square my shoulders. He grins at the motion, clearly amused.

"I have two more places on my list for today. If these don't work out, I'll have to search elsewhere."

"One of them is going to work," he says confidently.

We fall into step side by side. My heart stutters when his fingers brush mine. I itch to reach out and grab his hand, to hold it in mine, but I know we can't dare. Not when there are loads of people in this town who know my dad and would unknowingly let something slip.

I look up at Hollis, his strong jaw shadowed with a day's worth of stubble, his floppy hair and eyes hidden behind a pair of sunglasses. Dressed in a pair of jeans that hug his ass and a shirt I'm pretty sure is glued on, he commands the attention of all nearby women. I can't blame them for looking. I would too if I saw him on the street of some random town. There's something about his presence, too, that draws people in. It's some sort of spark I know will help him and his band go far in this world.

I stall at the thought.

Whatever we are, whatever this is, is just starting. It's new, with no definition, but if it continues it could become something. Then what? He won't stay here forever. He'll go back to L.A., to his *real* life, to promoting and concerts, to clubs and other venues, while I'll be here doing what I always do.

I push those thoughts from my mind, refusing to dwell on them now.

Finally, we make it to the next apartment building. It's nicer from the outside, brick, freshly painted door and shutters, even the steps leading to the front are clean as if someone has dusted off leaves and debris.

As we walk up the steps, I feel Hollis's hand press lightly against my waist and I smile to myself.

I open the door and the foyer is lined with old black and white tile. It shines like new even though it's not. There's a door to my left, one straight ahead, and another on the right with a sweeping staircase also on the left leading to the upstairs apartment. I'm sure before this was turned into apartments it was a beautiful, large, family home.

"It's upstairs on the right," I tell Hollis and we begin to climb the stairs. "The landlord said he'd leave the door unlocked for us and he's downstairs in apartment two if we need him."

We reach the landing and I turn to the apartment on the right. There's another beside it, two across, and another on the end. With so many apartments on one level I have a hard time believing it'll be large enough, but we'll see.

I try the door and it's unlocked like the landlord promised.

We step inside and I'm pleasantly surprised by what I find. Original hardwood floors worn with age, but in good shape, cover the floors. There are windows facing the street and an alleyway, which isn't the greatest thing to look at, but it does let in a lot of natural light.

There are exposed brick walls throughout the apartment, and the kitchen and bathroom have been recently remodeled with granite countertops and new cabinets. The bedroom is small, but it has enough room for me to make do.

Hollis follows me through the space, not saying anything, instead letting me think through on my own.

I finally turn toward him and he stops. His black boots nearly touch my sneakers we stand so close.

"I think it's perfect."

He smiles at my words. "You sure?" I love how he

doesn't give me his opinion, not yet, instead wanting to hear what I have to say.

I nod, smiling as I look around once more. "There's room for my bed and stuff, a couch and TV, even a small dining table and chairs set."

"Sounds to me like you're already picturing yourself here."

"I am," I admit with a quiet giggle. "It's a big step."

"It is," he agrees. "If you think it's time, then it is."

I nod, feeling excitement build inside. "It's perfect. It's within walking distance from the studio, close to the restaurants, and I'm only a mile or two from Kira."

He places his hands on my hips, looping his fingers into my jeans to tug me against him. "And don't forget, in close proximity to me." He lowers his head, nipping my ear.

I shiver involuntarily.

A moment later his lips press softly to mine. For a second fear clenches my body, but then I remind myself we're here alone, no one is watching, and I can kiss him back if I want. I wrap my arms around his shoulders, standing on my tiptoes to get closer, and kiss him deeply. Kissing Hollis is different than kissing anyone else I ever have. With him, I feel safe, protected ... cared for. In the past I've always felt used, or as if something wasn't quite right.

He breaks the kiss, tucking a piece of hair behind my ear. His touch is gentle, almost reverent, as his fingers linger against the curve of my cheek.

"Should we find the landlord?" he inquires, backing a step away.

My skin feels chilled from his absence.

I look around again then give him a smile. "Yeah."

An hour later, I have a signed contract and the place is mine. I'm free to move in any time next week.

Hollis and I step outside. The sun is already setting, painting the old buildings in a golden orange hue.

I squeak when Hollis grabs my hand and tugs me down into the alley between my new home and the building next door.

"What are you doing?"

A moment later I get my answer when he cages me against the brick exterior, one hand on each side of my head, and kisses me deeply.

"Mmm," I moan, my hands flat on his firm chest.

His hands find my legs and he tugs them up around his waist to wrap around his hips.

His mouth moves over mine like we're writing lyrics to our own song. One only we can sing.

His tongue brushes mine and I gasp, grasping his shirt in my hands and tugging him impossibly closer.

The wall is rough against my back but I don't mind.

I've never been kissed like this before and I don't plan on asking him to stop any time soon. I feel as if he's devouring little bits of my soul, taking them and making them his before placing them back inside.

My hands glide up his chest to tug on the strands of his hair at the base of his neck. I don't normally dig the shaggy unkempt look but on Hollis it works. He makes rumpled and bedraggled look runway worthy.

It's entirely unfair someone can look so hot without even trying. I wake up and look like a demon.

He bites my bottom lip and I gasp, all thoughts disappearing. It's like he knew where my thoughts had strayed and decided he needed my focus returned solely to him.

I don't know how long we're in the alley kissing, but finally he releases me. We're both breathless. My lips feel swollen and bruised. I don't mind one bit.

"Do you have to go home yet?" he asks, his voice low and husky. His eyes fall to my lips and he rubs his thumb against them. They're tender, but I don't mind his touch.

I shake my head.

He cracks a small smile. "Come to the hotel with me."

"But the guys..." I hesitate.

"They already know about you. The nosy bastards figured it out without me saying a word." I can tell he's irritated by this fact, but they're also his best friends so he can laugh about it.

"I don't know..."

"We can watch a movie or something. Nothing more," he explains, seeing where my mind is going. "We can order a pizza too—or whatever you want from room service."

I think a moment longer before nodding. I'm not ready to go home yet. Spending more time with Hollis sounds nice. As much as I love kissing him, I enjoy hanging out with him even more, which shocks me. I never expected to like him. From the moment he walked out of my bathroom in nothing but a towel I'd made up my mind to hate him.

But the Hollis I know is impossible to hate.

We walk back to the hotel, too worried to hold hands, but close enough our fingers graze often. Some people, mostly college girls, eye him up and down. He's hot, so it's expected, but word has also gotten around about the new band in town recording their album. While most people in this town are over it and don't care, The Wild is like a new shiny toy to be played with and admired.

I don't know how famous people do it—enjoy being gawked at like a specimen under a microscope. Heck, even I've been gawked at and had paparazzi follow me even though I'm literally the most boring person on the planet. I don't understand the obsession people have with celebrities, wanting to know every single detail about their lives, where they go, who their friends are, what they eat—give them a break and room to breathe. I saw a pap follow my dad into a public restroom once—he stormed out a second later and gave management a mouthful.

Hollis and I reach the hotel and ride up in the elevator together careful to stand apart and not say a word.

When he opens the door to their suite my mouth falls open.

"Whoa, this place is cool."

Fox's head whips over in our direction from the couch when he hears my voice.

"Yo, Mia, what are you doing here?"

"Hollis invited me for pizza and a movie."

"Sweet—as long as it's not a chick flick."

I fake a yawn. "Pass."

"Can I keep you?" Fox jokes, making a kissy face at me.

Rush strides out of a room then in only a towel. As he passes Fox, he whips it off and smacks him with it.

Hollis slaps his hands over my eyes, but it's too late, I already got an eyeful.

"Pretty sure she's already taken dude."

"Rush," Hollis hisses. "cover up, man."

"What? Afraid she'll see what I'm packing and come running?"

"It was impressive," I admit with a laugh.

Hollis growls and mutters, "Don't make me remind you what's really impressive."

I give him a sly smile as he lowers his hands. "I don't know, sounds enjoyable."

His eyes darken with desire.

"Not here," Cannon warns coming into the room.

"Yeah, down boy," I tell Hollis. "I'm here for a movie. If you don't feed me I might bite."

He lowers his head and whispers in my ear, "I wouldn't mind."

I can't help but smile. Patting him on the chest, I say, "Now go order my pizza, peasant."

All three of the other guys bust out laughing. "Peasant? More like he's your bitch," Fox chortles.

Hollis shakes his head, but his lips quirk in amusement. "What kind of pizza do you want?"

"Pepperoni."

"A pepperoni pizza for milady coming right up," he says bowing theatrically before slipping away.

I sit down on the couch beside Fox and swipe the remote from him.

"No chick flicks," Rush warns coming out of his room to join us. At least he's wearing pants now.

"What is it with you guys and chick flicks?" I mutter. "Afraid a little kissing and romance will make your dick shrivel up and die?"

"They're boring," Rush defends.

"Mhmm," I hum. "Keep telling yourself that."

"Don't listen to him," Cannon speaks up. "He's bitching because he cried at *Titanic*."

"It was *one* tear," Rush defends in mock anger. "And Jack shouldn't have died. He was the best character in the whole damn movie."

Cannon smirks at him as Rush sits on my other side.

I log into my Netflix account. "We're going to watch my favorite movie of all time," I warn them.

"If Reese Witherspoon is in it giving legal advice I'm out," Rush warns, raising his hands.

I snort. "Nope."

I click the movie and the guys all breathe a collective sigh of relief. Pussies.

"Jurassic Park is your favorite movie?" Fox asks, sounding surprised.

"Dinosaurs and Jeff Goldblum ... um yeah, it's my favorite movie."

"You have a crush on Jeff Goldblum?" Rush asks with amusement.

"Duh, have you seen him? Or listened to him speak? He could read me the dictionary and I'd happily sit there and listen."

Rush chuckles. "How does Hollis feel about that?"

"How do I feel about what?" Hollis asks, stepping back into the room. He gets a disgruntled look when he sees Fox and Rush beside me, but then shakes his head as a determined smile takes over his face.

He strides over to me and I squeal as he picks me up and sits down with me in his lap.

"Mia, here, has a crush on Jeff Goldblum," Fox explains.

"Really?" he asks, eyeing me with surprise.

"Why is this shocking?"

"I don't know," Hollis admits. "I guess it's unexpected is all."

"Can we watch the movie now?"

"Wait, we need popcorn," Cannon says in his gruff voice, hopping up.

I don't know why but I'm still always surprised when he opens his mouth. He's broody and quiet all the time. When he shows any bit of enthusiasm for something it takes me by surprise.

As the movie begins Cannon pops popcorn in the suite's kitchen making the room smell like buttery goodness.

"I can't believe you guys have popcorn here," I mutter to Hollis.

He chuckles, the sound rumbling against my back as he holds me tight. "Only because Cannon is a mother hen and went to the grocery store the day after we got here to make sure we had everything we needed."

"Better to be a mother hen than to starve," Cannon defends from the kitchen.

"Shh, I want to watch the movie."

Hollis pinches my side and whispers in my ear, "You started it."

We're all sucked into the movie and startle when the phone rings—the front desk letting us know the pizza is here, since the delivery guy isn't allowed on this level.

"I'll go get it," Hollis says, lifting me off his lap and depositing me back onto the couch.

He slips out, the door clicking shut behind him.

It feels like he's gone forever, but he finally returns with four boxes of pizza. He lays them on the coffee table with the lids open and we all grab a slice of the one we want.

Once again, he picks me up and sits me in his lap.

Between the pizza and the movie, I find myself fighting to not fall asleep.

Fox notices and grabs a blanket holding it out to me. I drape it over myself and therefore Hollis. If he's hot he doesn't complain.

I have to admit, I've enjoyed hanging out with the guys. It's nice to do something outside of the studio, and now I'm even more curious for what they have planned tomorrow.

Hollis begins to comb his fingers through my hair and I warn softly, "You're going to make me fall asleep."

"Then go to sleep," he says huskily.

"I have to drive home."

His lips find my ear. "Stay here."

"You know I can't."

"Say you were at Kira's again," he pleads.

I find myself torn between doing what I want and what I should do.

"Fine," I agree, giving in at last.

I feel his smile rather than see it.

EIGHTEEN

Hollis

I carry a half-asleep Mia to my room and give her one of my shirts to change into for the night. She gives me a nod of thanks before I slip out of the room. I'd love to stay for the show, but I saw the way the guys were eyeing me and know I have to talk to them.

I make my way to where they're sitting in the suite's living room. I remain standing, because it makes me feel better.

"Are you sure about this, man?" Cannon asks. "Mia's a cool girl. We like her," the other guys nod in agreement.

But she's Hayes's daughter," Fox pipes in. "You could screw this whole thing up."

I want to get defensive and angry, to rage at them, but I know it's the wrong reaction to have.

"I'm sorry," I say, meaning it. "Mia is ... I like the way I feel when I'm with her. I feel like me, a me I forgot even existed. I've let the little bit of fame we've received go to my head. She brings me back to reality, grounds me. I tried to stay away, to fight what I felt, because I knew the position I could put us in if I pursued anything with her, but fighting it became impossible. For both of us. I'm not asking for your approval, but I am asking you to respect my actions. I'm doing this because I care about her, not because I'm being reckless."

Cannon's jaw is clenched but he sighs and says, "We've noticed the difference in you. I didn't think it was possible but she's mellowed you out."

"I think we've all mellowed out," I retort.

Fox snorts. "There's not much trouble to get into in this small town."

I crack a smile. "It's never stopped us before."

"I've definitely *not* mellowed out," Rush smirks.

I glance at him. "Last I checked you were only sleeping with one girl. I think it counts as mellowed out."

He looks shocked, as if just now realizing he's only been with Kira since we got here.

Cannon looks at me, leaning forward with his hands clasped. "We can't ask you not to see her, but fuck, man, be careful. If you get a wandering eye cut her loose immediately."

My jaw snaps closed with an audible click. I know I

deserve him saying that. I've jumped from girl to girl the last few years, but it still irks me because Mia is different and I'm different with her. But it seems like that counts for nothing, not when there's more proof of my manwhore behavior.

"You don't need to worry about that," I finally say.

He raises his hands innocently. "I'm not trying to piss you off."

"I know," I admit. "But don't talk about her like she's just another girl I'm going to grow bored of. She's not. She never was."

Cannon shrugs. "Good. It's about time you grew serious. Ever since she came into the picture you've been more focused on music too, and in my book that's a good thing." He stands and stretches. "Now, if you don't mind, I'm going to bed."

He leaves and I look at the other two. "Do you have anything to say?"

Fox tilts his head. "She's a nice girl. Don't fuck this up. I'm not saying that because she's Hayes's daughter, but because she's too good to be strung along by you. If you care about her, keep proving it."

I'm irritated by his words, but again I know I deserve them. I deserve worse.

Rush leans back in his chair. "You know I never judge."

With the conversation finished I slip back into my room.

I pause, leaning my back against the closed door.

Across from me, sprawled beneath the crisp white sheets of the king size bed is the most beautiful woman in the world. She lies on her stomach, her arms wrapped around the pillow beneath her head, with her red hair billowed in a wild torrent of flame. My too large shirt falls haphazardly off one of her slender pale shoulders. Her lips are parted with sleep, her chest rising and falling softly with each breath. She looks comfortable, and too good, too kind, to be in my bed.

I take off my boots and hook my thumbs in the back of my shirt, yanking it off. I let my jeans fall on the floor and get in bed.

I roll over, facing Mia. She looks impossibly peaceful. I wish the dream world could claim me so easily.

My mind however, decides to dwell on things I shouldn't. I can't help but wonder if by caring about Mia, I've inadvertently set myself up for failure, destined to fuck this up and become a miserable bastard once more.

If I ever break her heart, I'll never forgive myself.

I'M STIRRED FROM SLEEP BY THE FEEL OF LIPS ON MY NECK.

This is nothing new.

The lips trail over my chest and then back up, sweeping over my cheek.

"Wake up, sleepy head," a voice murmurs.

I stifle a yawn, forcing my tired eyes open. I don't know when I finally fell asleep last night.

Impossibly blue eyes meet mine. "There you are," Mia breathes.

Mia.

I give her a small smile. "Sleep well?"

She nods, climbing into my lap to straddle me.

My eyes widen in shock. "Are you wearing panties?"

She gives me a coy smile. "No."

"Fuck," I groan, fingers digging into the skin of her thighs. "You're trying to kill me, I know it."

Her lips tilt up on one corner. "Sounds tempting, but I think you're more useful alive." She winks and my eyes go wide as her hand slips beneath my boxer-briefs.

This Mia is not something I'm used to.

"Do the mornings make you horny or something?" I choke out as her hand wraps around me.

She bites her lip and shrugs. "Maybe, but we haven't been alone in a while and..." she trails off.

"I know," I breathe.

She lowers her head and kisses me. She sucks my bottom lip between hers and lets go.

Fuck, I'm not sure I can handle this version of Mia. She's a siren, a temptress, and I'm ensnared in her web.

My t-shirt dangles loosely on her small frame and with her hair a tangled mess I swear she's the most beautiful thing my eyes have ever beheld. I could write a million songs about her and I've never had the desire to do that before. I thought one song would be enough. I've been sorely mistaken. Nothing, no amount of words in the entire universe, in any language, spoken in any tongue, is enough to encompass everything Mia is.

"We shouldn't do this," I warn. The words grate on my throat as I reluctantly speak them because I very much want this. "The guys—"

"I'll be quiet," she promises.

I narrow my eyes. "Are you challenging me?"

She bites her plump bottom lip, her eyes sparkling. "Not at all, Mr. Wilder."

My hands find her waist, my fingers digging into her skin as I fight to calm myself. With a few words she manages to undo my control and it's not fair.

In one smooth movement I have her flipped over on her back as I hover above her.

"Miss Hayes," I hum, "you are very, *very* dangerous."

She grins and leans up to whisper, "I know."

I kiss her, slipping my hands beneath the shirt, pushing it up her body. She lifts her arms for me to remove it, but instead I tie it around her hands. She narrows her eyes and pouts.

"You might think you have the control here, but I do, always," I warn her with a stern growl before I kiss her.

She melts into my kiss, her body like liquid.

I palm one of her breasts, using my other hand to keep myself braced above her.

Her body rises against my hand, her back curving above the mattress.

Her creamy skin looks even lighter against my tanned

hand—her skin impossibly soft against the roughness of mine.

We're opposites in every way—I'm hard to her soft, loud to her quiet, dangerous to her safe—but we click like two puzzle pieces snapping together, there's no denying it.

"I think you like it when I can't use my hands," she breathes, her voice no more than a husk of what it normally is.

"Only because you threaten to make me lose control before I'm ready and I *always* plan to take my time with you," I vow.

Her breath stutters out of her in a gasp. I grin as I kiss her. I love shocking her.

Kissing the shell of her ear I confess, "You were meant to be worshipped." *By me,* I leave unspoken.

Her impossibly blue eyes meet mine and they seem to read what I didn't say and say *I know* back.

I take her chin between my thumb and forefinger. I tilt her head up, lowering my mouth over hers. The kiss is soft, slow, it's us taking our time memorizing the feel of one another. It's one hundred percent *real* and it rocks me to my core.

I never knew it could be like this, never *wanted* it like this, but with Mia I can have it no other way. She isn't someone I want to fuck and kick out of my bed to never see again. She's someone I want to wake up to every day, who I want to hold, to cherish. A part of me is terrified if I step outside of this bubble I'll go right back to my manwhoring asshole ways, but I have to believe I'm strong enough to not fall into that dangerous trap again. Whatever this connection is between us, it can't be broken easily.

Her hands fight against the confines of the t-shirt, but I'm not finished with her yet.

I told her she was meant to be worshipped and I meant it.

I've been a selfish lover in the past, only caring about my own pleasure, but not with Mia. With her, I need to make sure she's enjoying herself. I can't be a selfish bastard anymore.

I have to be better.

Not only in bed, but a better person all around.

Someone worthy of the light Mia possesses.

I tear my lips from hers and she whimpers, quieting when I kiss my way down the elegant arch of her neck. I suck the skin where her neck meets her shoulder. It'll probably leave a mark, and I growl with satisfaction at the thought of my brand left on her unblemished skin.

Moving lower I kiss her breasts, swirling my tongue around each pert pink nipple.

Her back arches off the bed and I smile against the satin of her skin.

I trail my lips down her stomach and a tiny gasp releases from that gorgeous mouth when my tongue reaches her center. I grin against her.

Hazy blue eyes blink down at me, her breasts straining as she inhales harshly. Her pale skin is slightly damp with perspiration and her lips tremble as she struggles to stay quiet.

I slide my fingers into her pussy and her body clenches around them.

"Hollis," my name a prayer on her swollen lips.

Watching her lose control could quickly become my new addiction.

Her fingers wiggle and I know she longs for nothing more than to touch me. I finally have mercy on her and move up her body, untying the fabric from around her wrists. I growl in her ear. "Next time I'm handcuffing you."

She moans and I can't help but smirk.

"And if you fight me on it," I add in a whisper, "I'll spank you."

She blinks owlish blue eyes up at me. "What if I want you to do it anyway?"

"Do what, Mia?" I ask in a stern tone, wanting to make her say it.

"Spank me," she whispers, the words barely audible.

"Where have you been all my life?" The words tumble out of my mouth.

She bites her plump bottom lip, red and swollen from kissing, and says like the fucking siren she is, "Waiting for you."

I can't help myself, I devour her lips like I'm starving and she's my only form of sustenance. Her hands delve into my hair, tugging and pulling, before her nails rake down my back leaving their mark.

I don't mind. Mia can mark me in any way she wants. I welcome it. I want her mark on me, her scent clinging to my skin for days after.

Her hand slides down my abs and pushes my boxer-briefs down my hips. I get rid of them completely and then her hand is on me, sliding up and down slowly, her thumb rolling over the tip as she looks up at me batting her eyes innocently.

I growl into her ear, "You pretend to be innocent, but I see you, I know you. Like calls to like."

She smirks, the slightest tilt of her lips. "Maybe I've been waiting for you. You make me feel safe."

"Fuck," I gasp.

There's nothing overtly sexy about her words but hearing her say she feels safe with me is everything I never knew I needed.

"My turn," she purrs, pushing me off her to roll over.

Her eyes connect with mine as she strokes me and then she lowers her delicious mouth to my cock. My eyes roll back in my head and I reach down, holding her hair back to watch. She doesn't look back up at me, instead giving all her attention to my dick.

"Jesus Christ," I curse, fighting not to make noise.

I've never cared about bothering my friends with my exploits before, but I'll be damned if they hear any of this. Mia is mine, and I won't have them giving me knowing smirks or picturing her naked. I might punch one of them. I wouldn't be sorry either.

I tug on her hair, and she hisses between her teeth, but doesn't ask me to stop.

A little bite of pain always leads to more pleasure in my experience.

When I can take no more, I pull on her hair again until her mouth lets me go with a pop.

"I'm going to fuck you now, and if you try to scream, I'll gag you."

Her eyes sparkle and her lips lift in a coy smile.

Fucking temptress.

I grab a condom, rolling it on and give myself a few hard pulls. She watches all of my movements, never taking her eyes off me.

"Do you like watching me touch myself?" I ask in a husky voice.

She bites her lip, those blue eyes of her eyes giving me the answer I need.

I grab her hips and yank her toward the end of the bed.

Leaning over her body I remind her with a whisper, "You scream, I gag you. Understood?"

She nods.

In one smooth movement I'm inside her and I literally sigh in relief. It's been torture waiting to sink into her warm pussy.

Her lips part with a breath and I can't help but wonder if she's feeling the same.

"Harder," she begs, and I curse under my breath.

This girl will be my undoing.

I oblige her, more than happy to do so.

She whimpers and presses a hand over her mouth to stifle any noise she makes.

I want to tell her it won't be enough when I make her scream, but I can't find the words to speak. I can feel the tendons in my neck sticking out as I fight to keep myself quiet too. I feel like a teenager again, struggling not to get caught. There's something exciting about it—the desperation to stay quiet.

I lower my head to the crook of her neck, pressing my lips to her sweat dampened skin. We'll both need a shower after this and if she even thinks for one second, I'm letting her shower alone she's sorely mistaken.

"H-Hollis," she pants, her nails raking down my chest. "I-I'm—"

"Fall baby," I breathe. "I'll catch you."

Her eyes nearly roll back into her head as she falls over the edge into blissful pleasure. Her tight pussy squeezes my cock and with a groan I follow her over, helpless to stop it.

"Mia," I exhale against her skin, kissing her collarbone.

"I know," she, brushes her fingers through my hair. "I know," she repeats.

I pull out of her, getting rid of the condom. I then lay back down beside her, both of us struggling to regain our breath.

I recover first and haul her naked body over my shoulder.

"Hollis," she hisses. "What are you doing?"

I smack her bare ass and she jolts. "Washing your sexy body, that's what I'm going to do," I warn her, setting her down in the bathroom.

She watches as I turn the shower on, letting it warm, before I pull her inside. I don't have any fancy smelly girly shit, so she'll have to make do with my soap—which might undo me, knowing she's going to smell like me all fucking day.

I watch the water sluice over her breasts and she smirks.

"Like what you see, Wilder?"

I force my eyes to meet hers. "You know I do."

She wraps her arms around my shoulders, standing on her tiptoes.

"I've never had shower sex," she confesses. "Care to show me how it's done?"

My body roars to life once more at her words. "You fucking bet."

MY LEG BOUNCES RESTLESSLY IN THE STUDIO AND I CHEW ON the side of my nail. I'm never like this, but replaying every moment between Mia and me this morning has me on edge considering her father is in the same room as I am. If he knew what I'd done to her ... I'd be a dead man right now.

Beside me Rush bumps my leg with his and grinds out, "Stop looking like a guilty motherfucker, *please*. You're going to get us all in trouble."

I let my finger drop from my mouth. I know he's right, and if Rush—Rush who's the biggest manwhore of all of us—is calling me out, then I know I look bad.

This feeling of guilt is strange for me. All of this is new for me and I don't know how to handle it yet.

Rush gives me a look and then eyes my restless leg. I groan and force it to stop bouncing—not an easy task might I add.

At least Hayes is distracted enough not to notice my odd behavior since Cannon is in the recording booth laying down some bass guitar.

He nods his head along, tweaking things on the board, muttering to himself. If my thoughts weren't so distracted by Mia, it would be entertaining to watch. He gets so in the zone nothing else exists.

"Chill," Rush reminds me, and I curse silently in my head when I realize my leg is moving yet again. I put my hand over it, literally holding it down.

Pathetic.

The door to the studio opens and like a fucking dog waiting for its master my head whips in that direction, a smile already lighting my face as I expect Mia, but instead my mouth falls open in shock as the other three members of Willow Creek stroll in like musical gods.

"Holy shit," Rush mutters beside me.

We've never met the rest of Hayes's band before. We know *of* them, but we've never actually met them in person.

In the front is Maddox, wearing a shirt with a printed hedgehog on it—and if the rumors are true, he's hiding a live one somewhere on his person—and in his back pocket, his ever-present drumsticks. I don't know what it is about drummers that they refuse to go anywhere without them—Rush himself always has a set with him.

Next through the door is Ezra, his black curly hair hanging past his ears and his eyes crinkled with smile lines. He's the bass guitar player for their band and he stops, watching Cannon in the booth, arms crossed over his chest and his head moving to the music.

Pushing his way into the room behind Ezra is their singer Mathias, Maddox's identical twin. He wears a perpetual frown—having been dubbed the *moody bastard* by the media. I've always thought there was more to him than the media portrays—something haunting in his gray eyes like a man who's weathered a nasty storm, seen things no one else should.

Hayes holds up a hand for Cannon to take a break and swivels in his chair toward his bandmates.

"What brings you guys here?" he asks, crossing his hands behind his head.

Maddox tilts his head. "Thought we'd come check on our replacements—see how they're fairing."

Mathias snorts. "No one can replace us. We're the best for a reason."

Maddox shrugs. "True."

Hayes shakes his head. "This is Cannon in the booth, Hollis, Rush, and Fox." He points us all out.

Cannon steps out of the enclosed room, not wanting to be left out, I'm sure.

"What have you got so far?" Ezra asks, eyeing all the controls and instruments.

Hayes pushes a few buttons and one of the songs we've almost completed begins to play.

The three guys listen, their faces betraying nothing.

"Not bad," Ezra says when it ends.

"It'll do well," Maddox adds.

"It was okay," Mathias mutters, and coming from him that sounds like a glowing endorsement to me.

"Still think I'm crazy?" Hayes asks with a smirk.

Mathias snorts. "You've always been crazy—this changes nothing."

"Crazy," Maddox agrees. "But maybe not totally insane."

Hayes shrugs, crossing his hands behind his head. "I'll take it. You guys gonna hang for a while?"

"Why not?" Mathias asks, crossing his arms over his chest. "Let's see what you newbies got," he challenges, eyeing each of us.

"I've never felt so intimidated in my entire life," Rush mutters under his breath. "I think I might piss myself."

We pull more chairs in from other parts of the studio so there's enough seating for all of us. It certainly gets crowded in the small room, hot too, but no one complains—it'd be suicide when these guys are who they are. Any advice they deem to give us could be invaluable.

Cannon heads back into the booth, and I can tell even the big guy is shaken by the appearance of Willow Creek. Fuck, these guys are our idols—we've looked up to them practically our whole lives—admired their music, their drive, everything.

The room is quiet while Cannon plays, I think the three of us are afraid to speak—plus if we do speak, Mathias is likely to kill us with a glance. The guy has this deadly edge to him. He's the complete opposite of his identical twin who bounces in his seat like he couldn't keep still if his life depended on it.

Having the guys there definitely makes for an interesting recording session—we screw up more than usual but listen carefully to their advice. After all, having all four guys in the room is a rarity we have to appreciate. Even Mathias grunts some advice to me about controlling my pitch so I don't overdo it and strain my vocal cords.

I don't even realize how late it's become until Mia shows up with Kira, both dressed casually for our evening out. I have no idea what my friends have planned—they refused to tell me. They didn't want me to spill the beans to Mia.

"Hey, Dad," Mia chimes, bending to kiss Hayes on the cheek. She then greets the other three guys with hugs and hellos.

"So, you found a place?" Hayes asks her. "I got the pictures you sent. It looks nice."

"Yep." She nods stepping aside and shoving her hands in the back pockets of her jeans. I know her well enough to see it's a nervous gesture. "I put the deposit down. All that's left is to get some furniture and move in." She lets out a breath. I know a part of her is still questioning whether she's doing the right thing by getting a place of her own. In the end she'll see it's for the best. She's been stretching herself too thin for too long driving back and forth—I admire her love for her family that kept her staying an hour away.

"We'll get it taken care of," her dad assures her in a calming tone. "What are you doing here, Kira?" he asks Mia's dark-haired friend.

"Mia and I are hanging out tonight," she tells him, pointedly leaving out the part where the four of us are involved as well.

"Ah, well have fun. Don't get in too much trouble," he warns Mia with a laugh.

"Never do," she laughs back, but then her eyes meet mine and I swear she winks.

I nearly groan as my mind flies back to the details of this morning. It was all I could think about until Maddox, Mathias, and Ezra showed up distracting me.

Time feels like it's passing in slow motion as we wrap up and head out. The girls pile into Mia's car and head off —the plan is for them to circle back to the hotel's parking garage. That way we can all ride together, but with her dad and the others lingering around we have to make it look like we're not hanging out.

The guys and I walk down the sidewalk toward the hotel. For some odd reason I feel nervous—it's dumb, I've hung out with Mia plenty and this is hardly a date.

I don't understand how this one girl has me entirely unwound, but it's not an entirely unpleasant feeling.

The guys and I stroll into the garage and find the girls waiting for us, leaning against Mia's little red car.

Rush goes up to Kira, putting his hands on her ass and pulling her into an X-rated kiss.

Mia shakes her head, laughter playing on her lips as she looks at me. I fight a smile, questioning whether I should go up to her or stay where I am. I'm not good at this part. I've never *done* this part before.

"Don't be a dick, man," Cannon mutters, pushing me forward. I nearly stumble over my own two feet like a moron.

Recovering, I stride up to Mia.

She tilts her head back to look up at me. "Any hint as to what we're up to yet?"

"None," I sigh.

"All I can say is if there are strippers involved, I'm out." She holds up her hands, laughter in her eyes.

"I doubt there are strippers."

She raises a brow.

"Okay, there's a chance there are strippers."

She laughs, shaking her head, and I don't know whether to love or hate the way her laugh makes me feel.

Cannon motions for us to pile into his Land Rover. Somehow Mia and I end up in the very back. My legs are squished, but it's not entirely unfortunate since she ends up plastered to my side. Her soft curves press into the hard planes of my muscles and it makes me smile. Opposites in every way, and yet we fit.

The drive takes at least an hour before Cannon parks at some golf place. How on earth the guys found this is beyond me.

I groan in relief when I stand on solid ground again and can stretch my legs. They're stiff from being in one position for too long.

"So ... we're playing golf?" Mia asks, blinking up at the lit sign.

Fox shrugs, leaning against the side of the black SUV. "Golf, food, booze, what more could you ask for?"

"Hot chicks," Rush interjects, "but Hollis and I got that part covered." He flicks his finger from Kira to Mia. "Unfortunately, that leaves the two of you alone—too bad, so sad."

Cannon pulls out a cigarette, placing it between his lips. "If I want a girl, I'll find one."

"Maybe you should. You're getting too grumpy, Grandpa. I think your joystick needs a rub down."

Cannon gives Rush the finger and I stifle a laugh.

Mia shakes her head and mutters, "Boys."

"Offended princess?" I joke.

She chokes. "Hardly. I've heard much worse. I grew up on a tour bus, remember?"

"I bet you heard some things then." Suddenly I pale. "Did anyone ever—"

"God no—they knew better than to do that. My dad would've killed them and smiled while doing it."

I reach out to her, unable to stop myself, and wrap a red curl around my finger. Her breath stutters, her eyes flicking from my finger to my face, her lips slightly parted.

"I don't like the idea of anyone touching you," I admit. "Not like that."

"My body is mine to do with as I please," she says, shoulders squared. Ever the fighter, but she doesn't back away from me.

"I know—but you deserve to be worshipped not used."

She gasps slightly at that, almost like my words have hit something in her.

The others begin heading inside the building, but I don't want to move. I want to stay right here, in this parking lot with her, in this moment where I can feel something shifting.

Even if she walked away from me right now, never spoke to me again, I wouldn't be the same person I was before.

She reawakened a part of me I lost sight of.

Now, having it back, I won't let go again—I only hope I get to hold on to her too.

I stand there, wondering whether I should reach for her hand or do something, like a nervous teenage boy all over again.

She saves me from doing something stupid by pointing over her shoulder. "We should go in."

"Yeah—yeah, right."

We walk side by side into the building. The others are waiting, someone having already paid, and we head to a bay on the top level.

Fox, bouncing on the balls of his feet, starts entering everyone's names into the system.

"What is this?" Mia asks, taking a seat on the couch

beside Kira and Rush—I take the empty spot next to her. "Like bowling but golf?"

"Yep," Rush says, stretching his arm behind Kira. "Prepare to go down Little Hayes."

"Little Hayes?" she snorts, shaking her head. "Surely you can come up with a better nickname than that?"

"Eh, I like it and Red, too."

"Done," Fox announces.

"I need a drink first," Rush blurts, looking around to order. "How the fuck do you place an order here? The computer? A waitress?"

"You're asking us?" Kira laughs. "You brought us here."

"Fuck," he groans. "I'll be back. No one take my turn. I'm winning."

He eyes each of us before he heads off to ask someone.

"I'm first anyway." Fox grabs a golf club and lines up to play.

I've never played golf on a golf course, or done anything like this, so I'm sure I'll make a huge fool of myself.

Fox makes a big deal of testing his swing and God knows what else before he finally hits the damn ball. It soars up and away and when it lands it's pretty fucking far away. He turns to us and bows. "That's how it's done." He points at me. "Your turn."

I stand and shake my head.

"Good luck," Mia says with a smile. She sticks her tongue out slightly and rolls her eyes as if to say this is going to get crazy.

If I know my friends, which I do, it's not going to be crazy—it'll be insane.

We're a competitive bunch.

I take my turn, cursing when the ball doesn't get anywhere close to the distance of Fox's. Fox chortles from the couch, clutching his stomach as he points and laughs.

"Asshole." I give him a shove as I pass him on my way to sit on the opposite side.

"An asshole who's going to beat you."

Next up is Cannon who does as abysmally as me. I feel a little better to not be the only one who sucks at this.

Rush, now back from getting beer for everyone, comes the closest to Fox's range, Kira squeals and barely hits the ball, and then it's Mia's turn.

She stands up, her jeans hugging her ass. She smiles at me over her shoulder and winks.

She grabs the golf club and stands to take her turn. She adjusts her stance, takes a few practice swings, and then hits the ball.

It goes up, up, up and—"I believe I'm winning now," she says to Fox before taking a dramatic bow.

I sit, open-mouthed, wondering what I witnessed.

Mia plops down beside me and I turn accusing eyes in her direction. "You've done this before," I state.

She shrugs. "I'm basically a pro at mini-golf."

"This isn't mini-golf."

She laughs. "My dad golfs some—I was the only one of us kids to take an interest in it so when he went, he'd usually take me. I got good at it."

"How good?" I pry.

She presses her lips together to hold back her laughter as Fox takes his second turn, mumbling under his breath.

"I was the only girl on the golf team in high school."

"You golf, do jiu-jitsu," I tick off on my fingers, "anything else I should know about you?"

"If I'm angry throw Reese's cups at me and walk away slowly."

"Noted."

Fox throws his club down and storms back to the couch, picking up his beer.

"He's a sore loser," I tell Mia.

"I can tell," she says in an amused tone.

I take my turn, doing better than last time, but it's clear this game is between Mia and Fox.

I sit back down and grab a beer. Appetizers are brought out and I dig into those too. Food, alcohol, and the prettiest girl at my side almost makes up for not being good at this.

Luckily, I'm highly talented when it comes to *important* things.

Kira takes her turn and this time Rush helps her—and by helps her, I mean he makes sure to press his crotch into her ass and feel her up.

Beside me Mia shakes her head and mutters, "Those two are perfect for each other." She takes a sip of beer and glances at me. "They're two of a kind."

"Really?" I ask.

"Rush is a total manwhore and Kira is a self-proclaimed womanwhore. Honestly this is the longest I've ever seen her use the same guy. He must be pretty great in bed."

"Not as good as me," I mutter.

She raises a brow, stifling a laugh. "I didn't know you went both ways."

"Not what I meant," I grumble.

She laughs. "That's how it sounded."

"You know what I meant," I snap.

"I do, but torturing you is way too much fun."

"You're so mean to me," I tease. "I'm wounded. Truly."

"Get used to it."

I could get *too* used to it and that's what scares the shit out of me. I could get used to her teasing, to the feel of her hand in mine, to waking up to her every day. I can't wrap my head around what it is about her that has me hooked, but I think it's not just one big thing but a million little ones.

NINETEEN

Mia

"I can't believe my dad conned you guys into helping," I hiss to Hollis as we carry boxes up the steps to my new apartment.

It's taken me three weeks to get everything I need and be ready to move in.

In that time, I've spent more time with Hollis in his hotel suite than I'd care to admit. But he makes my toes curl and I find myself craving him more and more.

When he whispered in my ear this morning that he was thoroughly going to enjoy christening every inch of my apartment ... I might've shown him exactly how much I was looking forward to it.

Hollis gives a gruff laugh. "He said our sorry asses

needed to do something decent—apparently that means not recording but building furniture and carrying boxes. What's in this, by the way? It's really fucking heavy."

"Books," I answer.

"Books?" he repeats as we reach the landing. "Do you need so many?"

"Knowledge is power. Also, they make excellent weapons when they're heavy enough, you might want to watch your head if you piss me off," I say sassily and bypass him into the apartment.

My dad and Cannon are putting together a stand for the TV while Fox and Rush put the dresser together. They've already managed to get my bed built, two tables, and a desk. I have to say, I'm impressed. Who knew musicians could be so handy?

I set the box I'm carrying down on the counter and Hollis follows suit.

Boxes litter the entire space—labeled carefully to make unpacking easier.

Hollis and I head back outside to my dad's Range Rover to get more boxes. All the seats are down to make room for all my stuff—it's not like anything except one box would fit in my tiny car.

"How are you feeling about being on your own? Ready for your first night alone?" Hollis asks, pulling a box toward him. I stare at his bicep as it flexes.

"Well, I'm not going to be alone—am I?" I tease.

He grins. "Not if I have anything to say about it." He sets the box back down in the trunk and pinches my side.

I squeal and scuttle away.

"Mia?" I sober, and Hollis's smile falls as we turn.

"Oh, hey, Uncle Maddox."

Maddox tips his head in Hollis's direction. His eyes are narrowed suspiciously, but he's easy going enough I know he won't say anything—but he will be watching now. "How are you, Hollis?"

"Doing good," Hollis says, his voice higher than before.

"Need some help?" Maddox asks, motioning to the boxes.

"Sure," I reply, taking the box Hollis was going to take next and shoving it into Maddox's waiting arms. "The apartment is up the stairs and to your right."

"Mhmm," he hums, looking from Hollis to me. Finally, his eyes settle on Hollis and stay there. "When Hayes skins you alive for touching his daughter ... you better hope you have a guardian angel on your side."

"Uncle Maddox," I hiss.

"It's only a friendly warning, surely you know how your dad will react." He shrugs. "I won't say anything."

He heads inside and I hang my head, groaning out loud.

"Do you think he really won't tell?" Hollis inquires.

"He won't say anything. Maddox is pretty chill, except when it comes to his own kids."

"It's not like we were even kissing. I *touched* you. How'd he know?"

"I don't know," I force out.

But I do know. When Hollis and I are alone, we both can't help but have stars and hearts in our eyes.

Hollis looks up toward the building. "I can't believe I'm admitting this, but your dad scares the shit out of me—forget the fact I technically work for him, he looks like he could cut me in half with one look."

"Then don't piss him off," I mock, patting his chest.

"Devil woman," he mutters.

I can't help but crack a smile. "Hmm, has a nice ring to it. Mia 'Devil Woman' Hayes."

He shakes his head and reaches for another box.

"You know what else has a nice ring to it?" he asks, and from the dangerous glint in his eyes I know I'm in trouble.

"What?" I ask breathily.

"You gagged by my cock shoved deep inside that naughty mouth of yours."

I choke on air while he disappears inside with the box.

I shake my head and reach for something to carry, already plotting how to get him back.

THE APARTMENT IS EMPTY, ONLY I REMAIN SINCE HOLLIS HAD to leave with the others in order to not raise any suspicions. I survey the space. The guys got all the furniture together and even helped me put things away—Hollis *tried* to put my lingerie away, but I stole the box from him while he laughed.

Curtains and blinds hang from the windows sheltering

the space in a quiet darkness. A colorful rug rests beneath the simple black leather couch and wooden coffee table. I made sure to get muted furniture because I wanted to add pops of color throughout with pillows and other accessories. Since it's dark outside I have the lights turned on and the lamps add a nice warm glow.

I can't believe this place is mine. Moving out was a hard, difficult decision for me to make, but it was time. With school, work, and practically my entire life here it made sense. I've been too scared to do it in the past, but it was time I shoved it aside and took the leap.

I take a shower and change into a pair of gray sleep shorts and a tank top. Padding into the kitchen I fix myself a drink, knowing Hollis will be here any minute.

Sure enough, ten minutes later there's a knock on my door.

I open it and find him standing there with a goofy smile and a bag of takeout.

"Delivery for Her Royal Highness Devil Woman."

I shake my head. "Get in here." I tug on his shirt and he stumbles inside. I close the door with my hip, clicking the lock back into place.

"Eager to see me?" He smirks.

"Nah, it's the food I'm excited for. You're a mediocre bonus."

"Mediocre," he scoffs. "I'll show you mediocre again, and again, and again," he whispers huskily in my ear.

"Promises, promises. Let me see some follow through."

He narrows his eyes.

In a flash he's tossed the takeout bag onto the counter and has me lifted over his shoulder.

"Hollis," I squeal, the air going out of my lungs a moment later when my back hits the couch.

He grabs something from his pocket and in seconds one cuff is around my wrist and the other is secured to the metal leg of the couch.

My jaw drops. "Did you handcuff me to my couch?"

He smirks from above me. "If I remember correctly, I told you the first time we fucked I was handcuffing you. I didn't make good on my promise yet, so now I am."

"You're unbelievable."

"Unbelievably charming, sexy, bad ass, should I go on?"

"Only if you want me to kick your dick."

"Nah," he shakes his head, "I have much better uses for my cock and getting kicked is not part of the plan. But," he palms my breasts, "I definitely have plans to fuck your tits later."

Warmth floods my body and my pussy clenches at his words. "I hate you."

He shakes his head. "You wish you did, baby."

I shake the cuff. "Are you going to let me out of here."

He pretends to think. "Nah, I think I'm going to leave you there for a while."

"Hollis!" I shriek, thrashing against the couch, but whatever handcuffs he got are the real deal and I'm not going anywhere until he lets me. "Are you going to let me starve?"

"Nope, I'm going to feed you. But first I'm getting you naked."

My breath stutters at his words. Me, naked and vulnerable, handcuffed to the couch while he feeds me.

His golden eyes grow serious. "If at any point you want me to stop, all you have to do is say so, don't be afraid with me. This is about pleasure," his voice purrs.

"What do you have planned?" I choke out.

"Nothing too crazy .. yet."

My body shivers at his words.

He hooks his fingers into each side of my sleep shorts but doesn't take them off.

"I'm going to undress you now," he says huskily.

"O-Okay," I stutter out.

He slips my shorts off and grins. "No panties?"

"I knew I wouldn't need them."

Air hisses between his teeth and he shakes his head.

I've rendered Hollis Wilder speechless—quick, someone give me an award.

A moment later his shit-eating grin is back in place and he tilts his head. "I hope you're not fond of your shirt."

"Why?" I ask hesitantly.

He doesn't answer with words. Nope, the jerk grabs the thin fabric in both hands and *rips* it off my body.

He lets the shredded garment fall to the floor with a smug smile.

"I'm going to slap that smile off your face," I grind out —fighting not to let him see how fucking hot I actually found it.

"Ooh, feisty," he jokes.

His heat disappears from my bare body and in the blink of an eye I can't even see him, but I can hear him in the kitchen poking around.

Minutes tick by.

More.

I'm desperate to see what he's doing, but with my left hand cuffed to the couch I can't sit up to see him and my only other option is rolling face first onto the floor. Buck-ass naked.

I'm stuck.

I know it.

He knows it.

The bastard is enjoying this.

I don't know how long he keeps me waiting there, but it feels like an hour when he returns with one of the takeout cartons and chopsticks.

I never learned how to use them, but as he brings a bite to his lips it's obvious he's a pro.

He's ditched his shirt, unbuttoned his jeans and tugged the zipper down a bit.

"No underwear?" I challenge like he did.

He smirks. "I knew I wouldn't need them."

Sweet baby Jesus we're dangerous.

He sits down on the coffee table and holds a bite out to me.

"You were serious?"

"Yup," he says, shaking the piece of chicken. "Eat up. You're going to need your energy."

I take the bite, glaring at him.

"You can look at me like you hate me all you want. Your body says otherwise."

Sure enough, my hips are angled toward him and I have no idea how they got there. I can feel wetness beginning to seep out of me.

He takes another bite before holding one out to me.

I can't help but notice how long and strong his fingers are. I didn't even know fingers could be strong—but yeah, Hollis's definitely are.

He takes turns feeding himself and me until the box is empty.

"Still hungry?" he asks.

I shake my head. I'm not hungry for food anymore—but him? Yes, please.

"More for me then." He shrugs and disappears once more.

I press my free hand over my mouth to stifle my protest. I can't let him know his little game is getting to me.

I can't see him, forcing all my other senses to become laser focused.

I hear the scrape of chopsticks against a container. His feet shuffling across the floor. He clears his throat.

He's eating, standing in my kitchen without a care in the world, and I'm handcuffed naked to my couch. This was not how I foresaw the first night in my place going.

"'Sure you don't want more?" he calls from the kitchen.

"I'm sure," I reply, my voice thankfully stronger than I thought it would be.

Like before, he takes his sweet time. Even from here, unable to see him, I can feel the smugness rolling off of him in waves. He craves power and right now he's in the ultimate power position.

The more time passes the faster my heart beats, thumping in my ear. It becomes so loud it drowns everything else out and I nearly jump when he appears in front of me.

"Is that ... are you eating ice cream?"

His eyes sparkle as he licks the spoon clean. "Yes, and I'm not sharing."

He stands above me, his large body blocking the light, and eats his ice cream savoring every bite.

When it's gone, I squeak as he turns the bowl upside down, letting the cold melted liquid spill over my belly. There's not a lot of it, but enough.

"Whoops. How clumsy of me. Let me clean it up for you."

I expect him to go to the kitchen and get a wet towel.

Stupid me.

He drops to his knees beside me, and lowers his head using his tongue to swipe the dripping liquid from my body.

My breath stutters out in little wisps of air. "Delicious," he remarks, his mouth moving lower, past my belly button.

He gently opens my legs and I nearly rise off the couch when he licks my pussy. He lifts his head grinning at me, because I can't go anywhere. I'm trapped here, but let's face it I wouldn't move even if I could.

My hips begin to rotate, and he locks them down so I can't wiggle around.

I whimper and press my right hand against my lips to quiet myself. After all, this is only my first night here—the last thing I need is my neighbors complaining about the noise.

His fingers join his mouth and I nearly sob.

I reach down needing to touch him, but I can't reach him with my one hand and I can't *move* to get to him. Bastard.

"H-Hollis," I stutter, as he moves his fingers faster, hooking them inside and hitting that special spot. "Hollis, oh my God, please ... no ... more ... *oh my God.*"

I don't even know what's coming out of my mouth at this point. Honestly, I could be speaking Elvish because my brain is officially fried.

My orgasm hits and lights sparkle behind my eyes. My legs shake and my whole body practically convulses with it. I've never in my life had such an intense orgasm and that's saying something because Hollis is pretty fucking good at this whole sex thing. If the music thing doesn't work out for him, he could definitely teach classes on how to give orgasms.

He stands up and gets rid of his jeans.

I nearly whimper when he strokes his cock.

His amber eyes turn to liquid gold. "You like watching me touch myself," he states.

I nod anyway.

"I like you watching me," his voice is a husky whisper.

"But I told you I was going to fuck those gorgeous tits of yours and I meant it."

He picks his jeans up off the floor and pulls out a tiny key.

"Don't think I won't handcuff you again if you don't listen," he warns.

I hold still as he unlocks the cuff and it falls away from my wrist. I rub at it as he frees the cuff from the couch.

He holds the cuffs in one hand and reaches out with his other to take my mine. He helps me to stand—I start to protest, to tell him I don't need his help, but as I stand I notice my legs are trembling and I *do* need him.

He releases my hand and uses his to drag down the side of my body, settling at my hip. I look down at his tan hand splayed against the pale color of my skin. He rubs his thumb in circles.

I stand on my tiptoes and he groans, lowering closer to me.

"I want to unravel you," he growls, "but it's *you* who is unraveling *me*."

He crashes his lips to mine, stealing my breath, my thoughts, my very being.

I don't know who I am or even *what* I am. When he kisses me, I cease to exist. I'm simply matter, bending to his will.

Without breaking apart he sweeps me up into a bridal hold and carries me to the bed, laying me down. He pulls away, his face still close to mine. "I plan on fucking you in every part of this place, but first we're marking this bed."

Sweet baby Jesus this man.

He steps back, admiring every inch of my body. He reaches out, trailing his fingers ever so lightly, barely the graze of a feather, over my collarbone, then down one arm, the other, over each of my legs, my feet, back up my torso. He glides his fingers under each of my breasts, down to my belly button.

He leaves for a moment and returns with a bottle of lube. Before I can ask what he's doing he tips the bottle, dripping it over my body.

I swallow thickly at the heat in his eyes.

"Push your tits together," he commands, there's no room for arguing with him.

I do as I'm told, his eyes flashing with delight.

"Beautiful," he murmurs. "Absolutely perfect."

His big body crowds over me, shadowing me. I want to reach out to touch him, to run my hands along his biceps and strong shoulders, but I know if I move my hands I'll be in trouble—the devilish part of me wants to see what he'd do if I disobeyed him, but right now I'm too intrigued by what's to come.

He strokes himself, a sly smile tipping his lips.

Yeah, yeah, I like to watch. Sue me.

I'm pretty sure any sane red-blooded woman would enjoy watching Hollis pleasure himself.

I watch him, my eyes never straying as he rubs his thumb over the tip.

He lines up his pelvis with my breasts and looks into my eyes. He doesn't say anything, he doesn't have to, I see it all. It scares me, the depth of emotion in his eyes, because it's something I never thought possible or expected from him.

I never expected this thing between us to mean something to either of us, especially him, but it's become so much more.

When he begins to fuck my breasts I'm not prepared for the amount of pleasure I feel. Especially when his eyes roll into the back of his head. Watching Hollis lose his control because of *me* has singlehandedly become one of my favorite things.

He's this beautiful beast of a man and I can bring him to his knees.

Never underestimate our power as women. We can make a man bend to our will if we want—and I *want*. Hollis might think he's in control now, but not for long. He can have his way with me now, but I *will* have my way with him, I'm biding my time.

"Fuck, you're gorgeous," he grinds out between clenched teeth.

The veins in his neck strain and sweat beads on his brow.

"Do I make you feel good?" I ask.

"Fuck yes," he answers on a rasp.

I can't hide my pleased smile.

"Fuck," he groans. "I need to be in your pussy now."

He starts to pull away, to get a condom, but I lock my hands on his wrist.

"I'm clean—are you?"

"I got tested before we ever ... I wanted to be sure," he admits.

I nod. "I'm on birth control."

"Fuck, that's the best thing I've ever heard."

He moves down my body and I spread my legs, he settles between them and hooks his arms around my legs, lifting them up.

I gasp as he plunges into me. He doesn't even give me a chance to brace myself before pulling back out and seating himself firmly inside me once more.

"Holy shit, being inside your bare pussy feels so good."

His thumb finds my clit and he begins to rub it in slow deliberate circles, so at odds with his fast and relentless pace, but I soon find myself facing an impending orgasm and I'm afraid it might be as earth-shattering as the one he gave me earlier, and if it is I might not survive this night.

My legs begin to shake and he holds on tighter.

"Not yet," he tells me. "Hold on a little longer."

I whimper.

Does he want me to murder him?

"Almost," he says through gritted teeth.

"Hollis, I need—"

"Now," he declares.

He pulls out just as my orgasm shatters around me. He grips his cock, groaning as his cum spills over my pussy and thighs.

This is hands down the most erotic thing I've ever seen in my entire life. His eyes are closed, he's completely lost in bliss, as his pleasure spills over my body. My orgasm continues to tingle through me as the last of his cum falls in little drops onto my stomach.

"Fuck," he curses, lying down on the bed beside me.

I stare up at the ceiling at a loss for words.

I was content with my boring, monotonous life, and then Hollis Wilder showed up rattling the very foundation I'd built my life upon. He changed the landscape, molding it how he saw fit. There is no going back now.

TWENTY

Hollis

Waking up with a curvy redhead curled into my body is something I could get used to. Scratch that—not *a* curvy redhead, but *this* one.

Her head rests on my bare chest, one pale arm thrown over my torso. She sleeps soundly; like I'm the most comfortable thing she's ever laid her head on.

I can't help but stroke my fingers through her soft hair. She makes a little sound in her sleep causing a smile to slip across my face.

I never thought I'd find anything to make me feel content, definitely not *someone*.

But laying here with Mia is the only place I want to be.

I feel whole, like all the scattered pieces of myself have finally been assembled.

She gives me hope I could be something more, something better.

Eventually I manage to extract myself out from under her without stirring her.

I find my jeans and tug them on before padding into her tiny kitchen. The place might be small, but in only one day she's already managed to make it homey and leave a trace of her personality in every room.

I open the refrigerator and pull out the carton of eggs.

Cooking is not my forte, but I know she'll be exhausted from last night since we couldn't keep our hands off each other, so I'm willing to try. It might not be the most delicious thing ever to grace her taste buds, but I think I can at least make it edible.

I cook the eggs and make some toast. It's not much, but it's something. Once it's made I rummage around in her cabinets looking for a tray. I finally find one and fix plates for the two of us on it along with glasses of orange juice.

Carrying it to the bed I rouse her from sleep.

She blinks blearily at me. "What time is it?"

"Almost ten," I admit. "I wanted to let you sleep. We were up late."

"Mhmm," she hums, sitting up. "You made food." She eyes the tray of food I hold.

"I thought you'd be hungry."

"I am," she says, getting comfortable. Her breasts are on full display, she doesn't bother trying to cover herself up, and I have to suppress a groan because suddenly the last thing on my mind is eating these eggs.

I settle into the bed beside her, with the tray between us.

"I've never done this before," I admit.

"Eat breakfast?" she jokes.

I crack a small smile. "Make a girl breakfast. Spend the night. You're getting me to break all my rules."

She laughs. "Funny, you're doing the same with mine."

"What do you mean?" I ask, desperate for her to elaborate.

She shrugs. "I was ... fine before you came along. My life wasn't exciting, sure, but I felt fulfilled. I always swore I'd never date or be involved with a musician, but then you happened. I fought it, but..." She blushes, ducking her head so her hair falls forward to hide the pink hue in her cheeks. "I was attracted to you the first time I saw you—don't get me wrong, I still thought you were an arrogant, condescending asshole, but I thought you were hot."

I laugh at her words. "Is that all I am to you? Man candy?"

"Maybe." She winks. "It's funny," she continues, "I haven't had the most exciting dating life, but I have dated ... they all turned out to be jerks masquerading as nice guys. I pegged you as a jerk and ... you're not." Her eyes connect with mine. "You're one of the most genuine people I've ever met."

I chuckle, taking a bite of toast. "I think that's the nicest thing anyone has ever said about me."

"You're not who I thought you were."

I sigh. "Babe, I *was*. I was exactly the guy you thought I was then. The morning I met you ... your dad had driven through the night all the way to D.C. to haul our sorry asses out of a club. Some girl I didn't even know the name of was sitting in my lap. I would've fucked her that night," I admit, and it kills me it's true. "I felt like the music, the fame ... I thought I was doing what I was supposed to. What I'd seen in the media growing up. I wanted that. I wanted to live the typical live fast, die young lifestyle. Then we got here. I met you. Your dad. This town. All of it slowed me down. No one giving a fuck about us, it humbled me. I don't want to be that guy anymore. I don't want to live without abandon, I want to live with a purpose now. I want to make great music, tour the world, and hopefully..."

"Hopefully what?" she prompts.

"Fall in love ... but I'm afraid I already have."

She gasps, it's only a small sound, a bare intake of breath but it's there.

"Hollis—"

I shake my head, my hair flopping over my forehead. "Don't say anything. You don't ... just don't."

She grabs my chin and forces me to look at her. "Shut up and listen you idiot."

"Yes, ma'am," I say, but it's distorted.

"I don't know where this is headed. I don't know if you're my boyfriend, and even if you are, there's a lot we need to discuss. I have another year of college after this, you have your band, and you're going places, Hollis, I know it. But right now, none of it matters, because I've never felt like this for another person. I feel safe with you. I laugh with you. I argue with you. We're not perfect, neither of us, but it doesn't stop me from loving every moment we spend together and loving you."

Holy shit.

She releases my chin and I sit there dumbfounded.

Mia loves me.

I think—no, I *know* I love her too.

It makes no sense. It's absolutely illogical.

But I do.

We do.

I guess love ... it can't be defined. It can't be forced.

It can only be felt and there's no controlling when or how or who you love.

You just do.

I lean over and kiss her.

Not *her*.

Mia.

The girl I love.

I'm kissing the girl I've fallen in love with.

I've never been in love before—lust, infatuation, sure I've felt that, but never love for someone who wasn't family or a friend.

She angles her lips over mine, her fingertips light against the stubble on my cheek. I could kiss her for the rest of the day and night and never tire.

Pulling away, I keep her from moving with a hand on

the nape of her neck. Our foreheads are pressed together and I look into her eyes.

"By the way, I'm totally turned on by the prospect of you calling me your boyfriend."

She throws her head back and laughs. "You mean it doesn't send you running in the other direction?"

"Once, it would have. Not with you."

She smiles, it's a small shy smile, one she usually only reserves for me.

"I don't know how to tell my dad," she admits.

I wince. "He's going to be pissed."

"He's going to murder you," she corrects.

I sigh. "If you want to tell him, we can. I'll do what you want."

She shakes her head. "Not yet. I want us to keep this between us for a little while longer. I need to think of a way to explain it to him, so he understands this is serious, *before* he goes off and doesn't listen to a word I say. I don't care if our friends know, but my dad ... you see how he is. He's *so* overprotective. I don't want him to do anything stupid."

"Like kill us?" I joke—but it's a legitimate concern.

She nods. "He can be ... spiteful."

"What happened?" I asked.

"Let's just say this one guy I was dating cheated on me and he had his car impounded."

"Yikes."

"That's not the best part."

"Well, shit," I curse, running my fingers through my hair.

"He had it crushed."

"Fuck."

"Yeah." She shrugs with a wince.

"He's going to castrate me," I groan. "Pick out my eyes and put my head on a spike."

She scoots the tray out of her way and rolls toward me until her body lays over mine, the sheets tangled around her. "I'll protect you." She kisses my bare chest. "He might hurt you, but he'd never hurt me."

"You'll be my human shield?"

She laughs. "Yes."

I stare down at this amazing girl, this amazing girl who loves me despite my flaws, despite all the bad shit I've done.

I don't know what I did to deserve her, but I swear I'll do whatever it takes to keep proving I'm worthy of her.

Rolling away from me, she drags the tray back to us and begins to eat.

"Halloween is in a few days," she says, completely changing the subject. "If you're my boyfriend you better get a costume."

"Why?" I ask hesitantly.

She shrugs daintily. "There all kinds of things going on downtown. Parties. Pub crawl. You name it and it's probably happening. The guys should come too."

"How are we going to get costumes that quick?" I grumble.

"Amazon Prime that shit," she says like it's obvious.

"What are you going as?" I ask.

"Wouldn't you like to know?" She smirks with a glint in her eyes.

Something tells me whatever she has planned is going to torture me.

TWENTY-ONE

Mia

Hollis practically lives at my apartment now, but I kick him out and force him to get ready for Halloween night at his hotel with his friends, while Kira and I get ready here.

I didn't want him seeing my costume.

I love Halloween. It's my favorite holiday of the entire year. I plan my costume a full year in advance, going all out. There's something about becoming a whole different person for one night I find intriguing.

Kira curls my hair, taking her time to make sure it's perfect. My hair has a natural curl anyway, but I need this to be sleek and sexy curls.

After she's done with my hair, she weaves ivy through it, before moving on to my makeup.

When she's finished, it's my turn to help her.

I do her makeup first, going for a grungy sweaty look—it sounds gross, but it's necessary—and I even go as far as to add some fake bruising, cuts, and dirt. I braid her hair and then we're both ready to change into our costumes and make the final transformation.

Me into Poison Ivy, and her into Lara Croft.

This year, we both decided to play into our natural looks when it came to our costumes.

I wiggle the sheer green tights up my hips, before slipping into the leotard corset type garment I spent hours gluing ivy to. I even added green sequins to it so when the lights hit it, it shimmers. Finally, I grab my pair of matching green platform heels and put them on.

"How do I look?" I ask turning to Kira.

She tugs down her crop top and appraises me. "You look like a stripper."

"That's what I was going for."

"Then you nailed it."

"You look hot," I tell her.

She grins. "I wouldn't tell Rush what I was wearing. Homeboy better cum in his pants when he sees me," she says, turning to my floor length mirror and playing with the loose strands of hair framing her face.

I have no doubt he will. Her top is fitted tightly over her chest and amplifies her tiny waist. Her black shorts hug her ass, add in the straps on her thighs with the fake guns ... yeah, Rush is going to lose his mind. She looks like the gaming character brought to life.

"You look hot too you know," she tells me, pouting her lips at her reflection. "Sexy Poison Ivy is a look I dig on you."

"Too bad it's not every day appropriate," I quip.

"It's probably good for Hollis's heart, though," she cackles. "He's going to choke on his tongue. I still can't believe you guys made it official. I just wanted you to get laid, not go and get a fucking boyfriend."

"What about you and Rush?" I counter. "You guys are together all the time."

"Yeah, for sex." She shrugs. "His cock is exclusively mine, and my pussy is exclusively his—that's as far as it goes now. My personal thoughts are mine to keep. I don't need to know where he grew up, how many siblings he has, or even his favorite color. As long as his dick can make me orgasm, I'm all about it."

I shake my head. Those two are so clueless it's not even funny.

"I'm going to text Hollis to see if they're ready," I tell her, and she waves me away.

Our plan is to meet in their hotel lobby and go from there.

Me: Are you guys ready?

Hollis: Yeah—you seriously call dressing up like this fun?

Me: Yeah. Stop being a wuss or no puss for you.

Hollis:

Me: ;)

"They're ready," I announce.

"Just let me put my shoes on." She sits on the edge of my bed to lace her hiking boots.

My place is close to the hotel, so we walk, especially since parking is a nightmare.

We step into the lobby and I feel thankful for the cool air. It might be the end of October, but the weather has stayed unseasonably warm. There have been many Halloween nights when it has snowed, but tonight won't be one of them.

Kira and I find an empty couch in the hotel lobby to sit on and I text Hollis to let him know we're here.

A few guys eye us in the lobby, but nobody approaches. I'm with Hollis, so I don't care, but if I was single, it would frustrate me to no end. Why is it hard for guys to make the first move?

Kira plays some stupid game on her phone, completely oblivious to everything around us. Now that she has Rush on cock-anytime-I-want speed dial she's not scoping out the place for a male body to spend the night with.

I sit back in the chair, impatiently waiting for the guys to grace us with their presence.

I spot them approaching from around the corner where the elevators are and my jaw drops.

"Oh my God." If I wasn't covered in five layers of makeup I'd rub my eyes. "What are you guys wearing?"

"What's it look like?" Hollis asks, flicking the stuffed animal *hedgehog* Velcro-d to Cannon's white t-shirt. In the back of his pocket is a set of drumsticks. I take in the sight of the rest of them. Fox—shirtless with a brown leather jacket and worn jeans riding low on his hips, a microphone clasped in one hand, a cigarette in the other. Rush wears a truly *awful* curly black wig with a white t-shirt, black leather jacket, and jeans.

Finally, I look at Hollis.

Backwards baseball cap, white tee, light blue shirt tossed over it with the sleeves rolled up, and khaki pants.

"You did *not* dress as my dad," I groan.

He grins. "Yes, I did."

"I'm going to kill you. Literally murder you in your sleep."

Kira stands, holding up her phone. "I'm *so* posting this on Instagram. Smile. Or don't. I don't care."

The guys lean in together and she snaps her picture.

"You won't hurt me," Hollis says. "You like me too much."

I roll my eyes. "I wonder why."

"You look hot as fuck—Poison Ivy, right?"

"You know your comics?" I raise a brow.

"A little bit. I used to be a *bit* of a nerd when I was younger—then I discovered girls." He shrugs.

"I can't believe you're going to make me leave this hotel with you dressed as my *dad*. You do realize how creepy this is right?"

"You say creepy, I say hysterical."

"I should ditch your ass," I grumble.

"Aw, you'd never leave me hot stuff." He throws his arm around my shoulders playfully.

"I can't believe I go all out with my costume and you dress as Joshua Hayes, my freaking *father*."

"Hey, I put a lot of effort into this," he defends, as the group of us heads outside. He lets his arm drop and I instantly miss the warmth of his touch even if I know we have to watch ourselves in public settings.

"Mhmm, I'm sure it was extremely difficult to scrounge up all that."

"It was, believe me, babe."

"I need a drink," I sigh.

"Isn't that what a pub crawl is for?" he quips.

"Exactly."

AFTER TWO HOURS OF STROLLING AROUND WE END UP AT A restaurant a block up from the hotel. The back deck and patio area is packed with people dressed in all kinds of costumes. Zombies, Marvel characters, there's even an Indiana Jones—but who's getting the most attention of all? The dickwads dressed as Willow Creek. All night people have walked up, immediately knowing who they're dressed as and remarking on the creativity of it, then asking for a picture.

Hollis keeps flashing me a smug smile every time it happens.

I, in turn, roll my eyes every time.

What's worse is I know my dad and the other guys will get a kick out of this when they hear about it.

I don't know what's worse—Hollis gloating, or the inevitable gloating coming from my dad.

Kira and I push our way through the crowd, finding a table large enough to claim. Since most people are standing, there are empty tables—and I'm *starving*, so if I don't eat soon, I'm about to go super villain up in this bitch.

Menus are already on the table and I pick one up. I've eaten here a million times, but I look anyway.

The guys eventually manage to make it through the crowd—Rush now walking around with the hedgehog in his wig. I honestly want to glue the stuffed animal to one of their faces simply for irritating the shit out of me.

"We can't go anywhere with you guys," I grumble.

"Someone sounds jealous of our *brilliant* costume idea," Fox sing-songs.

I narrow my eyes as he sits down on the opposite side of the table. "Yeah, I'm *very* jealous you all dressed as my dad and uncles. Bravo."

Hollis takes a seat beside me and smacks a drunken kiss against my cheek. I frown and pretend to rub it away, to which he laughs. "Well, *someone*, my girlfriend might I add, wouldn't tell me what she was dressing as so it's not like I could match you or anything."

"Shh," I hiss, looking around to see if anyone heard him say that.

"You could definitely rock a red wig and heels," Fox chortles.

Hollis grunts. "I was thinking Batman or something—but I could definitely rock heels if I wanted to."

I throw my head back and groan. "Remind me again why I like you guys?"

"Because we're awesome," Fox says.

"And hot," Rush chimes in.

"Because I have a big dick," Hollis adds.

Cannon, as per usual, keeps his mouth shut. He merely reaches over and picks the hedgehog carefully out of Rush's wig and puts it back on his shoulder.

Cannon is the type of person who thinks if he doesn't have anything worthwhile to say then there's no point in adding to the conversation. I admire him for it, but I also want to punch him in the face because it can be highly annoying when he ends up going a whole hour not saying a word. I'm convinced he's not entirely human.

A waitress manages to make it through the crowd and we all order drinks—we've already had several tonight, but it's *Halloween* and I want to let loose. Yeah, I'll have a killer hangover in the morning, but whatever. That's a regret for tomorrow's me to have to deal with.

Hollis snatches my menu from me.

"Hey," I cry, making a grab for it.

He holds it out of my reach. "Don't you already know what you want?"

"Well, yes, but I was holding that. You don't snatch things from people, it's rude."

He playfully bites my earlobe and I swat at him.

"Stop being a pest because you're perturbed by my costume."

"It's not even a costume!" I cry. "It's *clothes*."

"I'm pretty sure everyone who has stopped us for photos disagrees with you."

I frown.

"What's really wrong with you?"

"She's hangry," Kira replies.

"Hey," I snap.

"See," she defends. "You can't let her get hungry. Anybody got a Snickers?" she jokes.

"Don't worry, babe," Hollis grins, "we'll get some food in you."

"We'll get some food in you," I mimic. "Oh my God, I am hungry."

I face plant on the table. Hollis laughs heartily beside me.

When the waitress returns with our drinks Hollis orders several appetizers before we give the order for our meal.

"I am still pissy about your so-called costume," I mutter under my breath.

"I bet you won't have a problem when you take it off of me," he jokes.

I spit out my drink. "Hollis," I chide.

"So, what? You can be a goddamn vixen in bed but can't talk about sex in public? Please. It's not like there are children around." He lifts his bottle of beer to his lips, giving me a look like I am crazy.

Which I am, but...

"My dad," I remind him softly. "I can't have someone overhearing and it getting back to him somehow. With social media you never know."

Hanging out? I can play that off. I'm allowed to have friends, but we just can't risk being too promiscuous in public until he knows.

"A vixen, huh?" Kira inquires.

"Shut up." I hide my reddening face. "I hate all of you."

"What'd I do?" Cannon voices.

I throw my arms wide. "It speaks!" I shout. "God, my head hurts."

"She's crashing from the buzz high," Kira explains.

"Kira," I groan.

"What? It's the truth. You do this every time you drink. You're super fun to start with and then your inner bitch unleashes and I want to strangle you. Do you expect me to lie?"

"Why do you let me drink then?" I snap back. "Oh, Jesus—you're right. Someone take me home."

"Nuh-uh." Hollis drapes his arm over the back of my chair. "We're not going anywhere until you eat. No more of this either." He picks up my drink and sets it aside. "Water from now on. You got an aspirin?" he asks Kira.

She rolls her eyes. "Does it look like I can carry anything on my body?"

"Um ... no."

"Exactly. Let her eat, take her home, give her some

medicine and tuck her into bed like a good little boyfriend," she instructs.

"Kira," I hiss.

"I have more than going to bed on my mind," he says with a wicked grin.

Clearly, he's not listening. I think the alcohol we've consumed has given him a loose tongue.

Thankfully the appetizers come, and I can stuff my face before I shove my fist in my boyfriend's face—after all, this whole relationship thing is new for us, and I'm pretty sure punching your boyfriend, hungry or not, is frowned upon. Plus, I'd hate myself for it later. Even *if* he should get knocked down a few pegs—the cocky bastard.

Hollis tries to swipe a cheese fry off my plate and you bet your ass I swat his hand away. "Get your own fries." I grab my plate and hold it away.

He laughs uproariously. "I thought we could share."

I point a finger in warning at him like I'm scolding a small child. "No."

Even the other guys snicker—naturally I give them all glares for it.

I drink the water the waitress brings me. I guzzle it down, not having realized how my mouth turned into a cotton ball from all the alcohol. This is the only night of the year I let myself go all out. Any other time I drink, two is my limit. There's a reason for it too—I'm a mean drunk, obviously.

"More water?" Hollis asks.

"Yes, please."

"Give me a fry."

"There's a whole platter! Why do you want mine?" I whine.

He levels me with a look.

"No." I hiss like a cat at him.

Oh my God, I am officially out of my mind.

Hollis busts out laughing. "God, this is the most entertaining fucking thing ever." He stands and pushes back his chair. "One water coming right up."

Before I can speak the sneaky nut-waffle swipes *three* of my fries.

I bare my teeth at him, but he merely dances away and through the crowd.

I grab another chunk of cheese fries—I deserve triple the amount for those three he took—and take two potato skins, and some chicken tenders. Yeah, I ordered a meal, but I'm starving and need food in my belly *now* before I turn into a real witch.

Hollis returns with *two* glasses of water and slides them both over to me before he sits down.

I sip slowly at the water this time, trying to make it last.

By the time our food comes, I'm stuffed, and ready to fall over asleep. I end up sitting with my head on Hollis's shoulder while he eats, my heavy eyes threatening to drift closed.

"I think Halloween was better with candy than alcohol, at least where you're concerned," he jokes to me.

"Mmm," I hum, neither in agreement nor disagreement. I've officially reached the point of not giving a fuck. I like this place.

He chuckles, his laugher rumbling against my ear.

"I'm sleepy," I mumble.

"I'll take you home," he promises.

"Mmm."

Waiting for him to finish eating *and* get the check to pay our massive bill takes so long I nearly come alive long enough to go off on management—which it's not the restaurant's fault there are a bunch of drunk adults in costumes demanding food left and right.

And more alcohol—always more alcohol.

Once the bill is paid and leftovers boxed up—you bet your ass I'm going to want snacks later—Hollis takes my hand and starts to lead me away.

I stumble in my heels and quickly pull those suckers off.

"You can't walk barefoot," Hollis scolds.

"I have tights on."

"That's barely anything."

"My feet hurt," I complain. "I can't walk home in these."

He lets go of my hand and I barely have a moment to blink before I'm slung over his shoulder and carried down the deck of the restaurant and on to the street.

"We're going to the hotel and you're staying there," he says. "Your apartment is close, but this is closer."

His tone implies *argue with me and I'll spank you.*

Unfortunately, now I only want to argue with him.

"Take me home you buffoon." I beat at his back. "I'm going to throw up if you carry me like this," I warn. "Although, this costume is vomit inducing as it is. You're lucky I didn't retch all over you the moment I saw you."

He smacks my ass.

Outside.

In the public.

"Hollis!"

He spanks me again. Harder this time.

I decide to shut my mouth as we reach the hotel and he carries me inside and to the elevator.

I'm sure it's a sight to see someone dressed as Joshua Hayes with a drunk Poison Ivy over his shoulders—a Poison Ivy, might I add, who's carrying two boxes of leftover food dangling from a plastic bag hooked on her index finger.

Halloween—it brings out the freaks in all of us.

Cannon and Fox get on the elevator with us—Kira and Rush no doubt going back to her place.

Lucky bitch.

I want to be in *my* apartment but my boyfriend has this annoying habit of doing the complete opposite of what I want.

He carries me into the suite, straight to his room and deposits me in the bathroom.

"I need to pee," I whine, tearing at my costume.

He sighs. "Hold still."

I turn my back to him and he works slowly to undo the ties of the corset.

"This get-up made your tits look fucking amazing, but holy shit this must be a torture device."

"You have no idea," I admit.

He finally gets it loose enough to help me wiggle it off.

I'm completely naked except for the tights as I stumble to the toilet.

I don't even have the capacity to yell at him to get out while I pee. He's not paying attention though. Instead, he's turning the water on and filling the large soaking tub. There's some bubble bath and salts provided by the hotel and he dumps those in too.

I finish peeing, flush the toilet, and wash my hands.

"What are you doing?" I ask.

He glances at me over his shoulder as he reaches down testing the temperature of the water.

"Running you a bath."

"Why?" I ask.

"Why?" He repeats incredulously. "You've been walking around in heels for hours, you have to be tired."

My lower lip trembles with the threat of tears. "You really do love me."

He looks at me like I've lost my mind—it's a possibility. "I thought we'd established my love already—despite your hard-headed crazy personality, despite my stupid asshole self, I love you."

If hearts can swoon, mine does.

"Get in," he commands when the bathtub is almost full. He shuts off the water waiting for me to climb into the warm water.

I'm already naked—having kicked off my tights when I used the potty.

I take the two steps up and step down into the large soaking tub. A sigh escapes my lips at the pleasantness of it. Whatever bubble bath or salts the hotels provides smell like lavender and mint. I inhale the aroma of it with my eyes closed.

"Are you getting in?" I ask Hollis, cracking open an eye.

He shakes his head. "No, I want this to be about you."

There's a tiled area around the tub where some decorations sit like the vase of bath salts and framed art. Hollis strips down to his boxer-briefs before sitting on the ledge behind me, dropping his legs in the water at my sides. Before I can ask what he's doing now he reaches down and begins to massage my knotted shoulders.

"Oh my God that feels *amazing*," I practically moan.

He kneads the tightened muscles in my neck and shoulders as my head lolls to the side. I hope he knows he's going to have to carry me out of his bath and straight to bed. I'm going to be worthless after this.

After he massages as much of my back as he can get to, he then proceeds to carefully disentangle the ivy from my hair. Once it's all out he grabs a washcloth, wets it, and puts some soap on it. He instructs me to hold out my arms for him to scrub. I let him and then he proceeds to lean over me to clean my breasts before moving to my back.

Once I'm sparkly and clean to his specifications he orders me out and wraps me in a large warm towel. It feels like a soft expensive blanket, not a towel meant for drying.

I inhale the scent of whatever softener the hotel uses lingering on it.

I twine my arms around him, leaning my chin on his chest to tilt my head up at him.

"I love you," I murmur, my eyes heavy with sleep.

He smiles down at me, pushing my hair back. "I love you too, beautiful girl." He presses a small kiss to my lips. "Go get in bed. You have to be sleepy."

I obey his orders, dropping the towel on the floor before climbing beneath the silky sheets completely naked. I hear him pull the drain on the tub and then the squeak of the shower nozzle turning. The sound of the water hitting the tile floor acts like a sound machine and I'm asleep before he returns.

TWENTY-TWO

Hollis

Another day in the studio. Everything is coming together perfectly and it won't be long until we have an entire album completed. It'll take a few months to get everything fine-tuned and perfect, but the base is there and it's fucking *good*. I'm proud of us.

I come out of the recording booth and Hayes swivels in his leather chair to face us.

"I want you all to perform a gig Friday night."

"Where?" Rush perks up—no doubt picturing a big venue. I can't lie and say I'm not thinking and hoping the same.

"Griffin's."

"Griffin's? Never heard of it," Rush frowns. "Where is it?"

"Three blocks from your hotel."

"Oh." Rush's shoulders sag.

"Don't sound so disappointed," Hayes chuckles amusedly. "Small sets can lead to bigger things. You all have done a decent job of building a fan base, I'll give you credit, but you have a long way to go. It's time to be humble. The minute you think you're bigger than you are is the minute you fall. Never take anything for granted." He turns to meet each of our eyes. "I want to see your success last a long time—if you get cocky it won't. It's as simple as that. Fame can come overnight but can also disappear in the same second."

"What time?" I ask

"You all go on at seven," he answers me. "You'll do *two* songs—no more. I'll be there, don't even think about doing more. You want to tease people. Get them excited for what's to come but give them too much and they'll move on. Maddox, Mathias, and Ezra will be there too. We'll also be monitoring your behavior. Think of this as a test in school. You fail—you flunk and don't graduate."

For one of the first times in my life I feel nervous at the thought of performing. We're going to perform in front of *the* biggest band in the United States, even to this day—hell Willow Creek has practically conquered world domination. They're the band every current and new group aspires to be. They're fucking *legends*.

"We've got this," I say, trying to brush aside my nerves. "No problem."

The words sound cocky, let's face it I'm the king of cocky, but I say the words more for the guys than myself. I can see the worry on their faces.

If Cannon is the dad of our group, then I'm the leader. Not because I'm the boss, I'd be happy to let someone else take the reins on that one, but I'm the reason we started our band in the first place. I thought it would be cool, I had a decent voice, and after a while they gave in to my pestering and found they liked music as well.

We've grown a lot since those days—we were only in middle school after all.

It's been over fifteen years since we started this venture. We were young, we still are, but fuck it's amazing to see it come full circle.

"We'll have fliers made and posted around town," Hayes continues. "Griffin's has live music every Friday, and there's usually a decent crowd, but I want to see the coffee shop be standing room only." There's a warning in his eyes and I swallow thickly.

In other words, don't screw up, be likable.

Great.

Softening, Hayes adds, "I've seen potential in you all from the start. I've seen it grow every day we've been in here, in the studio. But you can't lose yourselves. You have to remember where you came from."

Rush presses his lips together. Out of all of us, his story is the most tragic. Sometimes I don't know how he's dealt with it all—but I guess that's where the excessive drinking, partying, and women come into play.

Hayes claps his hands together.

"Let's get back to it."

I COLLAPSE ONTO MIA'S COUCH, SITTING BESIDE HER WITH A beer in one hand and a dinner plate in the other. I was shocked when I showed up and Mia had prepared dinner for us. Homemade lasagna. *Yum.*

She curls her legs under her and swirls the wine in her glass. She looks tired, lost in thought. I feel much the same, but suddenly my problems seem minimal compared to whatever is bothering my girl.

"What's wrong?" I ask her.

"Nothing. I'm tired," she admits. "School was exhausting and then I had work."

She worked at The Sub Club all afternoon and evening, now is the first I'm seeing of her today, and she still managed to make dinner? She's my hero.

"We should've ordered in," I tell her.

She smiles at me, but it doesn't quite reach her eyes. "I wanted to make dinner."

"Are you sure you're just tired?" I ask her.

She shrugs. "No."

"What is it?" I press. "Talk to me, babe."

"It's my dad," she sighs. "I hate keeping this from him. I can't even tell my mom because she'll blab to him."

"We can tell him. Any time," I insist.

Yeah, it fucking scares me to admit to Hayes I'm banging his daughter but fuck it I *love* this girl—he'll see that, he has to.

She shakes her head. "I want to wait a little longer. I feel like if he gets to know you more on his own maybe he'll be quicker to accept ... *us*."

I hate to tell her, but I don't think *anything* will get him to accept there's an *us*. She's his daughter and no guy is ever going to be good enough, least of all me. I fucking deserve for him to hate the idea of Mia and I together—after all, when we first arrived here look at the situation he found us in. To him, we're nothing but stereotypical musicians chasing any available pussy that falls in our lap. There's no way to explain how this place has changed my point of view, how Mia has, fuck how even *Hayes* has changed me. Anything I can say to defend myself will sound weak and pathetic—an excuse to cover my ass.

"Okay," I agree, trying to hide my relief.

My biggest fear about telling her dad is no longer about him dropping us, or even hating me—it's the fear he could be the reason I lose her.

Joshua Hayes is her father, a guarantee in her life.

I'm the guy she's only known for two months.

I'm replaceable. He's not.

I brush a strand of red hair behind her ear, taking in the sharp lines of her cheekbones and full lips. She's focused on her food, but from the slight jump in her cheek I know she's aware of my touch.

I've never known anything like this. I want to believe it's special, different, but what if I'm wrong. Inexperienced isn't a word I'd use to describe myself, but it's exactly what I am when it comes to relationships. I know nothing and it scares me shitless.

I glide my thumb around the shell of her ear and she shivers. My food lays forgotten in my lap. I want to look at her, memorize every feature. She looks over at me and doesn't cower from my scrutiny. Instead, she looks right back, and I almost jolt physically, because I see the same fear in her eyes.

I hate this feeling of being on solid ground together, but the minute we think about letting other people in on this, important people, suddenly the ground is quaking and we're falling endlessly into the unknown.

But if I'm going to fall with anyone I choose her, always.

I force myself to stop staring at her and turn my attention to my food.

"This is fucking delicious," I tell her, and I mean it too.

She smiles. "My mom taught me how to cook—I'll confess, it's rare I make an entire meal anymore, I don't have the time, but I enjoy cooking when I do.

"I can't cook worth a shit," I admit. She knows this.

"I should teach you sometime."

I laugh at the idea, but say, "I'd enjoy it."

I'll admit, my mind is imagining her teaching me to cook leading to a loss of clothes and dirty kitchen sex.

She smirks, knowing exactly where my thoughts

strayed. I can't help myself. I'm a dirty bastard and I've finally found my equal.

Mia's innocent in many ways, but my God she's adventurous. Never, not once, has she balked at anything I've wanted to try. I love how open she is, and her trust in me is astounding.

She turns the TV on and changes it to ... "Are we seriously going to watch National Geographic?" I ask with an upturned brow.

She glances over at me offended. A speck of tomato sauce clings to her lip. I reach over and brush it away with my thumb and she licks her lips.

"What's wrong with National Geographic?" she retorts, the pleasure that previously flashed in her eyes at my touch vanishing.

"I mean ... it's ... like educational, right? Boring?"

She glares at me, her mouth parted aghast. "What?" I defend.

"Don't judge me for liking to learn about dead things."

I snort and turn my attention to the screen. "Ew, what the fuck is that?"

"It's an Egyptian mummy," she explains. "It's a documentary on how they used to prepare the bodies. Did you know they used to insert a tool through the nose to liquefy the brain? They'd then tip the body forward so the liquid brain could pour out of the nose."

I gag and hold up my hands. "I'm trying to *eat*, Mia. Shut up. That's disgusting."

"I find it fascinating."

"Freak," I joke.

"Says the guy who enjoys tying me up."

"That's *fun,* not freaky," I defend.

"And this is intriguing. Maybe if you listened, you'd learn a thing or two—oh wait, your brain is already liquefied." She flicks my forehead.

"Hey, that hurt." I rub the spot.

"Aw, poor baby." She mock pouts. "Should I kiss it and make it better?"

She leans over and kisses the spot before I can retort.

As she settles back down, I say, "I'd rather you kiss my cock."

"I thought you liked when I sucked it?"

I choke yet again, this time on an actual bite of food.

So, this is how I die—choking on a piece of lasagna because my girlfriend has shocked me. I'll be mocked forever in hell.

"Could you stop choking over there?" she retorts playfully. "I'm trying to watch my show."

I finally manage to swallow the food and take a sip of beer. "You are insufferable, woman."

She grins back at me like the cat that ate the damn canary.

I'm the canary.

"'Bout time you got a taste of your own medicine."

By the time we finish eating and I wash the dishes—she cooked, the least I can do is wash the damn dishes—her torture of a show finally ends.

She calls me a pussy no less than twenty times.

She has a point. I officially have one of the weakest stomachs ever, since I can't stop gagging any time one of the ... *things*—okay, *mummies*—appears on the screen.

"You know," I begin, "I think it's kind of wrong the way they take them from their burial place. Isn't it sacred or some shit?"

"Yeah." She shrugs. "But it's history."

"Couldn't you study it, document everything, and learn what you needed to?" I reason. "Why remove everything? I don't get it."

"I guess as humans we can't help but be curious about what came before us. How they lived, how they died, and part of that discovery is sharing as much as you can with others."

She turns her body toward me, one leg curled under the other. She rests her elbow on the back of the couch, her wine glass dangling loosely from the tips of her fingers.

Her red hair glows with a golden hue from the light in the apartment and her eyes are warm, welcoming, *loving*.

I haven't told her yet, but I told my mom about her. I talk to my mom as often as I can, which admittedly isn't enough. But the last time we spoke I had to tell her about Mia. I couldn't *not*. She actually cried on the phone, and admitted she thought I might never settle down, seeing as I'm twenty-five. I'm still young, I told her, but the excuse seemed feeble. She begged me to bring Mia to meet her, but I know it'll be a long while before I can visit my mom —and what if, by then, Mia's decided she's sick of me?

It's laughable, how I went from woman to woman every day and night, and now I'm worrying about *her* growing tired of *me*.

The tables have turned. It makes me regret every nasty thing I've ever said to a girl to get her out of my bed. Okay, maybe not *every* word—some of those girls were certifiable.

I take a drink of beer as we sit there, looking at one another. It's a strange thing, this sitting in silence and not needing to fill it. With Mia there is no need for idle chatter, being with her is enough.

She finishes her wine and leans over to set the glass on the coffee table. She stretches out on the couch, laying her head in my lap with her hands clasped beneath her chin. She yawns, her tiredness an almost physical presence in the room. Even with her living close to work and school, she's running herself ragged. I think it's commendable that Arden and Hayes want their kids to work and not have everything handed to them, but the selfish part of me wants to beg Hayes to take care of her because I hate seeing her tired all the time. But I know Mia would swat me to within an inch of my life if I dared say a thing. Not only would it give us away, but I know she values working hard and wants to work for everything she has.

I brush my fingers through her hair and her eyes drift closed.

"Your dad told us today we're playing at Griffin's this Friday. You been before?" I ask.

"Of course—I'm from here, remember?" she jokes.

"You and Kira should come."

"We wouldn't miss it," she vows.

"Your dad will be there. Willow Creek too. I'm ... nervous," I admit.

It feels like a weak thing to admit. Nerves are pointless. They do nothing but hold you back, but I am nonetheless. It's a small venue, sure, and we've done larger, but when your mentor and his bandmates are going to be watching, and judging, it's a whole new ball game.

"Don't be," she says. "My dad would've never signed you if he didn't love you guys. You should hear the way he talks about you guys to my mom—he's like a proud papa. I think he might think of you guys as his sons, but he'll never admit it to your face."

I snorted. "I doubt it."

"You'd be surprised," she says, stifling another yawn. "He's a total softy. My mom wouldn't have fallen for him otherwise. Did you know when I was like ... two or three, I can't remember, he invited my mom to his birthday party and told her to bring me—it was at a Chuck E. Cheese."

I laugh uproariously picturing Hayes in a fucking Chuck E. Cheese for his birthday.

"For real?" I ask.

"For real," she echoes.

"He can be scary when he's pissed, but he's really a big kid. You should be more afraid of that poor cub who bit you."

I groan, tossing my head back. "I'm never going to live that down. It was a *scratch*," I defend. "I didn't even want to go to the fucking hospital, but the guys lost their shit. They thought I might get rabies."

"You can't get rabies if you already have it."

I pinch her side and she giggles.

How quickly I've come to love that sound, to crave it and expect it as surely as I expect the sun to rise in the morning.

"You should go to sleep," I tell her, concerned when she yawns yet again.

As much as I'd love to strip her down and fuck her right here, I know she's not up for it. She needs to rest.

"Not yet," she says.

"Okay," I give in.

I brush my fingers through her hair, massaging her scalp as I do.

"That feels good," she murmurs.

I keep going.

I don't know how much time has passed but eventually I look down and see her eyes closed, her lips parted with sleep. Her chest rises and falls with each breath. Her eyes roam behind her closed lids, already in a deep enough sleep to be dreaming.

As gently and as carefully as I can, I maneuver out from under her. I slide my arms under her small body and lift her to my chest, carrying her to her bed. She already has the sheets turned back, making it easy to lay her down and cover her up.

She rolls to her side and doesn't stir.

I strip down to my boxer-briefs before climbing into

the bed beside her. I spoon my body around hers and she wiggles her butt against me.

I groan as she settles.

Her hair tickles my nose, smelling faintly of honey and some kind of flower.

It's the sweetest, purest, kind of torture there is—holding her like this.

It wasn't long ago that I dreamed of having one night with her, for surely only one would be enough. Now I worry forever won't be enough time to love her fully. The way she deserves.

TWENTY-THREE

Mia

Kira, Dean, Willow, and I clasp hands pushing through the crowd at Griffin's. People grumble at us, but once they notice who we are they shut up. It's standing room only inside, patrons even spilling outside the building. I don't think I've ever seen this kind of turn out at Griffin's and my boys deserve nothing less.

Finally, with me leading the way, we make it near the stage. No one is performing yet, but the crowd buzzes with eager anticipation.

I spot my dad, standing with Willow's dad Maddox, Mathias, and Ezra. They're lined up against the wall, arms crossed, looking like an imposing force and not the goofballs I know them to be. Well, except Uncle Mathias. Goofy is not in his vocabulary.

My heart races with eagerness at the prospect of seeing The Wild perform. I've only seen clips online, and they're amazing, but live is always better. Thanks to my dad's job I'm privileged enough to have seen some amazing music acts growing up.

It bothers me, though, that I can't cheer for Hollis, or kiss him when he's finished. Not with my dad standing nearby, and not with the millions of people watching online courtesy of cellphones ready and waiting.

This town might be used to rock stars, but that doesn't mean they won't snap a pic of them and sell it to the highest bidder. Money is money after all.

The lights begin to dim and the ruckus of voices quiets to a murmur.

The guys take the stage—they're all dressed simply in jeans and t-shirts. My eyes find Hollis immediately and he smiles at the crowd. I know he's seen me, that he wants to acknowledge me, but with my dad only a few steps away it's impossible.

Keeping our relationship a secret from my family is tearing me up inside, but I also know how overprotective my dad is. After the kidnapping when I was young he's always felt more of a need to make sure I'm safe. Whether that's in the literal sense of slapping a helmet and pads on me before teaching me to ride a bike or threatening to ruin any guy who hurts me. It doesn't matter that I'm twenty-two almost twenty-three, all he sees when he looks at me is a little girl in pigtails and overalls who was such a daddy's girl. He's afraid if I fall in love, he'll somehow lose me, but I would never let that happen. He's my dad, not by blood but by choice, and nothing, and no one, can change my mind. He'll always have a special place in my heart reserved only for him and I'll always be his little girl. I wish he could see that.

Hollis wraps his hands around the microphone. "How's everyone doing tonight?" His voice booms through the room.

There are cheers and he smiles that slightly cocky but blinding smile of his. He chuckles and runs his fingers through his hair. I think I hear a girl sigh dreamily. I don't blame her. He is dreamy—even if he can be absolutely infuriating at times.

"This is our first time playing at Griffin's," he continues. "We hope it won't be our last."

More cheers erupt and he glances over his shoulder at the guys giving a nod.

They start playing and the crowd goes crazy singing along and dancing. They don't even know the words but they sing anyway, wanting to be a part of this night. Hollis plays to the crowd like a seasoned pro. They might not have done stadium tours but he's no stranger to being in front of a crowd. He knows how to draw them in, how to cater to them.

I find my dad and uncles in the corner nodding along to the song. Maddox drums the beat, banging his hands against his thighs. I grin, pleased they all approve. Even

Mathias has a surprised look on his face and whispers something to my dad.

"They're good," Willow yells beside me in order to be heard.

"I'm glad you guys could come out," I say back.

"It was difficult to pull Dean away from his Pokémon cards, but I managed," she jokes with a wink.

I throw my arm over her shoulder and hug her to my side. "I've missed you."

She hugs me back. "Missed you too, girl."

Between school and work, I've wanted to spend my free time with Hollis, which has meant sacrificing time with my friends and family. They have their own lives too, so even if I reach out, meeting up is difficult. I lucked out Willow and Dean could come tonight.

The crowd sways to the song and the four of us join in—Kira making crude gestures at Rush, which makes me want to run the other way.

She's open at all times with what she wants. I'm not. If I confessed to her what Hollis and I do behind closed doors she'd either faint or smack me on the butt for a job well done.

Forget it, she'd never faint. Nothing surprises her.

The song ends and already the guys are damp with sweat from the lights and the press of heated bodies in the small space. If Griffin's ever starts charging people to attend these things the place will make a fortune.

"We're going to slow it down with this one," Hollis says, leaning into the microphone.

The notes of the guitar fill the air before Hollis begins to sing.

"I don't know how to prove this to you,

so I put pen to paper, my heart on my sleeve,

bleeding out for you. Here I stand, just a man telling you this is real.

This spark isn't a flickering ember, it's every star in the sky.

I'll give you the world.

I'll give you me,

if you just see this is real.

I'm here to stay, to make you mine."

My heart stutters in my chest. He's singing our song. The one he wrote for me. The vows he made to me before I even understood that's truly what they were. I feel tears prick my eyes and I clasp my hands beneath my chin as I sway to the song.

Seeing other people respond to the song makes me happy—knowing the words Hollis poured out on the page straight from his heart can connect with other people is awe-inspiring.

I want to glance over at my dad and uncles, to see what they think, but I can't take my eyes off of Hollis.

His eyes connect with mine and he offers me a smile. Just as quickly he's moved on, playing to the crowd.

I'm desperate to touch him, hold him, kiss him, show him how much I love him.

Who knew listening to a song written for you was such a turn on?

"I want to give you the world,

whatever you ask it's never too much.
Anything it takes to make you mine.
Please believe me when I say,
this is real.
Oh baby, this is real."

Every word pierces my heart making me fall more and more in love with him. Despite hearing the song before, there's something different about hearing it now after all that's changed between us.

"You tamed my wild heart,
it belongs to you,
forever and only you.
You ensnared this devil with your angel eyes.
Baby, this is real.
My heart bleeds for you.
Everything I am, everything I will be
belongs to you.
Only you.
Only you, baby.
Believe me when I say,
This is real."

The last note lingers in the air for a moment, time suspended, before the crowd breaks out into raucous cheers.

"That's all for tonight," Hollis says. "Thank you for coming out to see us."

I watch as all four guys slip from the stage and disappear into a back room.

Joining hands again, Kira, Willow, Dean, and I plow our way through the crowd and outside.

November has bled the last of the heat out of the air and I revel in the chill as it pierces my heated cheeks.

"Are we waiting for them?" Willow asks, her blonde hair blowing around her shoulders from the wind.

"We can," I say. "They might be a while."

My dad strolls out of Griffin's, my uncles too, and strides over to us.

"Let's get dinner," he announces. "The guys can meet us there once they can get away."

"Wood-fired pizza?" Willow asks, lighting up.

"Whatever you want." My dad reaches over and ruffles her hair affectionately.

I'm pretty sure he thinks all us kids are still in the single digits and play with dolls and toy cars.

It's not a long walk from Griffin's to Woody's—unfortunate name, I know—the local wood-fired pizza restaurant.

We have to wait while they put a table together to accommodate the eight of us and the four more to come.

I want to text Hollis to ask him when they'll be here, but my dad's chosen to sit beside me and there's no way I'm risking him reading my text messages. This is not the time, nor the place, for him to learn about Hollis and me.

It's hard to sit beside him, knowing the lie I carry.

He's never approved of anyone I've dated and I know those ill feelings he's harbored before will be tenfold for Hollis.

I've seen the headlines, the pictures, everything that

exists before my dad met my mom, and I think when he looks at Hollis, he sees himself. But he can't see that Hollis can change like he did.

Part of me considers the possibility I'm naïve for thinking Hollis can change, but he *did*, he's proven it with more than pretty words. I've never even seen his eyes stray to other girls and believe me all the girls are looking at him.

By the time we've ordered the drinks and they've been brought to the table, The Wild finally appears. They stroll in, sitting at the end of the table.

"Hollis," my dad begins, and Hollis's eyes roll over to him, "I couldn't help but notice you sang your song." *My song. Our song.* "Does that mean you've decided to record it?"

Hollis's gaze drifts ever so subtly to me. "I have. Words from the heart should never be hidden."

"From the heart, huh?"

"Yes, sir."

"Who's the lucky girl?" My dad asks.

I choke on my water and my dad looks at me.

"Swallowed wrong," I croak.

Satisfied with my answer he turns back to Hollis at the end of the table.

"I don't want to say yet." Hollis shrugs. "I'm trying out this whole nice guy thing and that means respecting her right to privacy."

Kira's lips twitch with the threat of a smile.

The rest of the band is studiously glancing anywhere

but at me. Across from me, Willow eyes me shrewdly. I haven't told her about Hollis, the fewer who know the better, but I can see her putting two and two together.

"Can we order now?" I interrupt. "I'm starving."

"Yeah, I'm hungry too," Dean adds.

"Sure thing," Ezra says, signaling for the waitress.

We order our food and I swear it takes forever for it to be ready and even longer for everyone to eat.

By the time we leave, it's nearing ten o' clock.

"You have some explaining to do," Willow says, crossing her arms over her chest outside after our dads have walked away to wherever they're parked.

I shrug. "I don't know what you mean."

She narrows her eyes, tucking a piece of blonde hair behind her ear. "Don't lie. There's something going on with you and the singer. Am I right?" She aims her question at Hollis who lingers with Kira and Rush—Fox and Cannon already headed back to the hotel.

I look at Hollis and he raises a brow at me, his expression telling me the decision is mine on whether or not to share this with her.

"We're together," I confess. "But you can't say anything. My dad doesn't know yet. He can't." I grab her arm gently, pleading with her. If anyone should understand, it's her.

Willow rolls her eyes. "Believe me, I'll keep my lips sealed. Don't you remember how my dad freaked out over Dean?"

"He was pissed," Dean pipes up.

Willow appraises me. "It's our dads' job to protect us—

sometimes they go too far with it, and then it becomes *our* job to remind them we can make our own choices."

I feel Hollis's reassuring presence step up behind me.

"I know, and I'll tell him, we'll tell him, when I'm ready. I…" I pause and reach for Hollis's hand. "I want to enjoy this for a little bit longer."

She smiles. "I understand. I felt the same"

She wraps her arms around me in a tight, bone-crushing hug. "We have to see each other again soon—no more of these long stretches," she scolds.

"I know," I say in agreement.

I hug Dean goodbye too and watch them head in the direction of the nearby parking garage.

Hollis gives my hand a squeeze, and I turn around. Rush and Kira have vanished leaving only the two of us and passersby. The old-timey lights cast a warm golden glow in the night air. Hollis's hair flops messily over his forehead, several day's worth of stubble dotting his jaw.

"Hey, handsome, want to go back to my place?" I joke and he laughs.

"Is that your best pick up line?" he chortles.

"I wasn't trying to pick you up, so if it worked, then yes."

He shakes his head, fighting a grin.

"Come on, crazy girl. I've been dying to touch you all night," he growls the last part in my ear.

We head back to my apartment, and I barely get the door unlocked before he's picked me up and pressed my back into the wall. My legs clamp around his waist, my arms twining around his neck.

His lips devour mine, eager and desperate.

Clearly, tonight, pretending we don't care about each other, was as hard on him as it was on me.

I breathe him in, kissing him back with all that I have.

It's a frantic, aching kind of kiss, born of desperation and need.

A need so powerful we're both helpless to it.

My fingers delve into the soft locks of his hair. I hold on tight, not wanting the kiss to end.

His fingers edge under my sweater and I shiver at the feel of his chilled fingertips against my heated skin.

He deepens the kiss, his tongue sweeping inside.

His fingers skim higher, stopping at the edge of my bra. He rubs them back and forth tauntingly.

I feel like I'm burning from the inside out.

"Please," I beg.

I don't even know what I'm begging for.

He bites my bottom lip. "Whatever you want, it's yours," he pants.

His lips move down my neck and I remove my arms from around him. He pulls far enough away to let me take off my sweater and toss it aside.

Things become chaotic, our desperation making us frantic.

I claw at his shirt, pulling it over his head.

He unclasps my bra and it falls to the floor.

He sets me down and we both fumble to rid the other of their jeans.

Once everything is off, we stumble to my bed, tripping over the clothes and ourselves, but somehow making it without falling over completely or spraining an ankle.

The ache between my legs pounds in time with my heartbeat.

"Fuck me," I beg.

I don't care if I sound pathetic, I need him now and no part of me can wait.

When he continues to kiss me, I grow restless and push him onto the bed.

"I'll take matters into my own hands then," I declare.

He grins up at me.

"There she is."

"There who is?" I ask, taking his cock in my hand and stroking it.

"My vixen. I fucking love it when you unleash the part of yourself you keep so carefully chained. I love it even more that I'm the only one who gets to see it."

His words hit my heart and if I was the swooning type, I would definitely swoon right now.

"Shut up," I growl. "I need you in me *now*."

His big hands clasp my hips. "Take what you want."

I do.

I slide down on him with a moan as he stretches and fills me. I nearly weep with the feel of him. The part of me that felt empty only moments ago is now full.

"God, I love watching you fuck me," he murmurs, cupping my breasts.

I look down to where we're joined, mesmerized by the way his cock drives in and out of me. A moan escapes my lips and I place my hands over his on my breasts.

The girl who never let her hair down, who kept her nose buried in a textbook and never did anything fun, who believed boring was good, it was safe, has realized how wrong she was. Life's more exciting when you step out of your comfort zone—even if it means taking a chance on the guy you think is all wrong for you.

I press my hands to his solid chest and his roam my body, settling on my ass, rolling my hips forward onto him.

I moan, scratching my nails down his chest, leaving behind red marks. He hisses between his teeth.

I jolt when I feel one of his fingers pressing somewhere it should *not* be.

"Hollis, no," I warn, but it's weak sounding from my breathlessness.

"Do you trust me?" he asks.

"Yes, but—"

"Then fucking *trust* me, Mia," he growls, sitting up.

He rubs his finger round and round, kissing me while he does, distracting me.

As my body relaxes, he pushes his finger in slightly.

I gasp.

"Do you want me to stop?" he asks.

"I don't know," I answer honestly.

His other hand comes up to cup my breast and he lowers his head, taking a nipple into his mouth.

My eyes drift closed with pleasure and I moan as I slide up and down his length. He doesn't remove his finger and presses it in a tiny bit more.

Full.

I feel so full.

And I know with Hollis's wicked ways he wants more.

I can't catch my breath and my vision begins to blur. With a cry I bite down on his shoulder as my orgasm rolls through me. My whole body shakes as I lose control and he holds me tight, not letting go.

A moment later his carnal growl echoes through my ear and I feel his warmth seep into me.

We sit there, clinging to each other like a buoy in the sea.

My mind is lost. I can't think.

My body is damp with sweat, his too. Exhaustion seeps into my limbs.

Hollis moves first, brushing my hair away from my eyes. "I love you," he murmurs. "I thought it was impossible to fall in love, that I was above such frivolous things—then I met you. With you I've learned love, true love, makes all the difference in who we are. Love isn't silly, it's not something to be trifled with it … it's the most rare and valuable treasure we can ever seek as a human being and few ever find it."

"Wow," I breathe.

He kisses me, a slow and lazy kiss. He takes his time, our lips dancing together to a song only we know.

I cup his jaw and look him in the eyes. "I love you, too," I finally say. "I wanted to hate you, I still do sometimes," I laugh, rubbing my nose against his, "but it's still the impossible truth that I love you more than I knew was possible. All these years I've been chasing after this feeling, searching for it, but it wasn't the feeling I needed to find. It was you."

"You," he echoes.

TWENTY-FOUR

Hollis

I run, struggling to keep up with the impossible speed I've set on the treadmill.

Last night nearly killed me, being up on the stage, singing the song I wrote for Mia, and not even being able to look at her. A part of me wants to push her for us to tell her dad. This secret is weighing on my shoulders, the pressure painful every second I'm near him. As much as my mind wants to run wild, to think Mia's ashamed of me, I know it isn't the case. She's spoken of her dad's behavior in the past when she's dated, and she knows he'll be a thousand times worse with me.

Because I'm a musician ... and because my past escapades have been splashed across headlines.

But even if I could take it all back, erase it like it never existed, he'd never approve of my relationship with his daughter.

He's her dad, I can't expect any less.

It doesn't change the fact I'm in love with her. I've never known what it's like to be in love before, now that I have, it's a feeling I never want to let go of.

Love like this is the best kind of madness.

My feet pound against the treadmill, my body dripping with sweat. I feel like my body could give out any second but I still keep pushing.

"Get off the fucking treadmill," Cannon demands in his dad voice. "You're going to kill yourself."

"Maybe that's what I want," I growl at him.

He rolls his eyes. "Get. Off." He bites out the words.

I don't listen.

He slams his hand down yanking out the safety belt so it comes to an abrupt stop.

I fall, face planting on the rubber track.

"What the fuck man?" I glower at him, picking myself up.

"I had to save you from yourself." He shrugs, placing his hand on my shoulder and steering me away. "What's going on?" he asks in a lowered voice, leading me over to the water fountain.

I bend, guzzling down the water. Standing up straight once more I lift the edge of my shirt, wiping my sweaty face.

I let out a breath and stick my hands on my hips. "Mia's

not ready to tell her dad, but fuck ... it feels wrong spending all this time with him, having him *mentor* us and he doesn't know. He's going to be pissed if he learns how long this has been going on. It's going to be Thanksgiving soon and he fucking invited us to his house, man. Like we're family or some shit and all I can think about is him finding out there and stabbing me with the carving knife."

Serious, steadfast, always level-headed Cannon busts out laughing.

"He's not going to stab you," he chortles. The bastard even wipes tears from his eyes.

"He might," I grumble. "I am sleeping with his daughter."

"You didn't say fucking. I'm impressed."

I sigh. "Believe me, we fuck, but we also don't. It's different with her."

"There are feelings," he fills in.

"Yeah," I sigh, taking a seat on the bench.

He sits down beside me. I have no clue where Rush and Fox are, but I pray to God they don't stumble upon us to give their two cents.

Friends or not I'm not sure I could take it.

"The way I see it," Cannon begins, and I try not to roll my eyes at the tone of his voice, "Hayes is going to be mad no matter when he finds out. If Mia doesn't want to tell him yet, you have to respect that. He's her dad."

"He's our boss," I remind him. "He could—" There's fear in my voice, a shakiness, because my choices could ruin everything for my bandmates.

He holds up a tattooed-covered hand to shut me up. "I know what he could do. He can throw us out on our asses, refuse to work with us, I know the risks of your relationship with her. We all do. And believe me, I would've beaten you senseless if I hadn't witnessed the way you look at her. She's not another hook up to you. You love her." He shrugs, placing his hands on his knees. "We'll deal with whatever comes when it happens. But all I can say is, if he refuses to work with us because you're in love with his daughter then Hayes isn't the man I think he is."

I press my lips together and hold my fist out for a fist bump. He returns the gesture, cracking a small smile.

"It'll all work out, dude," he tells me. "Don't stress."

I want to believe him, I really fucking do.

IN A BLUR IT'S SUDDENLY THANKSGIVING. WE'VE BEEN HERE since late August.

Three months.

Three months that have completely changed my life.

In the big scheme of things three months seems like nothing, such a short blip of time, but I guess that's the thing about change—when it happens it happens, there is no appropriate timeline for it.

"How do I look?" Mia asks, coming out of the bathroom.

Her hair is curled, hanging down to slightly past her breasts. She's dressed in a tight pair of jeans with rips in the knees, boots, and a slouchy sweater. It's a simple, not dressed up look, but I still want to rip her clothes off and devour her.

"Fucking beautiful," I answer, my hands shoved into my jeans.

"You look nice too," she comments, taking in my button-down shirt tucked into my pants.

"I *am* going to your parents' house," I remind her. "I've got to look nice."

A worried look crosses my face and she frowns. She steps up to me, placing her hands on my chest.

"It'll be fine," she tells me for the hundredth time. "We'll tell him soon."

Soon. Such an ambiguous word. Soon could mean tomorrow or it could mean next fucking month. I want to get this over with. It's like this dark cloud looming above us.

I nod.

"I still can't believe he invited you guys to our house for Thanksgiving—that shows he likes you. I would've thought you all would've headed back home," she remarks.

I shake my head. "Too much work to do."

People don't realize how much work goes into creating an album. It's constant recording, re-recording, tweaking, changing, ditching songs and writing new ones only to start the whole process over again.

But it's worth it.

My phone buzzes in my pocket.

I pull it out, looking at the screen. "Cannon's here."

"Showtime." She smiles at me. With one look, she tries to convey that everything will be fine.

This is new for me, this nervous feeling. Normally I can't be bothered or worried about impressing someone. It's not like I don't know her dad, I spend more time with him than I do her, and I've met her mom, her siblings, and yet here I am, still completely on edge.

I follow her out of her apartment as she locks the door behind us. Cannon's pulled up right outside the curb and we hop in. Fox sits in the front with Rush stuffed in the third row.

"I can't believe I'm stuck back here," he grumbles. "I have long legs and my dick can't breathe."

Mia snorts as she buckles her seatbelt. "I can't believe you haven't named your dick."

"Oh, I have. His name is Crush. It rhymes with Rush and everyone who lays eyes on him ends up with a crush."

Mia laughs harder as Cannon pulls into traffic. "Need I remind you I've seen Crush and I don't have a crush on him?"

"Yeah, but you only saw him in passing. Not up close and personal. You'd change your mind if you saw him in all his glory."

"You have a framed picture of Crush somewhere, don't you?"

"Of course, I take it out every night and tell him what a pretty boy he is."

"The picture or your actual penis?" she asks.

"Both—can't have either getting jealous."

"Can we stop talking about Rush's dick," I grumble.

"You only want me to shut up because you're jealous, man. I can't help it I have an A-plus cock."

I slap my hands over my ears. "Enough," I mutter.

Mia, who's no help at all, snickers at my expense.

"That's enough, guys," Cannon speaks up.

I lower my hands. "Thanks, Dad."

Cannon sighs and mumbles something about not being a dad.

He's so a dad.

"Scold me all you want, my dick is still bigger," Rush declares.

Cannon turns the radio up, glaring at us in the rearview mirror while he does.

"Don't make me put you in time out," he warns. "If you're going to call me dad, then I get parental rights and that means a time out where you all shut the fuck up."

"Yes, sir." Rush mimes zipping his lips and throwing away the key.

We're quiet the rest of the ride and with each minute we get closer to Hayes's house the more nervous I get.

I don't like this feeling.

Hollis Wilder doesn't get nervous, ever.

I can sing on a stage in front of thousands of people at festivals and concerts, but I can't face my girlfriend's family for one small dinner?

Oh, how the mighty have fallen.

When Cannon turns onto the driveway my fight or

flight senses kick in and there's a moment where I consider opening the car door and tumbling out onto the street.

Mia reaches for my hand and squeezes reassuringly. I hate being like this. It's not me, but I hate him not knowing and I hate that I feel like no matter what I do to prove I love his daughter, that this is real, none of it will be enough.

Cannon parks his SUV outside the garage doors.

"It'll be okay," Mia whispers and daringly leans over to kiss my cheek.

The second we leave this car I'm not her boyfriend anymore and she's not my girlfriend.

Instead, I belong to Hayes, and it's not a feeling I like.

TWENTY-FIVE

Mia

My eyes want to drift to Hollis where he plays pool in the corner of the basement with my little brother.

At least Noah seems to be enjoying himself, hanging out with the guys. I'm sure it hasn't been easy growing up with two older sisters.

"I've missed you," my mom says yet again. "I feel like we never see you now." She frowns, her eyes sad. "I don't know what I'm going to do when you're all gone."

"You'll be fine," I assure her. "You have Dad and he's like twelve kids combined."

I know it can't be easy seeing your kids grow up and leave but she'll adapt.

"I hope I can visit more next semester," I continue. "I'll have fewer classes. Right now, with school, work, and…" I almost say Hollis but stop myself. "It's a lot," I finish.

"You seem happy, though," she remarks. "You're glowing."

I want to open up, to share with my mom how much Hollis means to me, how he makes me feel, but I can't.

My dad comes up, putting his arm around her. "This is nice," he remarks. "All of us together and the guys, too."

"They're cool," I say, looking over my shoulder at them.

Rush is giving Noah pointers while Cannon and Fox act as cheerleaders pepping Noah up to beat Hollis.

"We should eat soon," my dad comments. "Before it gets too late."

My mom turns in his arms. "I'll go check on things."

He follows her up the basement steps and I go over to the couch to sit with Addie. As much as I itch to go over to the guys, to put my arms around Hollis, to stand on my tiptoes and kiss him, it's not going to happen today.

My siblings are tattletales.

"What's up with you?" I ask Adalyn.

She looks up from her phone. "Nothing," she says in a tone that conveys it's definitely something.

"Are you texting someone you shouldn't?" I joke.

She looks over her shoulder, searching for dad most likely. "A guy from school," she whispers.

"Tell me about him," I encourage.

"He's … he's kind of a dork," she blushes. "Like, a total nerd, but I like him. He's been tutoring me after school in the library since I suck at math—that's how we met, and I really like him, but..."

"But?" I prompt.

"He's totally oblivious."

"You're texting him," I point out. "Surely he's not completely unaware."

She shrugs. "I told him to have a good Thanksgiving, he responded and I'm literally giddy because of it. I'm pathetic."

"You should tell him you like him," I encourage. "Guys are always so unaware. Don't be afraid to take charge."

"I don't know," she worries her bottom lip between her teeth. "I'll think about it."

Dad yells down the steps then, calling us all up to the table.

"Let me know how it goes—whatever you decide," I tell her.

We hop up from the couch and I see Hollis hanging behind so I do the same.

Addie looks back at me and I wave her on. "I'll be a second."

She hurries up the steps without a backward glance.

Rush, before starting up the steps, gives the two of us a look and pumps his hips.

"Don't do anything I wouldn't do." He winks. "And there's *nothing* I won't do, so have fun, children."

He runs up the steps after the others taking them three at a time.

I know we can't linger long before my dad will barge

down the stairs in search of the two of us, but Hollis doesn't give me a chance to voice this.

He closes the distance between us swiftly, grabbing my face roughly between his hands. He kisses me quickly, desperately. It's a bruising kind of kiss.

He lets me go and steps away. "I had to kiss you before I couldn't for the rest of the evening."

I touch my lips where they still tingle from his.

He flashes a cocky smile, pleased with himself for rendering me speechless.

"I know I'm a good kisser, but I didn't know it was possible to stun you into silence. I'm impressed with myself."

I snap out of my revelry. "I hope you go home and write about it in your diary."

"Oh, I will." He smirks.

"Is it pink and sparkly?"

"Of course—I even hot glued my name in sequins on it and the first page is marked with Future Mr. Mia Hayes."

I bust out laughing. "I can't handle you."

He growls lowly. "You can and you know it. You're the only one."

"True." I flash him a smile and hurry up the stairs with him chasing me.

"Gotcha," he says, his hands winding around my waist.

"Got what?"

Hollis's hands disappear instantly from my waist at the sound of my dad's voice.

"Got me," I say. "I started to fall and he caught me."

My dad looks from me to Hollis. "Thanks for looking out for her."

With those words he heads into the dining room with his plate.

Hollis and I both breathe an embarrassing sigh of relief. I lead him to the kitchen where my mom has everything laid out buffet style. We learned early on having everything spread out on the table only led to disaster.

I grab two plates handing one to Hollis.

We go around, piling food into little mounds onto our plates.

"You gonna eat all that?" he asks me in disbelief eyeing my plate piled high.

"Yes—are you judging me?"

"No, I'm impressed is all."

"Don't come between a girl and her Thanksgiving feast." I shrug and sashay from the kitchen. I hear him groan and feel his gaze zeroed in on my ass.

It's a little too fun torturing him when he can look but not touch.

Since everyone else is seated already this means I end up beside Hollis and I groan internally. He is *so* going to try to get me back for my little show in the kitchen.

My mom asks the guys about their music, listening intently as they explain their sound and vibe.

"We want our music to mean something," Hollis tells her and I bite my lip *hard* as his hand snakes its way up my thigh.

Thank God I'm wearing jeans and not a skirt or dress. Otherwise, he might not leave this house alive.

I kick his foot with mine and he squeezes my thigh in response.

He's in so much trouble for this.

"I think that's amazing," my mom says in response. "Music without meaning is just sound."

Beneath the table I shove Hollis's hand off of me.

He continues talking and eating like nothing is happening.

Oh buddy—if you play with fire you're going to get burned.

I let a few minutes pass and when he goes to take a sip of water, I place my hand on his jeans, right over his dick. I stroke it and he starts to choke.

"You okay?" Noah asks him.

"I'm fine," he replies, and I can't help the laugh that bursts from me at how high his voice has become. I find his zipper, easing it down slowly.

I smile triumphantly when his hand closes around my wrist stopping me.

"Don't even think about it," he whispers under his breath.

"You started it," I remind him, barely moving my lips.

He releases my hand and I go back to eating my second roll—carbs are life.

His knife drops on the floor and he bends to retrieve it.

I jolt in my seat when he caresses my leg before sitting up once more.

This is going to be the longest dinner of both of our lives. I'm sure of it.

AN HOUR LATER, I'M HOT AND BOTHERED—HOLLIS MORE SO—as I clear the table, bringing the dishes to the kitchen.

The rule is the guys have to wash and dry everything. Once I drop the last of the cutlery in the sink, I dash out of there as fast as I can. I know Hollis won't do anything in front of everyone, but my God I can't even look at him right now without wanting to combust.

Addie heads upstairs to her room and I join my mom in the family room.

She curls her legs under her, her hair the same shade as mine pulled back in a low bun. A few stray hairs fall over her face. I've always thought she was beautiful, and I hope I look as enchanting as her when I'm her age.

She rests her elbow on the back of the couch and her head in her hand.

"That Hollis is a good-looking guy," she remarks.

"He's okay I guess," I lie.

She smiles knowingly. "How long?"

I look over my shoulder and back at her with panic in my eyes. "You can't tell Dad."

"I won't." She raises her hands innocently.

I give her a look.

"*I won't*," she reiterates. "Believe me honey, there's a lot I haven't told your father over the years."

I raise a brow. "Really?"

"Are you kidding me? He's way too overprotective. If he had his way, I'd never leave the house."

We both laugh.

"So, how long?" she asks again.

"About two months," I say. "Less if you're asking when it became official."

"I haven't heard the best things about him," she admits. "But I also know how the media can be."

"It seems pretty accurate where he's concerned," I sigh. "He admits to it, but he's different with me. We talk. About deep things. Personal things. It's not like we have sex and that's it. We're ... a couple. God, it's weird to say but true."

She smiles. "I like seeing you happy—but you know you're going to have to tell your dad eventually."

"I know," I groan. "But you know how he is. He warned the guys to stay away from me. Like I'm some possession or something," I whine.

She gives me a motherly look. "He's your dad. In his eyes no one is ever going to be good enough for you. But this is your life, your choices, own them, sweetie. Tell him he can't control you—because he *can't*. If this is the man you want to be with, the one you love, be honest with him."

"I will, but not yet."

She pats my hand. "Do it soon."

It's as much a warning as it is a request.

"I will," I say again with more resolve.

TWENTY-SIX

Hollis

Cannon drops us back off at Mia's place after the fantastic Thanksgiving dinner we had. Mia's mom can cook like a goddess, that's for sure. It was also fun playing with Mia, even if I ended up being tortured in the process. Trying to hide my hard-on in front of her dad was not my idea of a good time.

I follow Mia up the stairs to her apartment, my hands on her hips and one thing on my mind.

She unlocks the door and I urge her inside kicking the door closed behind us.

Before I can kiss her, she puts her hands on my chest and gives me a shove.

She drops to her knees, tearing at my belt buckle like a mad woman.

"Oh fuck," I say as she starts on the button and slides the zipper down.

Seeing her like this, wild, desperate, on edge ... it nearly undoes me.

"Take your shirt off," she commands, fisting my cock in her hand.

She strokes it up and down.

"Shirt," she says again.

I tear at the buttons, getting them undone as quickly as possible.

As I toss the shirt aside, she finally, blessedly, wraps her mouth around me.

I throw my head back, saying a silent prayer.

I look back down at her, her thick dark lashes fanning her smooth pale cheeks. "You're so fucking sexy," I tell her, and I mean it too.

I think she's the sexiest girl I've ever met, and she doesn't even know it. She doesn't have to try to be attractive or get all dolled up, she already is. I'm drawn to *her*, her essence, her very being.

I put my hand in her hair, guiding her, and she gives me a look that says I better let go.

I lift my hands. "Sorry," I mutter and it's a throaty choked sound.

She releases me and tugs at my jeans and boxer-briefs. She slides them down and I step out of them, kicking off my shoes and socks in the process.

"You're wearing too much," I tell her.

"Shut up."

She takes me in her mouth again and all thoughts fly out the window.

She sucks me like I'm her favorite damn lollipop and when I'm about to cum...

"Why are you stopping?" I ask.

She looks up at me from the floor, wiping her mouth with the back of her hand. "That's your punishment for torturing me during dinner."

I narrow my eyes. "Need I remind you of the torture you put me through too?"

She grins wickedly. "That's what I was hoping for."

Aw, fuck.

I reach for her, pulling her up from the floor. In less than a minute she's naked before me and I bend her over the kitchen counter. She hisses at the feel of the cool granite, or whatever the fuck it is, against her tits.

"You like being punished, don't you?" I ask her.

Before she can answer I spank her hard enough to leave behind the imprint of my hand.

"Ooh, I like that," I growl and give her ass a squeeze.

She chokes out a soft plea.

I spank her again before I grab her hips and thrust inside her.

Home.

I'm home with her. Near her. In her.

I never knew what this was like, what you could

possess with another person. I thought people were crazy talking about love like it could change everything.

But it does.

I don't find myself looking at other girls or even wanting to because I have everything I could ever want with Mia Hayes. She's beautiful, smart, sassy. She makes me laugh and I *want* to spend time with her doing things other than sex, which is something I could never say before.

"Hollis," she breathes my name like a prayer, a plea.

I run my hand down her spine and she shivers, turning her head against the counter to look at me.

"Beautiful," I mouth.

She moans, the sound music to my ears.

Not being able to hardly touch her all afternoon, and then the way we both teased each other during dinner ... I'm not sure how long I can last.

I've been picturing her bent over in front of me for hours and now that this moment is here, my body wants to lose control, to fuck her senseless until we're both cumming, collapsing to the floor in an exhausted heap.

She rises up, wrapping one arm around the back of my neck. I grab her chin roughly and kiss her. Her tongue tangles with mine and I groan. She tastes sweet, like the caramel ice cream she had for dessert.

Her fingers tangle in my hair and she gives it a tug. I hiss between my teeth and feel her smile against my kiss.

I glide my other hand up her stomach, stopping at her throat.

"Do it," she pleads.

I squeeze her throat. Not enough to completely close her airway, but enough to make it difficult. Her eyes roll back in her head.

"Yes," she breathes.

I let go and she takes a breath, releasing it, before I squeeze again.

When I let go this time she murmurs, "I love you."

The trust glimmering in her eyes is nearly my undoing. She trusts me completely, to keep her safe, to bring her pleasure, to love her.

We are a beautiful madness, equals in every way.

"I've been waiting my whole life for you," I growl in her ear.

Her breath is a gasp—her eyes lust ridden.

She leans down over the counter once more, and this time I can't hold myself back. I pound into her with brutal force and she takes it, letting me lose control.

She falls apart a moment before I do, her legs shaking.

I hold her back to my front as we both come down from our high.

"Don't let go," she begs.

"Never."

I sit up in bed, looking down at Mia. Her red hair fans around her like a curtain as she lies on her stomach, hugging her pillow. Her lips are parted slightly and she gives the smallest of snores.

Reaching out, I trail my finger down her bare spine and she shivers in her sleep.

Her classes don't start back up for a few more days, so she gets to sleep in this morning before heading to the studio.

I don't have the same luxury. Hayes is a slave driver—okay, that's a lie, he's dedicated and there's a difference. We are too. We want nothing more than to get this album out.

I look at her a little while longer, noting the way her dark lashes brush the curve of her cheek. How she makes a small noise at whatever she's dreaming. She gives a small sigh and turns her head the other way.

Taking that as my cue, I get out of bed and shower before dressing for the day. It's cold as fuck out now so I tug a sweatshirt over my t-shirt and add a beanie for good measure. Living in L.A. for the last few years I'm not used to this kind of cold.

It's funny how I've basically moved into her place. She didn't ask me to, but it happened gradually. A toothbrush here, a t-shirt there, until most of my things slowly left the hotel and found their new home in my very own drawer. I spend most of my time here anyway.

I feel bad leaving the guys at the hotel, but not bad enough to take time away from Mia.

It already scares me thinking about going back to L.A. and leaving her here. She has school, a job, a life, just like I have one there, and I can't ask her to abandon that. I don't expect her to.

Long distance sounds like fucking torture but for her, I'll do it. I'll do anything. If I have to have my ass on a plane every weekend to see her, I will. She's worth it.

I haven't talked to her about this yet, after all we'll be here for a while yet. But it is something we'll have to talk about eventually.

I find a piece of paper and write her a note.

Gone to the hotel and then the studio.
I'll be waiting for my muse.
-H

I leave it on the pillow I use and then kiss her forehead before I go. I'll stop by the hotel first to catch up with the guys some and that way we'll arrive at the studio together.

I slip outside and into the chilly air, walking the few blocks to the hotel.

I slow down when I see Hayes unlocking the door to the studio. I silently curse the fact that the studio is on the same street as our hotel.

There's nowhere for me to hide so I pray he doesn't see me.

No such luck.

He looks up as he opens the door and smiles in greeting.

"Morning Hollis. You're out early and ... why are you coming from that way?"

Why are you coming from that direction? Huh, Hollis? Any other reason except you're fucking his daughter?

"I ... um ... decided to go for a walk," I lie. "It helps clear my head and I thought maybe I'd come into the studio early."

"Oh, okay," he says. "Well, get in here it's freezing." His breath fogs the air as he speaks.

I do as he says, breathing a sigh of relief my excuse was believable.

"Will the other guys be here soon?"

"No idea," I answer honestly. "I left a while ago."

I mean, it's not a *total* lie. I did leave the hotel a while ago.

"We can start with you first this morning," he says, turning on lights as he moves through the studio.

I take off my beanie, leaving my sweatshirt on for now, and head into the booth when he's ready.

Once I'm seated behind the microphone I feel at peace. I've always felt most comfortable with a mic in front of me.

I've never had stage fright like some people. I love singing. I love entertaining.

I don't know how long I've been recording—mostly re-recording parts that need work—when the other guys arrive. I get so in the zone when I'm recording nothing else exists.

By the time I'm done and taking a seat on the leather couch Mia arrives with a carrier full of coffee and a bag from Chick-fil-A.

"I brought breakfast," she announces, shaking the bag.

Maybe it's just me tooting my own horn, but I swear

ever since we've been together, she seems happier. Like she's glowing from the inside out.

"You're a saint," Fox says, taking the bag from her. "I'm starving."

He pulls out one of the wrapped sandwiches.

"There are two for each of you in there and one for me," she tells him.

"I fucking love you," he cries, taking out another before passing it on.

"Language," Hayes warns.

"Like you don't cuss," Rush chortles.

"Not in front of my kids I don't."

"What kids?" Fox jokes. "I don't see any kids."

"Yeah, I don't either," Mia pipes in.

Hayes merely shakes his head and takes the bag when it's handed to him. The bag finally gets back to Mia and she grabs her sandwich.

She sets the coffee carrier down and hands everyone their order. She ends up sitting in the chair beside her dad.

I unwrap my sandwich and start to eat, forcing myself not to look at her.

I hate this feeling, like I'm living a lie, like somehow what we're doing is dirty and wrong.

I'm in love with Hayes's daughter, the little girl he's vowed to protect, and my past goes against me. Nothing I've done proves I can treat a girl right, least of all a girl like Mia.

Honestly, I don't know why my own mom hasn't chewed me out for my past behavior. She's probably wanted to, but she knows I'm stubborn and won't listen to her nagging.

She was giddy when I told her about Mia. I want nothing more than for the two of them to meet. Mia would love her, and in return she would love Mia.

Hayes and the guys are talking about the songs and changes they think we should make. I interject my opinion here and there, but my mind is in another dimension. I'm not invested like I should be.

Mia's eyes catch mine and she gives me a small smile before spinning away, still working on her breakfast sandwich.

I devour my food. She savors hers. It's kind of cute how slow she eats. She's like that a lot, stopping to savor moments, to take in everything, never wanting to miss a single second.

I want to get up and touch her, to hold her hand, to kiss her.

I can't and it's killing me.

If I had ever stopped to imagine myself in a relationship, I would've been the one with the cold feet, not the girl, but here we are. I want her dad to know, for it to be out in the open and not this big fucking secret, but she doesn't want him to know yet.

And that means, I continue to hang in limbo, wondering if I'm really what she wants or not.

TWENTY-SEVEN

Mia

"Ooh, you're going down," I say to Rush, making finger guns and then pretending to blow out smoke.

"You wish, Little Hayes," he remarks, picking up his bowling ball to take his turn.

"You're going down, babe," Kira tells him.

He looks over his shoulder at her. "Aren't you supposed to be on my side?"

"I'm just fucking you." She shrugs. "She's my best friend. I choose her."

"I'll remember that," Rush begins with a wicked grin, "when you're begging me to lick your pussy."

A woman gasps and we look over to see her slapping her hands over her son's ears. "There are *children* in this establishment!"

"My bad," Rush apologizes, but he doesn't sound sorry at all. Kira herself is trying not to laugh.

I take a seat next to Hollis, Fox on his other side—Cannon has gone outside for a smoke break.

Hollis has been distant the last few days and I don't know why. I *suspect* why, but we haven't discussed it.

"Are you mad at me?" I ask, picking up a crinkle fry and dipping it in ketchup.

"No," he sighs, and the word is honest. His golden eyes meet mine. "I'm worried."

"About my dad?" I guess.

"Yeah," he confesses. "It feels wrong, him not knowing. I see him five days a week Mia. Sometimes even on the weekends if he's feeling particularly power hungry." With a sigh, he shoves his fingers through his hair. "He should know, Mia."

"I know," I whine. "I know," I repeat in a defeated tone. "I'll talk to him soon," I promise.

This shouldn't be so difficult, telling my dad, but I've always been one to follow the rules and going against him on this could cause a rift between us. I just want him to accept this without an argument and I don't see that happening.

He gives me a look.

"I'm serious. I will," I vow.

I know with my birthday coming up, and Christmas, I can't keep this a secret any longer because I want Hollis to be there for those things.

"We can do it together," he says reaching for my hand under the table.

It's so kind of him to offer and shows how much he's grown, that he's willing to stand by my side and face telling him together.

I shake my head as Rush cheers. "It's just a spare!" I yell at him. "I got a strike!"

Rush gives me the finger and the mother at the lane beside us makes a disgusted face and storms away—no doubt to report us to management, but I mean she's the one bringing a five-year-old to the bowling alley at eight at night on a Friday.

To Hollis I say, "I think it's better if I do it alone. Otherwise, he might kill you."

He laughs and it's good to see the light come back into his eyes. "Do you really think he'll resort to murder?"

I give him a look.

"*Right*," he drawls.

Fox leans over to Hollis. "Not that I'm eavesdropping or anything, you *are* right next to me, but um ... yeah ... Hayes would totally kill you. He probably will even if she tells him alone."

"Thanks for the boost of confidence, Fox," Hollis grumbles.

"Yeah, my dad's not *that* bad."

They both glare at me. "Okay, so he's overprotective.

But he's a father. It's his job. He'll get over it. I'm turning twenty-three in two weeks. I'm an *adult*. I make my own decisions and my dad can't tell me who I'm allowed to love. That's not the way it works."

"You go girl,' Fox says in a fake valley girl voice and high fives me. "You tell him."

"Hey, what does the fox say?" Rush butts in.

"Not this again." Fox rolls his eyes.

"Nobody knows what the fuck the fox says, but the Rush says it's your fucking turn, get off your ass."

"*See*," shrieks the mother from beside us, now returned with a manager. "They are *heathens*. They need to leave."

"Oh, clutch your damn pearls, Karen," Rush groans. "You've got a kid, so I don't know why you're so offended by the words *fuck* and *pussy*."

She stares open-mouthed.

The manager sighs and looks at us. "You've got to go."

"Are you fucking serious?" Rush stands up. At six-foot-six he towers over the poor manager who's probably still in high school.

"Um ... yes," the manager stammers.

"What's going on?" Cannon asks, returning with the scent of cigarettes clinging to him.

The manager turns to him and literally squeaks like a mouse. I can't say I blame him. Cannon is pretty scary looking even if I'm fairly certain he's a giant teddy bear. But with all the tattoos, piercings, and muscles ... yeah, he's intimidating.

"Is there an issue?" Cannon asks. "I'm trying to understand what's going on here?"

The woman turns to him. "I assume you're with this ... horrid bunch of hoodlums."

"Hoodlums?" Rush snorts. "Oh, Karen, you wound me."

"Stop calling me Karen," she hisses. Turning back to Cannon she says, "The use of crude language in front of children is disgusting. You should all be ashamed of yourselves."

"Maybe you should be ashamed for keeping your kid out so late," Kira pipes up, saying what I've wanted to say this whole time. She points and we all look to the table next to ours where the kid is passed out asleep in his chair, his head flat on the table at an angle that can't be comfortable.

"I ... I ..." the mother sputters. Not able to come up with a good argument she grabs her kid and calls for her husband who's been lurking God knows where—probably looking for a new wife since this one is psychotic—and hauls ass out of there.

"Does this mean we can stay?" Rush asks.

The manager sputters for a moment but finally answers, "Yeah, but please watch the language."

"Sure thing." Rush salutes him before sitting down once more.

"I always miss all the fun," Cannon jokes sitting down.

"Did you just make a joke?" I mock gasp.

"I can be funny ... sometimes." He shrugs, his shoulders stretching his leather jacket. "You guys always wait for me to leave to misbehave."

"Yeah, Dad," Rush starts, spinning in his chair with his hands clasped behind his head, "we know better than to act up in front of you."

Cannon shakes his head. "Not your dad," he mumbles.

"Stop acting like it then." Rush sticks out his tongue. "Still your turn Foxtrot."

Fox rolls his eyes. "All right Rushing River let me get right on that."

"That-a boy," Rush says, slapping Fox on the ass as he passes him. "Also, Rushing River is one-hundred percent going to be my stripper name."

"I'm going to throw this bowling ball at your head," Fox warns him.

"That's called murder, Foxhound."

Fox throws his hands up in the air in defeat before grabbing a ball and taking his turn. He gets a strike and turns to give Rush the finger—luckily no one sees.

Next up is Cannon.

I pick up my hot dog and take a bite. Hollis steals a fry off my plate and I swat him away. "Do *not* touch my fries, Hollis Wilder."

"But I love your fries." He smirks.

I narrow my eyes. "You're not talking about fried potatoes are you?"

He swipes another and pops it in his mouth. "Nope."

Fox returns and this time it's him snagging one of my fries. I frown. "If you guys keep eating all my food you're going to buy me more," I say in a tone with no room for argument.

"Sure thing." Hollis swipes another fry.

Fox takes another too and I waggle my finger back and forth. "Swiper no swiping."

He rolls his eyes, chewing *my* fry. "What's with you guys and the fox jokes today? You're on a roll."

"You're easy to rile up which makes it fun." Rush reaches over to ruffle his hair.

"Play nice while I'm gone children," Cannon says, standing to take his turn.

I pick up my hotdog and before I can take a bite I shriek because all of my fries are gone.

I shove the paper container my fries *were* in into Hollis's chest and he grabs it. "More potatoes, peasant, and make it snappy."

He stands and makes a dramatic bow. "Yes, my Queen. I live to serve."

"You," I point at Fox, "go get your own damn fries and make sure he does too. I'm *not* here to share." Fox sits there for a moment staring at me. *"Now."*

He scurries after Hollis over to the food part of the bowling alley.

Rush snickers. "Seeing Hollis whipped is hands down the greatest thing ever."

"He's not whipped," I defend.

"Oh, he's whipped all right," Cannon adds, sitting down once more. I check the screen to see his score. Rush and I are still in the lead and he's going *down*. I don't lose at bowling. Ever.

If I can't make it in the music industry, I could always become a professional bowler—if it's even a thing. Surely it is if people get paid to play football and basketball, right?

Kira takes her turn and then it's Hollis's turn—Rush takes it for him since he's not back yet, cursing when he gets a strike for him.

Then it's my turn.

I lift the bowling ball up, assessing the pins. I swing my arm back and let the ball go. It soars down the alley and...

"Strike," I scream, turning to Rush and performing my happy dance, finger guns included. "You're going down," I tell him for the thousandth time as I sit down. Fox and Hollis are back and the table is now covered in ... I pause to count the boxes of fries. "You bought twenty servings of fries, *why?*" I level my gaze on each of the boys.

"This way you can't say we're stealing yours." Hollis shrugs. "There are plenty to go around."

"Such a smart ass," I grumble. "But at least there are fries now."

I may or may not hoard three of the containers close to me. I only got a few fries out of my last order, so I'm making sure this time I actually get some.

"This is fun," Kira says, drinking from her root beer. "We should go out as a group more often."

I snort. "You're only amused by our childish behavior."

"True," she dips her bottle in my direction, "but it is fun, too."

I have to admit she's right. When I first met the band, I

never imagined I'd see them as anything other than a nuisance. Now, I'd call them friends. I guess it shows you should always give people a chance, even if at first they don't seem like your kind of people. Sometimes you find hidden gems. I found four of them and happened to fall in love with one.

It's funny, I've dated in the past, but I never told any of those guys I loved them. Even when I dated Will for six months, we never said those words to each other. I guess we both knew it wasn't going to last.

As much as my dating life has sucked in the past, I'm glad for it. It's taught me to respect myself and taught me I don't need a man to complete me—a good man is simply a bonus. Hollis is the best of the best, which still shocks me, but he's definitely one of the good ones.

I reach over and brush an errant curl from his eyes. "I love you even if you steal my fries."

He cracks a grin. "Is that so?" His fingers creep toward the hoard of fries I've taken.

I slam my hand down on his.

"Don't test me," I warn him.

"See, your mouth said one thing, but you really meant you love fries more than me."

"Not possible—but a tie maybe," I relent.

He smiles.

A while later the game ends, and we decide to head out.

Hollis follows me to my Audi and watching him

contort his large frame in my small car is more than amusing.

I open the driver's door to hear him cursing as his head brushes the top.

"How you can stand this clown car is beyond me," he grumbles, pulling the seatbelt across his torso.

"It's not a clown car, you're just large."

As soon as the words leave my mouth, I instantly regret them. My mouth makes a firm line, waiting for his remark.

"I can't help it if I'm *very* well endowed, Mia, thank you for noticing."

"I hate you," I growl, putting the gearshift in drive.

"Nah." He leans over, gliding his hand along my jean-clad thigh—thank God for winter and the necessity of jeans. "You love me and my dirty mouth and..." his voice lowers and he comes even closer until his mouth is pressed right against my ear. "You love every dirty little thing I do to you."

He's right, of course. "That may be true," I relent, "but it doesn't mean I still don't want to punch you in the nuts right now."

He grins from ear to ear. "But you won't."

I glance at him with narrowed eyes. "Don't test me, Wilder."

He chuckles and I pull out from the bowling alley parking lot.

"I'm not ready to go home," I confess.

"Me either," he admits quietly.

"Let's walk around Old Town for a little while," I suggest.

"It's cold."

"I'll buy you a hot chocolate," I sing-song.

"Well ... when you offer hot chocolate how can I say no?"

"You can't, it's that simple." I shrug.

The drive is short and I park on the side of the street near the entrance to the walking mall.

Hollis hops out, change already in hand to put into the meter.

I meet him on the sidewalk and he takes my hand, the two of us walking across the street together. His hand nearly swallows mine, the cold can't even reach it.

"My nuts are going to freeze off," he complains.

"Stop being such a baby. You have a coat on." I tug on his coat to demonstrate my point. "But don't worry, one hot chocolate coming right up for the big baby."

"With extra marshmallows?" he asks with a wicked grin.

"Of course—you don't think I'm going to share *my* marshmallows do you?"

"You already share your marshmallows with me." He looks significantly at my chest.

"Do you want hot chocolate or not?" I raise a brow.

"Yes, ma'am. I'll shut up." I give him a look. "Okay, I'll *attempt* to shut up."

I lead him over to the hot chocolate stand set up for the winter months. There's a fairly long line, which I guess shouldn't surprise me, even at this late hour. Downtown stays pretty busy in the evenings.

I shiver and Hollis wraps his arms around me, pulling my back to his front. I instantly feel his warmth fall around me like a blanket.

He bends his head and presses his lips to my neck. I tilt my head smiling up at him. I gasp then, as fluffy white snowflakes begin to fall from the sky. As one lands on his nose, he looks up too.

"It looks like the stars are falling," I breathe. "The first snow of the season is always the most magical."

"And the coldest," he retorts.

I look at him, at the flakes collecting in his hair and sticking to his lashes.

I turn in his arms and touch my fingers to his jaw.

I wish I could take a snapshot of this moment, to cherish it forever, but my memories will have to do.

"Magic," I repeat, capturing one of the snowflakes that lands in his hair and watching as it turns to water on my finger.

He bends his head and kisses me as the snow falls around us.

I forget all about hot chocolate, how cold the night is, and only focus on him and the feel of his lips on mine.

My hands fist in his jacket, holding him to me.

Cold stings my cheeks and still my lips do not leave his.

He breaks the kiss and brushes my hair away from my forehead.

"You're beautiful," he whispers, his breath fogging the air.

I hug myself to him, holding on. How quickly I've come to crave him, to need him.

I wonder if he can feel the beat of my heart against his, because it feels like it's going to beat out of my chest.

"Excuse me?" I turn to see the girl working the hot chocolate stand ushering us forward and I blush at the line forming behind us.

"Let's get that hot chocolate I owe you," I say, looping my arm through his.

We place our order and wait for her to hand us the Styrofoam cups.

Walking hand in hand we make our way down the walking mall. The trees are wrapped in twinkle lights and with the snow it's ... well, a fairy-tale come to life.

I lean my head against his arm and I feel him look down at me.

"Did you ever think this would be us?" I ask him.

"No," he admits. "For the longest time I didn't think I was capable of loving someone like I love you. At times I didn't think it existed. Then I met you—and I was instantly drawn to you. You didn't fawn all over me—you warned me you knew jiu-jitsu and fuck, I think I was a goner from that moment on."

I laugh loudly. "You mean to tell me, my threatening to kick your ass is what did you in?"

"Yep, that's exactly what I'm saying."

"You're so weird, Hollis."

He grins, his eyes twinkling as brightly as the stars and lights around us. "It's part of my charm."

"Insufferable bastard," I groan.

"But I'm *your* insufferable bastard."

"You're right." I agree lifting the cup of hot chocolate to my lips.

He takes a sip too. "This might be the best fucking hot chocolate I've ever had."

"But you still needed ten mini marshmallows?"

"Any less is for pussies," he quips.

I shake my head. We reach the end and turn around to head back.

"This place, this town," he begins, looking around, "it's pretty unique."

I look around. "Yeah, I guess it is."

"I could be happy here," he remarks. "Happy with you."

My heart stutters.

He looks down at me, his eyes serious. "We have a lot to figure out, Mia."

"I know," I breathe shakily. "It seems like an impossibility at times, you and me."

He shakes his head and stops walking. He tucks a piece of hair behind my ear. The snow is still falling even harder than before. "Impossibilities only exist to prove the possible, and we, Mia," he bends his head closer so I feel his breath against the skin of my cheek, "are most definitely possible."

He kisses me then. Slowly. Deeply. Until I completely forget the world around us.

I close my eyes, soaking in his words, holding them close to my heart and willing them to be true.

It's not until were tucked back, safe and warm in my apartment, that I realize we haven't been careful at all tonight.

Not once, did I think about the possibility of getting caught.

TWENTY-EIGHT

Hollis

The bell above the door at The Sub Club chimes as I head inside.

"Welcome to—oh it's you," Kira says, adjusting her hat. "Are you here to see Mia or get food?"

"Both, preferably. *I* wanted to pick up food from my favorite place in the world—Waffle House, but I was outvoted, so here I am."

She cracks a smile. "I'll send Mia out."

She heads into the back and I wait, hands stuffed into the pockets of my jeans.

"Hey," she greets with a small smile. Little pieces of hair escape her uniform's baseball cap and she looks frazzled.

"Hi," I say awkwardly. "I volunteered to pick up lunch for everyone," I explain.

"Face it, you wanted to see me." She smiles, pulling on a pair of gloves.

"That too."

I start giving her the order, because I *do* have to return with sandwiches, chips, and soda.

"You wanted Waffle House, huh?" she jokes, putting the first sub in the toaster oven.

"Kira told you?" I laugh when she nods. "What can I say, I love me some Waffle House. We haven't been back in too long."

"Yeah, because we rarely have time in the mornings," she reminds me, taking the sub out of the toaster. She starts adding the toppings before I can tell her—having already memorized what each of us orders.

"True, but Waffle House is an any time of the day kind of place. We should go tonight."

She raises a brow. "Are you asking me on a date?"

"Shit," I curse. "We've never been on an actual date, have we?"

"No, and I don't need one."

"I should probably take you somewhere fancier than Waffle House."

"I love Waffle House," she retorts. "I don't need fancy, Hollis. I never have and I never will."

"Okay—so Waffle House tonight then?"

"Yes, as long as you promise we never have to say

Waffle House this many times in a conversation ever again."

I grin. "Deal."

She finishes the sandwiches and fifteen minutes later I head out into the cold. I borrowed Cannon's car since my bike is useless in this frigid weather.

I wish I could've stayed longer, but she's working and Hayes will wonder what's taking so fucking long if I don't get back soon.

I don't bother driving back to the hotel garage and walking over to the studio. Instead, I park in the small lot in the back beside Hayes's Range Rover.

We sit down in the front area since there's more room to spread out than in the recording studio. Hayes joins us. It was awkward at first, spending time with him like this, especially after the way he found us in D.C. He's an icon, but a father figure nonetheless. I feel the need to watch what I say around him, wanting his approval of me as a person. I wanted that before I even had anything going on with Mia. Hayes is the kind of man who despite what he may have done in his past is a *good* person. You'd be an idiot not to want him to like you.

He'll never like you once he finds out what you've been up to with his daughter.

"How are you guys feeling about the album?" Hayes asks, grabbing one of the bags of sour cream and onion chips.

"It's the best music we've ever made," Rush says

honestly. "You can tell how well we work together and the lyrics flow."

"Yeah," I chime in, pushing away the sudden sickness in my stomach. "The singles we've released previously ... none of those compare to what we're doing here. I think we've really nailed our sound down and it's perfect."

"It's going to resonate with people," Cannon chimes in.

"Can you pass me those chips?" Fox asks, pointing at the bag of BBQ ones in front of me. I toss them to him.

"I think everything should be a green light to release your first single after the first of the year with a second around April. We should have things wrapped up for a summer album release."

The guys all smile, I try as well, but it feels too good to be true in a way.

We've been working for *years* to get here and now that it's all within grasp I feel sure I must be dreaming. To finally have a full album out there, to be able to actually tour, even if it's only as an opening act ... it's crazy. We've spent so long recording when we had the money to pay for it, performing at festivals for free, doing whatever we could to get our name out there.

I know we're damn lucky people started taking notice of us, which led to Hayes. Not everyone gets an opportunity like this.

All four of us have had our trials in getting to this point.

We've put our blood, sweat, and tears into our album, our music.

"Smile, Hollis." Hayes reaches over and claps me on the shoulder. "Dreams do come true, you know?"

Yeah, but at what price?

"What can I get y'all today?" Marge, a waitress we've had a few times before, asks. She's older, probably in her fifties or sixties, with graying hair and plump around the middle. "The usual?"

"Yep," we say simultaneously, not even looking at a menu.

She leaves to go get our drinks and call out our order.

"School is kicking my butt," Mia says, resting her chin in her hand. "I'm beyond ready for winter break. I fully plan to stock up on snacks and hibernate."

I crack a smile. "Can I get in on the hibernating?"

"Only if you bring your own blankets," she quips.

Marge sets down our drinks. "Thanks," I tell her.

"Yes, thank you," Mia says, picking up her straw and ripping the paper off.

"Do you want to do anything for your birthday?" I ask her.

"My family always throws a party. It usually turns into a big deal with my uncles, aunts, and cousins coming. You guys will be welcome to come too. Kira does."

I press my lips together. "Are you going to tell your dad *before* your birthday?"

"Yes," she sighs, giving me a look like I should give her

some credit. "I know I need to tell him about us and there's no way I'm having a family gathering for my birthday with him not knowing. I won't hide you from him anymore."

"Good," I say.

I'm still scared for him to know—fearing the worst, but I also know the best thing is for us to be upfront and let him know. He's her dad, he deserves to know and not be kept in the dark.

"Have you thought about what you want to do when you go back to L.A.?" she asks, barely meeting my eyes. "You're not going to be here forever."

"I know it won't be easy," I begin, "but I figure we can do the long-distance thing, and I'll fly here as much as I can. You can visit me whenever you want, I know you have school—but when you have breaks or something."

"Really? You still want to be together when you go back?"

My brows furrow. "Um ... yes. You thought I'd break up with you once I go back to California?"

She shrugs. "I figured you wouldn't want to be tied down with a girlfriend. Don't get me wrong, it's not what I *hoped* for. I want to stay together, but I figured going back to that ... environment, you'd want to be free to do as you pleased."

My hands fist on top of the table. I feel irrationally angry she assumed I'd end things so I could go back to L.A. and fuck my way through town.

"Don't be mad," she pleads.

"I'm not mad," I defend. "Okay, a little mad, but

mostly hurt. I thought you understood this is different for me. I've *never* had a girlfriend, Mia. Not even in high school—not even a silly elementary schoolyard girlfriend. I don't take what we're doing lightly. Yeah, I won't lie, I was attracted to you from the beginning and only thought about sleeping with you, but as I got to know you, I knew one night wouldn't be enough, not when you were the first girl I could picture myself having a future with."

"You see a future with me?"

"Fuck," I scrub a hand over my jaw, "I see it all—you walking down the aisle in a white dress, a house, kids, pets, all of it. I used to think I was the kind of guy who would never settle down. It wasn't something I thought I wanted or needed—then I met you and I realized when you find your person it changes your perspective on everything. Suddenly you want things you never wanted before. I want to be a better man for you. No, not *for* you—because of you."

She sniffles. "You made me cry in Waffle House. I hate you." She wipes away a tear.

I can't help but chuckle. "I didn't mean to get sappy on you, but it's true. Don't get me wrong, I see those things far in the future—I promise not to drag you into a church tomorrow, but I do see it. One day."

"I can see it too," she confesses on a whisper. "It scares me."

"It scares me too," I agree. "But I'd be more worried if we weren't afraid of this."

"I've never felt what I feel for you before ... and so quickly too."

I grin. "When it's meant to be it's meant to be, baby."

She tosses a napkin at me. "Don't be an ass."

I laugh and pick up the napkin. "Sorry, I had to lighten the mood. It got too serious."

She shakes her head. "I should punch you."

I rub my jaw. "And mess up this fine specimen? I think not."

She laughs, drying the last of her tears. "Thank you for making me laugh."

"Thank you for teaching me to love."

She starts tearing up again. "Stop it—Jesus I hope I'm starting my period and not just being a little bitch."

I laugh way too loud at her words.

"What's so funny?" Our waitress asks setting down our plates of food. My three plates to Mia's one is comical.

"My girlfriend is a comedian."

She looks at Mia and then turns to glare at me. "Then why is she crying?"

I hold my hands up innocently, my eyes threatening to bug out. "I was being *sweet* and she started crying."

"I really need some chocolate," Mia sighs desperately.

"Got any chocolate?" I ask just as desperately.

The waitress laughs. "We have chocolate pie."

"Bring one—two, stat," I add when Mia glares. "Actually, make it three, I want one too and my girl here needs two."

She hisses.

"Marge, save me," I plead with the waitress.

"You're on your own," she says. "But I'll bring you those pies."

"Make it snappy," I beg, clasping my hands and pouting my bottom lip.

She laughs as she walks away, clearly not understanding the urgency of the situation.

"I do *not* need two pies," she growls, swiping a piece of *my* bacon. She's looking for war taking my bacon like that.

"Then you can take one home for later. I'd thoroughly enjoy eating it off your naked body."

"Hollis!" She tosses the piece of bacon at me.

I gasp. "*Mia.* You do not waste bacon. This is blasphemy." I frown down at the piece of bacon, which bounced off of me and onto the floor.

"Then don't say such dirty things in public," she mumbles, her cheeks crimson. Her freckles grow darker as color floods her face.

"There is nothing *dirty* about me licking pie off your body."

"Ooh, sounds fun," Marge says, setting the pies down on the table.

"See Mia," I point to Marge, "even she thinks it sounds fun."

"If I had a piece as hot as you, I'd let you eat whatever you wanted." She winks.

"Marge," I mock-gasp. "You dirty minx."

"I might be getting older," she says, pointing to her

wrinkle-lined face and graying hair, "but this girl still knows how to have fun."

"I'm dying a thousand deaths and no one cares," Mia grumbles, sliding down in the booth.

"You should be used to my dirty mouth by now and everything I like to do with it."

"Marge, can we get to-go boxes," she pleads.

"We're not going anywhere," I tell Marge.

Marge shakes her head. "Oh, young love," she sighs, and heads to another table.

Mia covers her eyes with her hands and peeks out between her fingers. "You live to embarrass me, don't you?"

I grin. "It might be one of my favorite pastimes."

She sighs and sits up straight. "At least I got pie out of this."

"Pie makes everything better," I agree.

She pushes her food to the side and pulls the pie closer. I watch her wrap her lips around the fork loaded with chocolate and whipped cream, groaning with the erotic gesture.

She glares at me. "Are you making something sexual out of my pie eating?"

"I can't help it," I whine. "I have a dirty mind, you know this."

She shakes her head but I can tell she's trying her hardest not to laugh.

"Just eat your food," she commands.

"I'd rather be eating your p—"

"Do *not* finish that sentence, Hollis Wilder."

I grin. "I was going to say pie—did you think I was going to say pussy? Who's the dirty one now?"

"You're impossible."

"But you love me," I point out.

She gives me a smile—so I know I'm not entirely in trouble.

"For whatever unknown reason, I do."

I haven't gotten tired of hearing her say how she feels about me. I hope I never do.

We might be unexplainable, but what we have is real, and I'm thankful for whatever force out there put us in each other's path. I don't pretend to know where the future will lead us, and I've always been a live in the moment kind of guy, but right here, right now, it's safe to say I'm happier than I've ever been. And I think, no I *know*, I make Mia happy too—and her happiness?

It's the best damn reward in the entire fucking universe.

"FUCK, YOU LOOK HOT," I GROAN WHEN MIA OPENS THE door. "Forget going out. We're staying in."

She laughs, stepping outside. "It's Friday night, and you promised me a *real* date even though I said I didn't need fancy. Now, here I am dressed up, hair done, makeup on—that means we're going out."

"I don't know why I don't listen to you," I complain.

She passes me and starts down the stairs. I can't see the

way her dress hugs her ass since her winter coat hangs down long enough to hide it, but I know it's got to be *glued* to her curvy body. Tonight might kill me. I want nothing more than to grab her, drag her back inside, and show her exactly how much I love her.

"One day you'll figure out I'm always right," she sing-songs looking at me coyly over her shoulder.

"Fucking vixen," I whisper under my breath, trudging after her.

I lead her outside to Cannon's car and open the passenger door for her.

She raises a brow as she climbs inside.

"What?" I defend. "I can be a gentleman."

"Where are you taking me?"

"Ah, ah, ah—I'm not telling."

She crosses her arms and mock pouts. "Come on, tell me."

"Nope," I say adamantly.

"You suck."

"No, you do baby. I lick."

"Oh my God," she sighs. "There's no winning with you."

A few minutes later I park the car.

"Your hotel? You brought me to your hotel?" she asks in disbelief. "No wonder you wouldn't tell me where you were taking me. This is anticlimactic."

"How you doubt me." I shake my head. "Trust me, this will be worth all the effort you put into your outfit, hair, and makeup."

"Better be," she grumbles, and I crack a grin.

I hand the keys over to the valet, since we'll need the car to get back to her place. It didn't make sense to park in the garage tonight.

I take her hand, leading her up the stairs into the lobby. A fire roars in the fireplace and a few people linger around chatting and hanging out in the bar.

I pull her in for a kiss and that's when I notice a woman with her phone pointed in our direction. It could be entirely innocent, maybe she's checking for service, but something tells me she just got a photo of us.

I don't tell Mia, not wanting to spoil the evening I have planned, so I tug her toward the elevator and the moment we step on I push the button for the top floor.

"Are you seriously taking me to your hotel room? We should've stayed at my place. Besides, I thought this was supposed to be a real date," she rants playfully.

I shake my head, looking up at the mirrored elevator ceiling.

The doors open and I lead her down the hall. She tries to stop in front of the suite door, but I keep pulling her along.

"*Now* I'm curious," she says.

I smile.

I open a door at the end of the hall that leads to a set of stairs.

"After you milady." I step aside and sweep my arm.

She rolls her eyes. "You just want to look at my ass but jokes on you since I have my coat on," she snickers.

I shake my head. "Such little faith in me, but I am in fact an ass man. And a boob man. And—"

She slaps a hand over my mouth. "Don't finish that."

The stairs lead to another door which she pushes open and steps onto the roof.

"If you brought me up here to freeze my ass off, you'll succeed."

I take her hand. "Come on."

I lead her to the other side of the roof, and she gasps. "Hollis," she breathes on a whisper.

I open the door to the greenhouse, and she steps inside, her mouth parted in awe. Twinkle lights are strung from the ceiling and it's nice and toasty warm inside. I remove my coat and hold my hand out for hers. She slips out of it and just as I thought, she wears a skintight dress. It's black, with long sleeves and ends well above her knees. She wears a pair of black heels with red soles that do amazing things to her legs and ass.

I bite my knuckles and hiss. "Damn Mia. You look fucking sexy—I mean you always do, but ... *fuck*."

Her eyes heat and I can see her nipples harden through the fabric. Something tells me she's not wearing a bra, and from how tight that dress is? Yeah, I bet there aren't any panties involved either.

If she's trying to kill me, she's succeeding.

I push all my naughty thoughts out of my mind. There will be time for that later.

We have all night.

I drape our coats over one of my arms and with the

other I put a hand on her lower back, my fingers splaying onto her ass, and guide her through the greenhouse, stopping when we reach the table I requested. It's covered with a white tablecloth and set up with candles and a low vase of flowers. A bottle of wine waits for us—the food will be coming shortly.

"Hollis," she breathes. "Did you do all this?"

"Well, it was my idea, but I asked the staff for help. I couldn't exactly get all this up here without their permission."

She laughs as I pull the chair out for her, and she sits down.

A staff member steps out of the shadows and takes our coats before disappearing again.

I sit down across from Mia clearing my throat. I feel slightly awkward. I've never done anything like this before and I feel insecure.

Is it too much?

Not enough?

Does she think I'm going to propose or some shit?

What have I done?

I clear my throat again, pushing my worries aside and watching Mia as she looks around taking everything in.

"This is so beautiful, Hollis. I can't believe you'd do something like this for me."

When her blue eyes meet mine, they shimmer with barely contained emotions.

"I wanted our first official date to be something you'd never forget."

Her eyes have strayed around once more, but drift back to me. A smile tugs her lips. "You never do anything small do you?"

"Baby, there's nothing small about me."

She rolls her eyes and I chuckle.

"Are you ready for dinner, Mr. Wilder?" The male staff member steps forward.

"Yes, now would be great, thanks."

He nods and leaves.

Mia raises a brow. "Mr. Wilder? Hmm, I like the sound of that."

I lower my voice to a gravelly growl. "You can call me Mr. Wilder any time you want. Preferably naked. Tied up. Completely exposed and bared to me."

She twists in her seat and coughs, and I know I'm getting her worked up.

I love watching her get turned on, all the tells her body has. She's not even aware of them. Like the way her eyes darken, and she licks her lips. She also tends to tuck a piece of hair behind her ear or at least play with a strand.

"How did you think to do this?" she asks.

I shrug. "I didn't want to take you to a basic restaurant. I knew I had to get creative."

"This is incredible. Truly."

"I think you know by now I'd do anything for you."

"Why?" she asks, her head tilted, and eyes puzzled. "Why me? Why is this different?"

"I don't know," I answer honestly. "It just is."

She swallows and nods. "As much as I wish there

was a real solid explanation for this, for us, you're right. Some things are unexplainable. We're one of them."

I grab the bottle of wine, uncorking it, and fill each of our glasses. I'm not a wine guy, but tonight I am. I need something to take the edge off the nerves dancing just below my skin.

She picks up her glass, swirling the wine around before taking a small sip. I watch her movements. Everything about her is fascinating to me. She's like an intricate work of art I could stare at all day and still not unlock all its secrets.

"Why are you staring at me?" she asks, holding her wine glass partially in front of her face to hide.

"Because I want to," I answer honestly.

She blushes, hiding behind her hair.

"The dinner you requested, Mr. Wilder," the man returns, setting our plates down.

"Thank you," we both tell him.

"I'll be around if you need anything," he says, bleeding into the shadows once more.

Mia looks down at her plate. "This looks delicious."

"It does," I agree.

I requested steak, a lobster tail, asparagus, and a loaded baked potato.

"I didn't realize how hungry I was. I forgot to eat lunch," she admits.

"Why didn't you?" I question, cutting into my steak.

"Well, I worked at the sub shop and by the time I got

home I was so focused on getting ready I didn't think to eat."

"Eat up then. You're going to need your energy."

"For what?" she asks coyly.

"All the things I have planned to do to you later."

"Sounds promising."

"It's not a promise, baby. It's a fucking vow."

I swear she eats a little faster.

When our meal is done, and the plates are cleared away I stand and offer her my hand.

She looks at me speculatively. "What now?"

"Take my hand and you'll see."

She slips her pale hand in mine, and I haul her up into my arms.

"Tom," I call out to the staff member as I guide Mia over to where I want her. It's at the end of the green house, with the glass walls overlooking the city. "Now," I say as the night sky lights up with fireworks.

The music begins to play, and I bow before her—I might have a flare for the dramatics.

"Will this beautiful lady accept my offer to dance?"

"I might be inclined," she says, and I can hear the smile in her voice as I raise up.

I place my hand at her waist, clasp her hand in my other one, and begin to ballroom dance.

She gasps. "I didn't know you could dance like this."

"I couldn't. I watched a bunch of YouTube videos when I had time. I still can't tell you what dance this is, but I think it's a waltz or some shit. But hey, at least I can do it."

She shakes her head. "And the fireworks—is that you too?"

"Nope, but I knew they were going off in the park for the early Christmas festivities and I timed it just right. But the song, it's only for you, baby," I whisper the last in her ear.

She quiets then, listening to the song.

"It's the song you wrote for me, but it's…"

"Acoustic," I tell her. "I slowed it down, made it raw, more … real. And yes, baby, before you ask that is me on the guitar. I'm a man of *many* talents" I smirk at her.

She shakes her head, her fingers playing with the hair at the nape of my neck. "I can't believe you did all this for me."

I brush my lips over her neck. "I'd do anything to make you happy."

She pauses her eyes meeting mine and I can see how much this has meant to her. "This has been the best night of my life. I love you."

"I love you too, beautiful," I murmur.

"Can I kiss you now?" she asks.

"You can kiss me any fucking time you want," I tell her. I want to add *preferably on my cock, on your knees, naked*, but I don't want to ruin the moment with my dirty thoughts. Frankly, she can't blame me. She's too fucking sexy in that sinful dress and she knows it.

She raises up and kisses me just as the grand finale of the fireworks begin.

My hand flexes at her waist, desperate to get her home and show her *my* version of a grand finale.

I CLOSE THE DOOR AND TURN TO FIND MIA STANDING IN front of me. Her breasts strain against her dress as her breath grows ragged.

We stand looking at each other, taking the other in. The air grows thick between us. I itch to break the distance, to take her into my arms, but I'm captivated by her and can't move. I can barely fucking breathe.

With a shaky breath, like this is my first time or some shit, I hold out my hand to her.

She takes it and I pull her against my chest. I push her hair back, looking into her ocean blue eyes.

"I'm going to fuck you now, Mia. And then," I lower my voice, pressing my lips to her ear so she shivers, "I'm going to make love to you. I'm going to worship every inch of your body like you deserve. Because you're *mine*."

She shivers again. "I like the sound of that."

"Good." I crash my lips to hers, my hands on her cheeks, kissing her like a man headed to his death. I'm desperate, frantic, positively aching for her.

I drop to my knees and grab her leg, pressing kisses to the inside of her thigh before I meet her gaze. I slip my hands under her dress and start pushing it up. I keep pulling it up as I stand, revealing each delectable inch of her naked body, until she lifts her arms and it's off completely.

I bend and kiss her collarbone, murmuring into the skin of her neck, "I knew you were fucking naked under this dress. It's had me hard all night."

She puts her hand over my erection straining against the zipper of my dress pants.

"You must be ... *aching*," she says in a husky whisper.

Before I can blink, she drops to her knees and undoes my belt and button with speedy ease.

She looks up at me as she slowly, oh so fucking slowly, lowers the zipper.

She wets her lips and yanks down my pants and boxer-briefs. My cock bounces free and she grabs it, wrapping her delectable mouth around it.

"Oh, fuck. *Mia*."

Her name is a curse and a prayer all in one.

My heartbeat is a violent roar in my ears.

Swallowing roughly, I look down to watch her. Watching her might get me off more than the actual blowjob, though she's a fucking pro at sucking cock.

I unbutton my dress shirt and it falls on the floor.

"Stand up," I command, my voice hoarse.

As much as I'd love to cum in her sexy little mouth, I don't have plans for it tonight.

She does as she's told, her eyes heated.

Fast enough I could probably make the *Guinness Book of World Records* I'm out of the rest of my clothes.

"You're still in the heels," I pant, finally noticing. "God, that's fucking hot."

She smirks. "I thought you'd like them."

"Like them? I fucking love them."

I grab her ass and lift her up onto the counter. She shivers and wraps her arms around my shoulders.

I slip my hand between us finding her wet and ready.

I let out a low growl and kiss her, murmuring against her lips, "It makes you wet sucking me off, doesn't it? You fucking love it."

"I do," she whispers breathily.

"Naughty, naughty, Miss Hayes. Whatever am I going to do with you?"

She takes my face between her hands and looks me in the eyes. "I'm ready."

"Ready?" I ask, puzzled. My eyes widen in surprise. "Oh."

She nods.

"Are you sure? I won't push you."

She shakes her head. "I'm ready, and I want this."

I've been preparing her for weeks, dying to take that sweet ass of hers but she's been hesitant. I haven't pushed it, I never would pressure her into something she's not comfortable with, but I knew if she warmed to the idea, she'd love it.

"If you want me to stop, I will," I promise. "I might be fucking dominant at times, but you always have the last say. I won't do anything you don't want."

She nods. "I know. I trust you. I wouldn't do this with

anyone else." She rubs her fingers against my stubbled jaw. I don't think she even knows she's doing it. "Am I nervous? Of course, but I trust you," she repeats. "I know you'll take care of me."

"Hell yeah I will." I kiss her passionately, her tongue tangling with mine.

My fingers dig into her ass cheeks with bruising pressure as I try to hold myself back, to take this slow and be in the moment with her.

I tear my lips from hers, trailing kisses down her neck and sucking on her skin.

"I fucking love you," I growl. "So fucking much."

Her legs are tight around my waist, and I pick her up, carrying her to the couch.

I kiss every inch of her body, turning her over and doing the same.

I worship her.

I cherish her.

"I'll be right back," I tell her. "Don't move—I'll know if you do, and you know I'm not above spanking you."

She wiggles her ass and *moans*. That fucking sound. She's killing me.

I grab the lube from the drawer in her room and carry it back out to the living room.

She listened and didn't move but I give her ass a light smack anyway. A low throaty sensual moan leaves her, and I struggle to keep my composure.

I squirt out some of the lube, rubbing it on her tight virgin hole. After tonight it's *mine* and only mine.

Slowly, I rub my index finger against her, slipping it inside.

"Hollis," she begs. "Please."

"I know, baby." I bend pressing a kiss to the back of her neck. "I have to make sure you're ready."

She whimpers.

I remove my finger and press in with my thumb next.

She moans. "Hollis, I swear to God, I will kill you if you don't fuck me right now. We've been leading up to this for weeks, I think I'm ready."

"I fucking love it when you get bossy with me."

"I'll have to remember that." She looks over her shoulder at me on my knees behind her, the couch dipping with my weight.

Rubbing some lube on my cock I grab it at the base, lining it up with her tight hole. "This'll hurt at first, but then I promise it'll feel so, *so* good, baby."

"I trust you," she reminds me.

I slowly press into her, and she tightens.

I reach around her front, rubbing her clit. "Relax." I kiss her back. "You have to relax, baby."

She shudders a breath and slowly relaxes. I push in a little more.

I give her time to adjust before inching in all the way.

She gasps and I hold her hips. "Don't move," she pleads. "Not yet. Give me a minute."

"You tell me when you're ready. I want this to be good for you."

She nods and takes a shuddering breath. Gradually I feel her body relax, accepting the intrusion.

"I'm ready," she tells me. Looking over her shoulder she meets my eyes and adds, "I swear."

I inch out and back in, rubbing her clit to help her relax. "God, you're so fucking beautiful, Mia," I tell her. She looks like a fucking goddess beneath me, her vibrant red hair a fiery halo around her.

I gradually pick up speed as she adjusts, her low quiet moans tell me she's no longer hurting.

"I need to feel you," she begs.

I place my hand on her stomach, guiding her up until her back is to my front. We're pressed together tightly, not even a piece of paper could fit between us. My hand slides up to her throat and I hold it lightly. She leans her head back against my shoulder looking at me with heavy lust-filled eyes.

"I love you," she mouths, and I kiss her.

I will never get tired of those words leaving her lips.

My other hand continues to rub her clit and she takes a shuddering breath.

"Hollis, don't stop. I'm so close. I'm … I'm going to cum. I'm going to cum. I'm going to cum," she begins to chant.

Then, she falls apart around me, her orgasm so powerful I fear she might pass out. I hold her tighter and grit my teeth, my orgasm shooting through my body, rippling down my spine. I think I shout. Or curse. Maybe I black out. I don't know.

All I know is suddenly we're on the floor tangled

together. She's sprawled over my chest, our legs tangled together.

"Fuck," I curse. "That was…"

"I know," she sighs sleepily.

"Don't get sleepy on me now," I warn her. "I promised to fuck you and then make love to you. We haven't even gotten to the making love part."

She grumbles.

"Come on." Somehow, I manage to stand and lift her up with me. "We're going to shower first, then I'm laying you on your bed and showing you exactly how much I love you. I'm warning you now—it's a lot."

She hums. "I think I can stay awake for that."

"Good," I growl.

I sweep her legs out from under her and carry her into the bathroom. Not bothering to put her down while I turn the shower on. I wait a moment, check the temperature, and seeing that it's warm enough step inside before finally placing her on the cool tile.

The water sprays down on her and I can't help but watch the way it sluices off her breasts. She runs her hands over my abs and bites her bottom lip. "Are you going to fuck me in the shower too?" Her voice is begging, pleading with me.

I shake my head. "Not tonight baby. I can't wear you out before we get to the best part."

"You mean to tell me fucking my ass wasn't the best part?"

I shake my head. "No, making love to you will be. I've

never made love before—even with you, with loving you, we've always been so frantic and desperate for one another. But tonight, we do this slow. We take our time. We make it something we never forget."

"I think I just orgasmed again," she jokes with a smile.

"Oh, believe me baby, there will be plenty more of those tonight."

We rinse our bodies off; she washes me with her vanilla scented soap, and I return the favor—paying extra attention to her breasts and the curves of her ass.

Turning the shower off I grab a towel and dry her off then use it on myself.

I take her hand, looking at her as I pull her to the bed.

Her blue eyes are trusting, full of love.

I thought it was an impossibility anyone would ever look at me in such a way.

She lies down on the bed, and I stare down at her. Her hair fans around her, her breasts full, pale pink nipples begging for my attention. Her eyes are heavy-lidded, and she crooks one finger beckoning me closer.

I climb onto the bed, holding my weight above her. She grips my cheeks, rubbing her fingers against my stubble.

Lifting her head up, she presses a kiss to my lips. It's soft, sweet even. I cup the back of her head, deepening the kiss. Our lips move together like they were made for doing so. Her fingers delve into my hair, and I groan.

I slide one of my hands over her curves, down her side and gently spread her legs open further. My fingers find her center, already wet and ready. She moans as I begin to rub her, her lips parting on a gasp. She breaks the kiss, looking down and between us, watching the movement of my hand against her and then into her.

I watch as her eyes roll back, her breath comes out in small pants, and finally as she falls apart with a small aching cry.

Her hazy eyes slowly meet mine as she recovers from her orgasm. She reaches down, grabbing my cock and stroking it slowly.

"I need you inside me, please."

My arms shake, but I manage to nod.

She lets go and I guide myself inside her. Slow. Gentle.

Her lips part in a small O-shape and she grips my biceps.

I pull my hips back, moving in and out of her as slow as I can.

I kiss her lips, her cheeks, her forehead. I kiss everywhere I can reach, all the while making love to her. Something I've never done before.

I worship her, her body, her soul. I want her to feel, to see, how much I love her without words.

After tonight, if she's ever had any doubts about how I feel she won't anymore.

I kiss her deeply, the kind of kiss you feel in the deepest parts of your being. I mark her as mine and she claims me as hers.

We're cautious, gentle, taking our time and studying one another's body.

This isn't the frantic, desperate love-making, fucking,

whatever you want to call it, that typically overcomes us in our moments of passion.

This is real true love pouring out of our bodies and into the other person. She takes, I give. I take, she gives. It's a dance we seem to know well despite never having performed it before.

When the dance ends, we lie tangled in one another's arms, the sheets barely covering our sweat dampened limbs, trying to soak in what's transpired in this bed tonight.

The realness of it.

I kiss the top of her head which she tilts back to look at me. "That was beautiful," she whispers on a fleeting breath.

"It was."

For once, I'm at a loss for words, because I know without a doubt while my heart beats inside my chest, giving life to my body, it doesn't belong to me anymore. It's hers. It's always been hers, it was only waiting for me to find her.

TWENTY-NINE

Mia

I curl my body against Hollis's toasty warmth. I don't know how guys always manage to be so warm, like their own personal furnace or something. I lay my head on his shoulder and his arms wrap around me. He tucks his head close to mine.

My body is worn out, but my heart is full.

Hollis rubs his finger back and forth along my skin, grazing gently against my bare arm, and I can feel sleep beginning to beckon me. My eyes keep drooping closed, but I fight it, not wanting tonight to be over.

I can't hold it at bay for long and within minutes I'm dozing off.

I startle awake at the sound of my front door slamming open.

I sit straight up, Hollis doing the same beside me. If he's in here then...

"Who is that?" Panic makes my voice high, almost squeaky. "Did someone break in?"

I reach for my phone to call the police, but that's when I notice all the notifications. From my mom, my dad, siblings, Willow, Kira and the list goes on.

My mom's stands out the most to me.

Mom: Your dad knows.

Mom: Someone posted pictures. Video, too. It's gone viral.

Mom: He's on his way. He wouldn't listen to reason.

Hollis jumps out of the bed in less than a second, grabbing a pair of loose gym shorts from the drawer and yanking them on.

"Hollis—" I open my mouth to tell him I know exactly who this is barging in, but he holds up a hand to stop me.

"Stay here," he hisses.

"I'll do no such thing," I seethe, wrapping the sheet around me. "I'm not sitting in bed like a naked sitting duck for—"

"MIA! HOLLIS! GET YOUR ASSES OUT HERE *NOW!*"

"Oh my God," I gasp, tears springing to my eyes. I swear my heart drops right out of my body.

"Shit," Hollis curses, his panicked eyes meeting mine. I pass him my phone so he can see the messages. He quickly taps over to my Twitter app, and that's when the video pops up. It's grainy, but there's no mistaking it's us kissing on the rooftop of the hotel. It has to be from a staff member. Who else could've gotten up there? "Jesus Christ," he mutters, dropping the phone back to the bed.

He gives me a look that's a cross between panicked and resigned. He has every right to be mad at me, though. This is all my fault, because I was too scared, too weak, to woman up and tell my dad. I'm an adult. He has to respect my choices, but I just ... chickened out.

My dad is one of my favorite people in the world and I couldn't stomach the thought of him being mad or disappointed in me.

But now, I realize, by doing that I let Hollis down.

I shouldn't have hid him away like some dirty secret.

And now this is how my father finds out.

I tumble out of the bed, tripping over the sheet, but Hollis is already there giving me a hand to help me up.

My lower lip trembles. "He's going to hate me."

"No, baby, he's going to hate me," Hollis says, giving me a sad, resigned look.

I tighten my grip on his hand, but he pulls away, refusing to look at me.

I can feel him slipping through my fingers, literally.

He's shutting down. Pulling away. It's all my fault. I have no one to blame but myself.

"DO NOT MAKE ME COME IN THAT FUCKING ROOM!" My dad yells. "GET YOUR ASSES OUT HERE NOW!"

I've never in all my life heard my dad sound so ... *livid*. Irritated, sure. Mad, sometimes. But so angry he sounds like he's ready to commit murder? Never.

Hollis swings open the bedroom door, and immediately falls back into me, both of us crashing to the floor. He cradles his jaw and I look from him to my dad standing in the doorway.

His face is red, purple in places like he's forgotten how to breathe and is close to passing out. His shoulders are bunched nearly to his shoulders and one hand is still raised in a fist.

"You *punched* him," I shriek, horrified. "What is wrong with you?"

His eyes are wild, like a rabid animal, and in this moment, I don't know him. Not at all. He's certainly not my dad, the man who has raised me as his own.

"I told you to stay away from my daughter," he shouts, pointing down at Hollis. "I warned all of you she was off-limits. But especially ... *especially* you."

"Why?" Hollis asks. "Because she's too pure? And I'm what? Fucked up? A loser?"

"You're a *user*. You use people to get what you want and then you go on your merry fucking way. I was young once, fame went to my head, and you might think you've gotten a taste of it ... but you don't know *anything* yet—and I will not let my daughter get drug down a path pining for some asshole musician who will only use her for sex and God knows what else."

"Dad—"

"Shut up, Mia!"

I flinch.

"I want you gone," my dad tells Hollis. "You, your band, the contract is over. I'm done with all of you. Get out of town. I never want to see any of you ever again. I warned you what would happen." He wags a finger, jaw clenched tight. "I fucking warned you."

Hollis stands, helping me up. He opens his mouth to speak but I push past him.

"How dare you." I shove a finger into my dad's chest. "How. Fucking. Dare. You." I punctuate each word with another jab. "I know you weren't a saint in your past, but *you* changed—so I guess no one else can then? How fucking hypocritical are you?" I seethe, anger making me shake. Hollis gently holds my elbow to steady me, thankfully my dad doesn't notice. "Hollis is the best man I've ever met. He loves me, and I love him, and I refuse to let you of all people belittle our feelings. I'm not that little girl anymore that you need to watch over all the time. I'm an adult and I'm free to love whoever I want."

"Mia," Hollis begins softly from behind me.

"*No,*" I tell him. My eyes glued to my dad's I continue, "You have no right to be angry. You have *no* right to tell Hollis or anyone else they can't sleep with me, or date me, or *fuck* me," I add and he winces. "Because that's *my* choice. I choose who I share my time, my *body*, with. Not you. Never you." I take a breath. "You busting in here like a mad man is beyond ridiculous. If I have dragons needing to be slayed, I can do it my damn self. If I needed your help

I'd *ask*. I don't need you marching around, barking orders, like some Lord or King from the dark ages. You storming in here like this, unannounced, because you saw some things on social media proves how unhinged you are when it comes to your kids. I get it, Dad, I know how protective you got after what happened when I was a kid, but you have to learn to let go." I clasp my hands together, pleading with him to see reason.

He glowers, his jaw working back and forth but I can see the hurt in his eyes from my words. Did he really think I was going to side with him in this situation? I will not be told who I can and cannot love, like my virginity is up for auction to the highest bidder or something.

His eyes drift briefly to Hollis, then back to me. "He's not the guy for you, Mia. Not him."

Hollis stiffens beside me. I know that has to sting. He respects my dad, and I think he's grown to care about him. Having my father shun him can't feel good.

Tears prick my eyes—anger at myself for not telling my dad sooner and putting Hollis in this position.

Steeling my spine, I say, "You need to leave."

"I'll do no such thing. But you," he points a finger, one that's literally shaking from anger, at Hollis, "you can leave."

"Sir," he tries to speak.

"Shut the fuck up, haven't you done enough?"

"Dad!" I yell, my lips trembling. "Stop it. You're not being fair!"

"Hayes, I—"

"Mia," my dad speaks over Hollis again, "if you were so sure about this guy, you would've told me. You have to realize that."

"No." I shake my head. "You're wrong. This is the exact reason I didn't say anything to you! You blow everything out of proportion. Can't you see you're smothering me?"

I'm full-on crying now, there is no holding back the tears. I'm hurt—angry at both him and myself.

"Smothering you?" he retorts, rearing back like I've slapped him. "How the fuck do I smother you?"

I gape at him. "Do you need me to list it off?"

He runs his fingers through his hair, agitated. "Yeah, go for it, Mia. Tell me what an awful father I am."

"Dad! That's not what I—" I shake my head, my cheeks damp with tears. "I *love* Hollis and he loves me and that should be enough for you. I don't want to fight about this."

He snorts like this is oh-so-amusing. "You think this loser loves you?" Out of the corner of my eye I see Hollis flinch. I want to push, shove at my dad for saying anything hurtful about Hollis. He doesn't deserve that. "He's going to leave here, Mia. He's not staying in Viriginia. He's going to go back to L.A. and fuck his way through the city and I'll be the one trying to pick up the pieces when he breaks your heart. You're my little girl. I'm just trying to protect you."

"Protect me?" I snap back. "Or protect *you*?"

"What's that supposed to mean?"

"It means it's time for you to face the music—I'm an adult. A grown woman. I choose who I love and I picked

Hollis. You have to deal with it and if you choose not to then that's on you." His jaw works angrily back and forth.

"I can't ... I can't *look* at you right now. I'm too angry, and hurt, and ... just go, please, Josh."

I've never called my dad by his first name. He's always been daddy or dad. But right now ... I don't even recognize him.

He busted in here like a crazy person.

He punched Hollis.

He voided their contract.

He ordered the love of my life to leave. To leave this town, this state. Probably the whole country if he could make it happen.

I don't know if I can ever forgive him for this, for having the gall to think he can decide who I'm with.

He swallows thickly but doesn't move.

"*Go*," I seethe, my tone deadly. "You need to go."

I'm just ... done. Exhausted. Emotionally drained.

He backs away.

He doesn't say he's sorry. He just ... leaves. The door closing softly behind him. It's at odds with the way he busted in here.

A broken, ragged, sob leaves my throat and I drop to the floor as my tears pour out of me. Hollis kneels on the ground with me, holding me against his strong chest. My tears dampen his skin. He brushes his fingers through my hair murmuring over and over that it's going to be okay, but he doesn't sound so sure. I'm not either.

THIRTY

Hollis

I hold Mia the rest of the night, somehow managing to carry her to the bed. I cover us both with a blanket and she curls against me, pressing her palms flat against my chest as she sobs. Her cries break me. I don't know what to do or what to say. I don't think there's anything I *can* do.

I hate that I'm the one that put her in this position with her dad.

If I had never pursued her...

I don't care about him being angry with me, or saying the contract is over. None of it is important compared to how hurt Mia feels. I hate seeing her suffering. I'd rather take a knife to the gut than to ever witness this again.

After a while her cries grow softer, and she begins to hiccup.

"I'm sorry, Mia. I'm so sorry this happened. I never meant for any of this to happen. I didn't want ... I'd never want to come between you and your dad."

In a soft voice she says, "He had no right to say what he did. To show up like that, to act like your contract with him was nothing." She rubs at her eyes. They're swollen from crying.

I know how much she loves her dad, and cares about his opinion. It has to be devastating for him to find out about us through social media. I know she could've told him sooner, and that fucking sucks because maybe we could've avoided this thing, but then again maybe he would've acted like this no matter what.

We'll never know.

"He's your dad," I whisper, looking up at the ceiling. "He wants to protect you."

"He's protecting me from all the wrong things," she seethes. She raises up a bit, looking down at me. I have trouble meeting her eyes. "I know I should've told him about us a long time ago, I know he shouldn't have found out like this, but he would've still been mad, no matter what I had done." Her voice sounds defeated.

She lies back down and grows quiet. Eventually she drifts off to sleep. I hold her tighter than I did before, afraid any second from now she'll be ripped from my arms.

It's no less than I deserve.

I FINISH EXPLAINING TO MY FRIENDS ABOUT WHAT HAPPENED with Hayes, or early this morning, whichever. It's not important. They sit in stunned silence looking at me.

When I got here, they'd already seen our relationship splashed all over social media. Videos, various photos from different times, proving that as careful as we tried to be we got complacent and started slipping up too much. After the one video leaked, more and more people came forward with evidence of our involvement.

I'm sure Hayes is even more pissed off today than he was last night.

The articles vary in tone from headlines that say things like; *Hollis Wilder's new plaything is none other than Mia Hayes* to *A new power couple in the making? Get all the deets on Mia Hayes and Hollis Wilder's relationship here!*

The one I saw that pissed me off the most was an article that suggested I was only using Hayes to fuck his daughter.

"Fuck, man, are you okay?" Cannon asks.

I can't believe he's asking me that right now. I should be asking them that since I'm the one who fucked everything up.

"I'm fine." Looking away I add, "It's Mia I'm worried about."

The last thing I ever wanted was to drive a wedge between her and her dad. Sure, Hayes is over protective as hell, but knowing that Mia was kidnapped as a toddler it makes sense why he's the way he is. I can imagine something like that leaves a long-lasting impression on a parent.

"Would you mind calling Kira and having her go over and check on her?" I ask Rush.

She barely slept and I don't think she should be left alone today. She needs support right now—support I'm not sure I can be the one to give since I'm the reason this is happening.

"I'll call her now." He gets up, already fiddling with his phone.

I look at Cannon and Fox.

"I fucked everything up. I've cost us our album, and with Hayes's influence in the music industry our chance of landing someone else is slim to none." I shove my fingers through my hair in frustration. "But," I begin sadly, "I don't take it back. I would do it all over again. She's worth it."

"Good answer," Cannon says.

My head flies in his direction in surprise. "You approve?"

Sure, my friends have been supportive of my relationship with Mia, but I expected them to be pissed at me for fucking things up. I should've been firmer with Mia and insisted we couldn't keep it a secret for my band's sake. But I guess love makes us blind. I ignored the consequences even though I was very much aware of what they are.

"Yeah, I fucking do.' He coughs—stupid smoker's cough, the guy seriously needs to give them up. "Mia's been good for you. This fucking sucks, sure, but I don't believe it's the end for us. I refuse to believe that."

Fox grins, trying not to laugh.

"What?" I ask him.

He chuckles, while Cannon glares at him. "It's just that he's been working on all this Zen and meditation shit. Oh, and what else is it?" He snaps his fingers, thinking. "Oh, yeah, manifesting. He's manifesting our future too—you know picturing in his mind that we've already achieved certain things."

Cannon shakes his head. "I never should've told you any of that."

Trying not to laugh, I put my hands on my knees and stand.

"I'll get our flights booked back to L.A. for later this week."

"Whoa, whoa, whoa." Cannon holds up his hands. "You're leaving too?"

"I can't stay," I whisper, finally admitting out loud what I knew last night, why I didn't want to look Mia in the eyes. She would've known. She would've seen my resolve and talked me out of it, and I would've gladly let her.

"Why the hell not?" Fox asks, leaning forward. His hands are clasped tightly together, and his dark hair is a wild disarray. "Are you going to leave her?"

I nod, barely the jerk of my chin. I feel like I can't breathe admitting my plans aloud. "I won't come between her and Hayes. That's what would happen if I stayed. She'd choose me. She *chose* me. I won't have her regretting her actions because of me. Her dad is her dad and I'm ... replaceable."

"You know that's not true," Cannon says, looking at me sadly.

"She'll move on," I say, the words scratching at my throat like poisonous barbs. "And I will too."

Lies.

THIRTY-ONE

Mia

I open the door for Hollis and immediately start ranting. "I can't believe him barging in here like a lunatic. I am an *adult*. I can have a boyfriend. I can have sex and drink and party and do whatever the fuck I want and he can't say a thing."

Hollis stands in the doorway, rocking back on his heels.

"What? What is it?" I pause, walking slowly back toward him. "What's wrong?"

My heart drops to my stomach when he won't meet my eyes.

He works his jaw back and forth, looking down at his boots. Finally, he raises his head. His golden eyes are shuttered, closed off, not at all like him. "I won't come between you and your dad. I won't become someone you resent some day for driving a wedge into your family."

I feel he's stabbed me in the chest. I press a hand to my heart expecting to find a tangible wound there, but there's nothing.

"I would never resent you," I whisper.

"You would," he states. "Maybe not now, or even three months from now, but one day you would—I don't ever want to see that day come."

I go to him, grabbing his jacket in my hands. "How can you say that?"

"He's your dad, he's family. I'm ... I'm nothing." He ducks his head, refusing to meet my eyes.

My heart begins to race, panic freezing my limbs.

"Nothing? You're everything. How can you not see that?"

"Mia," he pleads, his tone begging. "Let me go."

My lip begins to tremble, and I can't catch my breath. *"No."*

"We're leaving. Going back home."

"*No*, you're *not*," I spit out between my teeth. "You are not running away from this like some coward."

"I'm not a coward!" He roars finally looking at me fully, letting me see the emotion in his eyes, the hurt, the pain, the fear, the *love*. "This is the hardest fucking thing I've ever had to do. The selfish thing to do is stay and for once I'm choosing the selfless road."

"You're *wrong*," I bite out. "*This ... this* is *selfish*. How can you abandon me now?"

"You'll forgive your dad," he says coolly. "You'll move on. You'll forget me. I'll become a story you tell one day, of the few months you spent with the lead singer of The Wild"

"Stop it," I beg, tugging on his jacket, almost shaking him. "That's not what's going to happen and you know it."

He looks away. "I'll forget you."

"Hollis," my voice breaks. "Don't lie to me."

He slowly brings his eyes back to mine, once more he's closed them off to me. His gaze is cold, hard, unyielding. "There were plenty before you and there will be many more after you."

"Stop lying," I beg, grabbing at his shirt. My hold on the fabric is strong. I won't let him be ripped away. Not when this was my fault. I know that. I know I should have told my dad. Sucked it up and stopped being so immature. But I was scared. I've never gone against anything my parents have said before. "Stop, *please*. Don't do *this*."

He closes his eyes and when he opens them, he says, "Don't be pathetic, Mia."

Don't be pathetic.

Those three words hit me like shrapnel, cutting into my skin and then burrowing into the most insecure crevices of my mind.

"You're trying to make me hate you, but it won't work," I tell him, shoving a finger into his chest. "You think you're leaving out of some sense of ... duty or justice or something *stupid*, but you're wrong. You're leaving because you're scared, because you don't want to fight this battle together. Don't you think I'm scared too?" I plead with him with my eyes, trying to get him to understand, to see sense. "You think by leaving I'm going to somehow magically forgive my father? That's not how forgiveness *works* Hollis. Forgiveness has to be *earned*. And you know what? I chose you. I choose you—every day."

His teeth clamp down. "Well, I don't choose you."

I gasp, a broken sob leaving me. He pulls from my hold on his jacket. I forgot I'd even grabbed it again after I poked him.

"Please don't go," I plead. "I need you."

He doesn't say anything.

He leaves and I listen to the sound of his boots hitting each and every stair. The door below opens and closes, just like the door to my heart.

THIRTY-TWO

Hollis

I hate myself.

I *hate* myself.

I fucking hate myself.

Lying to Mia, telling her I don't choose her when everything I've done is for her ... I don't think I can ever forgive myself.

I shove the last of my clothes into my bag and zip it up.

"You ready, man?" Cannon asks, poking his head in the door with a pitying look.

I hate that look. I'm the last person he should be pitying. It's my fault we're in this predicament.

"Yeah," I sigh, hauling my bag over my shoulder, and wheeling my suitcase behind me. A lot of my stuff is still at Mia's. After what I said, what I did, I couldn't go back for it. I didn't want it anyway. It'd only be another reminder of what I had lost. I figure she can do whatever she wants with it. Keep it, donate it, light it on fire for all I care.

"Are you sure about this?" Cannon asks me as the four of us get on the elevator.

"It's for the best."

He gives me a doubtful look.

I know Mia wants me to stay, fuck she'd already *chosen* me over her family, but I won't be the wall standing between them. I refuse to be that kind of guy.

"Maybe you should talk to Hayes?" Fox suggests.

I snort. "Yeah? And say what—sorry I willingly lied to you about the one thing you made me promise not to do?"

Rush groans, leaning his head against the side of the elevator. He's subdued, dejected and guilt eats at me for being the reason why.

"That might not go over too ... uh ... well."

"Ya think?" I glare at him.

"It just seems to me like," Fox pipes in, not to be left out, "this whole thing could have been sorted if the three of you—Mia, Hayes, and you—had just acted like fucking adults."

He's not wrong.

I think it's truly hitting all of us, now that we're leaving the hotel—leaving this town for good—just how screwed over we are.

My stomach roils.

I did this to them. To my friends. My selfishness cost them our dream.

The doors open to the lobby and outside we get into the waiting Uber SUV.

Their cars and my bike are being left behind. We didn't earn them.

We pile our bags inside and I take the front passenger seat, so I don't have to be beside any of them. Listening to their bickering or feeling their concerned but annoyed stares.

Luckily, they keep their mouths shut during the hour drive to the airport.

We unload our stuff and head inside, checking into our flights.

"This is where I leave you," I say, taking a step back.

"Wait..." Fox grins. "Are you going back for her? Are you going to make things right with Hayes?"

I shake my head forlornly. "No, I'm not going back."

"Where the fuck are you going then, man?" Rush asks, puzzled.

"Home," I answer.

"Uh ... so you are coming with us then?"

"No," I say adamantly. "I'm going *home*."

Cannon claps me on the shoulder, a toothpick is held between his teeth, a sign he's desperate for a cigarette. "Tell your mom hello for us. If you see my parents tell them I'll be home soon—and tell my sister to stop sending me pictures of random dicks and asking me to rate their attractiveness for 'research purposes'. Those are not the kind of naked pictures *I* want to see."

I snort, surprised I can find humor in anything. "Calista always did love fucking with you."

"Little sisters are annoying as shit," he grumbles.

I back away from them. "I'll be back in L.A. in a week or two. We'll do what we can to find new representation."

It won't be easy, but for them I'll grovel on my knees until I find someone else to take a chance on us.

"Are you sure you'll be back in L.A.?" Fox asks, tilting his head.

"Yes," I growl, irritated that they're being so pushy. I know they like Mia, but after all this I can't believe they're actually encouraging me to go back. I thought they'd hate us both for fucking things up. And yeah, they're definitely perturbed but hate doesn't seem to be what they're feeling at all. Maybe I'm trying to force that feeling on them? Because if I can convince myself they hate her, that my leaving is the best thing for them, then it helps lessen the guilt. "I'm not coming back here. She's better off without me."

"She's not," Rush says, almost angrily. "But keep telling yourself whatever you need to in order to feel better."

He turns and walks away, not looking back.

Cannon gives me a concerned look. "I'm sorry."

I sigh. "I am too."

"We'll see you."

Then him and Fox are gone too.

I'm alone once more, like I deserve.

I GET OFF THE PLANE IN NASHVILLE, RENTING A CAR, BEFORE making the almost two-hour drive to my hometown.

It's just as small as I remember, smaller than Mia's hometown.

Mia.

Why the fuck can't I stop thinking about her?

Because you love her.

I bang the heel of my hand against the steering wheel when I'm stopped at a stoplight.

Love is a pathetic, stupid emotion that makes you lose all of your common sense.

The light changes to green and I drive through it. Within five minutes I'm parking outside the trailer I grew up in.

When I was only fourteen-years-old I vowed to buy my mom a home one day. A real one. Not one with wheels beneath it.

She did her best, she took care of me all on her own, but I hated seeing her struggle. I wanted to make it all better.

I *will* make it better. I thought this was my chance to make good on my promises, but things change.

I hop out and haven't even made it to the trunk when the door bangs open, and she comes running out.

"I can't believe my eyes! Oh, Hollis, I'm so happy to see you." She launches herself at me and I chuckle, wrapping my arms around my momma.

She smells exactly like I remember. Freshly baked pies and sugar cookies with a slight tinge of grease from the diner she works at as a waitress. It's been too long since I've been home. I got so caught up in making my dream a reality, I forgot about my roots.

I set her down and look at her. She's still young, but there are small lines around her eyes and the corners of her mouth. She had me when she was only sixteen, and at forty-one she still looks amazing. Her hair is the same color as mine, pulled back in a sloppy ponytail. Even our features are similar. My eyes are the only thing I seem to have inherited looks wise from my dad. She wears her uniform for the diner and based on the time, she's probably only been home a few minutes. There's still flour dusted on her cheek.

"I missed you, Ma." I hug her again, not having realized how much I missed being able to hug my momma.

"I missed you, too." She squeezes me in only the way a mother can. "What brings about this surprise visit? Where's your girl?" she asks, looking behind me like Mia's going to pop out from behind the overgrown bush by the mailbox.

She looks back at me with a puzzled expression and I shake my head.

"Oh," she says, pulling away. She doesn't even need me to say it. A mother's intuition always knows. "Well, come inside. It's cold out here."

She pulls me inside and I leave my shit in the trunk for now.

Inside I sit down at the small kitchen table. It seems even smaller now that I've been gone. The whole place is miniscule. But it's home.

She bustles about the kitchen and hands me a cup of hot chocolate. We used to have hot chocolate every Christmas Eve and stay up watching all our favorite movies.

My mom might've been young when she had me, but she was the best mom ever. Still is.

She sits down across from me. "Tell me what happened. It must've been bad if you're here."

I groan, rubbing my hands over my face, but I open my mouth and fill her in.

By the time I reach the end, telling her what I told Mia, how I ... *left* her, I begin to cry. I don't even remember the last time I cried.

My mom gets up, coming around the table, and wraps her arms around me. I cry against her and when I compose myself, I ask her, "What do I do, Ma?"

It's been so long since my mother was the one I went to for advice. Probably too long, because if there's anyone in this world with the wisdom I usually need it would be my mom.

"What does your heart tell you?" She holds my face between her hands like she did when I was small.

"I can't listen to it," I confess. "She's better off without me."

"You're wrong, baby boy. You're so wrong." I swear tears shimmer in her eyes. "You have a beautiful soul and she's lucky to have you love her, just as you're lucky to have her. You know you did wrong."

"But her dad—"

"Is a dad. He's a parent. He's protective. What did you expect? He'll calm down, they'll talk, they'll forgive, and she'll still love you."

I try to pull my face from her hands, but she refuses. She just holds on tighter, trying to force me to see sense.

"I can't see how things will ever be good between him and me—I didn't listen to him. I couldn't stay away from her. If I'm to be with Mia, how can I expect her to deal with that kind of animosity?"

"Then fix it," she tells me. "Go to him. Explain how you feel about her—he'll see the truth in your eyes, and he won't be able to deny you. There's a lot to be said for being honest. I think too many people have forgotten that."

"I don't know if I can go back. Not after how I left things."

"If you wait too long you won't be able to," she admits. "You have to decide—do you want to live the rest of your life without the girl you love, or do you want to experience a joy so few ever truly find?" She rubs my cheek, her fingers grazing over the nasty bruise Hayes left there. "I take it he gave you this?" She raises a brow.

"It's no less than I deserved."

"Why are you determined to convince yourself you're not good enough for her? That you somehow *deserve* this?" Again, she gently touches the bruise.

"Because it's the truth. I slept with women left and

right. I used them. I drank too much. I partied too hard. I lost myself. I didn't know who I was anymore not until..."

"Not until her," she finishes for me. "She reminded you of who you've always been. *This* is you. This is my Hollis, the boy I raised to be a brilliant, loving, kind and caring man. Are you really going to give it all up, a future, because of one incident? Because that's not the boy I raised. My boy is a fighter, he goes after what he wants and doesn't give up. He would never cower so easily."

I wince. She's right. I *am* being a coward. Mia told me the same thing.

"I just want her to be happy," I confess.

Her voice is soft, tired sounding. "Why do you think you're not her happiness?"

THIRTY-THREE

Mia

"Happy birthday to me," I sing glumly, blowing out the single candle in the cupcake Kira set on the bar top in my kitchen. I rest my chin in my hand feeling glum.

Hollis is gone. Cannon, Rush, and Fox too.

The town suddenly feels so devoid of life—like something vibrant and essential has fled.

"Cheer up, Reese's cup," Kira says, hopping up on the counter with her own cupcake in her hand. She peels back the wrapper and takes a bite. "It could be worse." The words come out distorted around her mouthful of cake and icing.

"How could this *possibly* be worse? My dad hates me. He fired the band. He punched my boyfriend. And now my boyfriend is gone. Hell, my boyfriend isn't even my boyfriend anymore."

"Yeah, you're right. It can't get much worse," she says with a playful smile and a shrug. "But, girl, it's your birthday. You're twenty-three now. We have to do something to celebrate."

"I don't feel like celebrating," I tell her. "I'm staying home, eating chocolate ice cream with chocolate chips, and watching Netflix in my jammies. I'm not deviating from that plan," I warn, holding up a finger to halt any protests she might have.

"Fine," she grumbles. "Honestly, that sounds amazing. I miss Rush."

"You miss Rush?" I ask shocked, taking the candle out of the cupcake. I take a bite. Red velvet, my favorite.

"What?" she asks innocently. "He knows how to fuck—which is more than I can say for most guys our age. Do you have any idea how many men don't know what a fucking clitoris is—if they think they're going to orgasm and I'm not, they're sorely mistaken."

"Well, if you're staying, I think we should order pizza."

"Mmm, pizza," she hums. "I'll order it now." She does and then we pile on the couch, beneath several layers of blankets, and I put *Beauty and the Beast* on because I love the movie and for some reason it makes me think of Hollis and me. Clearly, I'm trying to make myself even more miserable.

When the pizza is delivered Kira jumps up and pays for it despite my protests. She insists it's my birthday and I deserve it.

Hollis is gone for good now. Never coming back.

Not mine. Not anymore.

"There were plenty before you and there will be more after you." His words echo through my skull.

He was lying, I know it, but it doesn't mean it hurts any less.

What we had, *have*, is real and nothing he does or says can convince me otherwise.

"Have you heard from him?"

"Who? Hollis?" I ask stupidly.

She smiles but quickly hides it. "No, your dad."

I snort. "God, no. I'm still mad at him. He's called, but I don't answer. I talked to my mom though. She feels awful. She tried to stop him from showing up here, but..."

Kira tilts her head. "But no one, not even your mom, can stop him when he's out for blood?"

"Yeah," I sigh. "He's something when he's angry."

In a soft voice she says, "Have you ever stopped to think maybe it's because you were kidnapped? Something like that has had to have lasting scars on your parents and dude's take shit like that harder anyway. They have to be the hero and protector, all that jizz."

"It's jazz." And my dad *did* mention the kidnapping as having a profound effect on him, and I can understand, but he needs to realize what's acceptable behavior and what's not.

"I like my version better." She grins, tucking her legs under her before grabbing another slice of pizza.

We pig out on pizza and ice cream before crashing in my bed—Kira claiming she's too full to make it home.

She falls asleep almost instantly, but I can't sleep. I keep thinking about Hollis, how I planned to celebrate today with him at my family's house like always, but instead I'm sulking with Kira.

Everything went from the best time of my life to the worst.

Eventually I get out of bed and run some water for a bubble bath. My bathtub is nowhere near as nice as the one Hollis had in his hotel room, but it works.

I sink down into the steaming water and sigh. My hair is tied up in a messy bun and I drop down into the lavender scented water as much as I can.

I never knew I could hurt like this. This ache deep in my heart and soul, like a vital piece of me is missing.

Hollis took a part of me with him, a part I'm never going to get back, one I'll have to unfortunately learn to live without.

When the water goes from hot to warm and then begins to cool even more I finally get out. My fingers are wrinkled little prunes, but I don't care. I pull on a pair of pajamas and pad back into my room. I lift the lid on my hamper to drop my towel in, but it hits the edge and falls to the floor. I sigh and bend down to pick it up.

My hand closes around it and my eyes narrow, spotting something shiny behind my dresser.

I reach for it and pull it out, finding a large rectangular wrapped birthday present.

I glide my fingers over the paper, my heart beating a mile minute, because there's only one possible person who could've hidden a present in this exact spot.

A large part of me wants to throw it away, to never see the secrets it holds, but I know deep down I'll never do that. I can't.

I rip open the paper and a card falls out.

I don't look at the gift, instead I read the card first.

In Hollis's scrawled handwriting it reads:

For the girl who had my heart from the moment she asked who the hell I was and warned me she knew jiu-jitsu. You own me, Mia Hayes, heart, body, and soul. I'm yours.

—Hollis

I press a hand to my mouth to stifle the sound of my sob.

I let the card fall from my fingertips. Finally, I allow my eyes to land on the present. It's a framed picture of the lyrics to the song he wrote for me. He's written out the words as neatly as he can, but it's still sloppy. In my eyes, it's perfect.

Laying on top of the frame is a small white box. I pick it up and open the lid to find a gold necklace with a small heart charm.

On the bottom of the lid he's written;

Now you can wear my heart around your neck, proof to anyone who dares second-guess that it belongs to you and only you. —H

I can't stop the tears from falling freely then.

I'm surrounded by tangible proof of how much he loves me and still I feel achingly alone.

THIRTY-FOUR

Hollis

I slide into the booth at Jerry's Diner where my mom works. It's one of my favorite places in this town. There's not a lot I liked about growing up here. I didn't care about being poor or even it being small—I just wanted more. I always wanted to be better, to be greater.

"What can I getcha?" I look up and break out into a smile.

"Alice, it's good to see you." I've already been here a few days but didn't venture out until today—instead choosing to stay home with my momma while she was off work.

"Is that you, Hollis?" she asks, squinting dramatically. "Your momma said you were back when she got here this morning, but I didn't believe her. I said there's no way that boy has been back and not stopped in to say hi." She plops her hands on her hips.

"I'm back, but not for long."

She clucks her tongue. "Shame. Well, is your order still the same? Fresh squeezed orange juice and five cinnamon pancakes?"

"You got it, Alice."

She taps her pen against her notepad. "It's good to see you, Hollie."

I groan. "I hate that damn nickname."

She grins. "Why do you think I like using it? I'll get this put in for you."

I wave at my mom behind the counter, and she waves back. I couldn't stand being stuck in the trailer by myself, and there wasn't anywhere else to go.

Alice drops off my orange juice and I take a sip. It's as good as I remember.

A few people come in and out, picking up orders or staying to eat a meal.

"Well, well, well look what the cat dragged in."

I look up at the sound of the voice. "Callie," I chuckle, as Cannon's younger sister Calista makes her appearance.

"My brother said you were in town. I thought he was lying, so I had to come see for myself." She quints at me, tilting her head left and right. "Yep, it is you. Still ugly."

I snort. Calista Rhodes has been humbling us all since she was a kid.

She slides into the booth across from me.

"Take a seat," I say sarcastically.

"I did," she retorts, sticking her tongue out.

She's five years younger than Cannon and me. At twenty she acts more like sixteen at times. I think it comes from growing up and chasing after the four of us.

"I heard you like to send your brother dick pics."

She busts out laughing. "Anytime some dude sends me a dick pic I forward it his way. I can't help it."

"You get a lot of dick pics?" I raise a brow. "You know Cannon would be pissed if he knew that's what it was."

"Versus what? Random peen off Google." She waves a dismissive hand. "I can handle myself. Now tell me, why are you back here? Out of all of you, I figured you were the one who'd never come back."

"Not Rush?" I retort.

Her eyes grow sad. "I didn't think he'd come back either."

"I wanted to see my mom," I tell her honestly. "How are your parents?"

"Marty and Debra are great." I give her a look. "*Dad* and *Mom* are great—better?"

"Much," I say, studying her. She looks the same as I remember, only a little older. She has the same dark hair and green eyes as Cannon, but where he's big and muscular she's short and curvy.

Alice delivers my order to the table along with an order for Calista.

"I'm not buying your breakfast," I tell her.

She pretends to pout. "Not even for your favorite not-really-yours little sister?"

"Nope," I laugh.

She shakes her head. "Always such a jerk."

"Always so nosy," I counter.

"True, true," she says, unrolling utensils from the napkin wrapped around them. She takes a bite of her eggs and says around a mouthful, "But you all love me."

"Actually, we find you annoying as shit," I joke.

"Ha, ha, ha," she fake laughs. "Oh," she says, and reaches for her bag. She pulls out an envelope and slides it across the table to me. "Make sure and give that to my brother—when he goes to open it record that shit and send it to me."

"What'd you do?" I ask, reluctantly taking the envelope.

She shrugs nonchalantly. "Nothing too bad. Promise. It'll be *hilarious*, though."

I glance down at the envelope. "It's not going to ... explode is it?"

She rolls her eyes. "Don't be stupid."

"I'm the stupid one?" I retort.

"*One time*—one fucking time," she holds up one finger, "I thought I had a penis. I was *two*. You have to let it go."

"No, never happening."

She groans.

"You asked to see mine," I continue.

"Oh my God." She covers her face. "Again, I was *two*."

"You still asked."

She picks up her plate. "I'm going to another table."

"Aw, come on. You know I'm only kidding."

She shakes her head. "One brother by blood—but I have three more I didn't ask for."

"At least you don't torment all of us like you do Cannon."

She grins and settles back down. "Only because you three would get a kick out of it, but Cannon is such a fucking control freak he gets all worked up over *everything*. He makes it way too easy and fun to mess with him." She takes a bite, chews, and swallows before continuing. "Honestly, he acts like the kind of guy who wears slacks, button ups, and ties to work. Not covered in tattoos and piercings."

"Hey," I shrug, raising my hands, "looks can be deceiving."

"Yes, they can be," she agrees. "Now tell me, why are you *really* back here?"

"I told you—to see my mom."

"What'd you fuck up so bad you had to come running back to mommy? Does this have something to do with that girl I keep seeing pictures of with you? Her name is Mia right?"

I sigh, knowing she isn't going to let this go. "Yes. Her name is Mia and I fell in love with her."

"You?" She snorts in disbelief. At my look she adds, "Oh my God, you're serious. You fell in love?"

"Yeah."

"What happened?"

"I fucked up, like you figured."

"Did you cheat on her? Sell nude pictures of her? Kiss her best friend?"

"No, not any of those."

"Then I can't see what could possibly be so bad." She pulls her dark hair back, securing it with an elastic.

"I got in between her and her dad. I won't let her choose me over her family."

She pauses with a forkful of food halfway to her mouth. "Why is it you think you're not worth loving?"

"I ... I don't know," I whisper.

"If you love her, and she loves you, that's all there is to it. None of the other shit matters. It'll all work out given enough time."

"I don't have time." At least, it feels that way. Not if I'm to find some way to fix this for the band. It feels like I can't do both.

She levels me with a look like she wants to smack me for being an idiot. "Then *make* time."

I mull over her words.

In my life, loving another, someone who wasn't family, or a friend, has been a fleeting whisper. Something I knew existed, but I could never seem to grasp. Then Mia came along. She wasn't a whisper, but a roar. A roar I felt all the way to my bones, shaking me to my core, utterly changing everything I've ever known and ever been.

I can't give her up. I won't.

I have to go back.

For my girl.

For me.

For *us*.

I GET IN THE TAXI AT THE AIRPORT AND GIVE HIM THE address.

Nerves make my palms sweat and I wipe them on my jeans. The guy driving the car keeps trying to talk to me, asking me if I'm visiting the area and whatnot, but I can't answer him because I'm freaking the fuck out too much.

Finally, we arrive, the gates mercifully open, and I get out of the car. "Wait here," I tell him.

He grumbles, but I know he'll be fine once he gets paid.

I ring the doorbell and wait.

It swings open revealing Mia's mother.

"Hollis?" she gasps in surprise. "What are you doing here?"

"Is … uh … Hayes here?"

She steps aside. "Yeah, he's in the family room."

Taking a deep breath, I head that way and pause outside of the large room, clearing my throat. Hayes looks up, his eyes widening in surprise at seeing me.

"Can I talk to you … sir?" I add.

I figure the best way, the easiest way, to go about this is to be respectful.

He looks like he wants to say no, but finally nods.

I take a seat in a leather chair across from where he sits on the couch.

"What are you doing here? I thought your sorry ass went back to L.A."

"I went back to Tennessee, actually," I admit, rubbing my hands together. "To see my mom."

He stares at me, waiting for more.

"I came back because ... because frankly, sir, I can't stay away from your daughter. I love her, I'm *in* love with her, and I don't see that changing ... ever. I'm going to marry her one day. You can hate me all you want, but I'm not leaving her. Not again. I shouldn't have left at all, but I didn't want to stand in between her and her family." The words tumble out of me like verbal vomit—it's not how I intended to say all this, but nerves have turned me into a babbling fool.

He stares at me, mulling over what I've said. "I don't know if I'll ever like you Hollis, not with my daughter, but I do accept the truth in your words and I believe you love her."

"I do," I breathe. "So much it scares me."

He cracks a small smile. "That's how you know it's real."

I rub my hands over my jeans, palms still sweaty. "I needed to come here before I see her. I wanted you to know this wasn't, and isn't, some fling to me. It's end game."

"Well," he sighs, holding out his hand, "I'll see you in the studio after the holidays then. I'll get the guys flown back out here on the next flight."

I take his hand, shaking it with a grin. "Really?"

"Don't fuck this up," he warns me. "I don't give second chances lightly."

"Meaning ... if I hurt Mia no more contract?"

He shakes his head. "The contract stays no matter what. I was ... pissed beyond belief before and not thinking rationally. But if you hurt her, as a father, I'll beat you to a pulp. It's a promise."

"One you'll never have to fulfill."

"I hope you're right," he chuckles.

I say my goodbyes and head out to the waiting taxi.

Time to get my girl back.

THIRTY-FIVE

Mia

He's not coming back.

That certainty feels like a cinderblock tied around my ankle pulling me under.

He's been gone a week, gone back to L.A., back to a life which doesn't include me.

I work, going through the motions, with Kira at my side. But my head and my heart is somewhere else—*with someone else.*

She keeps telling me one day it won't hurt so much—but she doesn't realize that's what I'm afraid of. I'm terrified of one day waking up and my first thought not being of his whiskey-colored eyes or rain shower smell. I'm scared of moving on, for the feeling of not having him to become normal.

I've read the card he left for my birthday more times than I care to admit. His written words proof of how real what we had was—*is*. How he can walk away from it, from me, makes no sense in my muddled brain. If I left him, it would feel akin to losing a limb. He's become such a vital piece of my life. I *love* him and he loves me, it's a truth that can't be denied. No matter what was said and done it can't erase our love like it's insubstantial. Love doesn't work like that—it's the most powerful emotion to exist and can't be brushed aside like a pathetic falling feather.

"Can you stop frowning?" Kira begs. "You're going to get wrinkles."

"I don't care."

Sadly, I don't care about much of anything at the moment.

She huffs out a sigh and doesn't say much more.

I'm sure she's getting irritated with me, but it's only been a week and I need more time to move on. A week can't erase everything I felt and experienced with him.

I still can't believe he's actually gone. Pathetically, I keep expecting him to walk in the door and order a sub, or to show up at my place with French fries, and every time he doesn't, I hurt even more.

I hate this hurting. I hate the aching.

But I take it, because it was real, and this pain is even more proof of how real it was.

"You're coming to my place, we're putting on something sexy, and we're going out," Kira demands, dragging me to her car and away from mine.

"Kira," I whine, trying to tug out of her hold. "I really don't want to go."

"Nope," she refuses. "You are *not* going back to your place to mope. You've done enough moping."

"I really haven't," I grumbled. "I think I have a month or two, maybe even longer, of moping left in me."

She rolls her eyes and opens her passenger door, all but stuffing me inside.

She gets in the driver's side, and I don't bother trying to make a run for my car. I'd only look pathetic, and she'd drag me back anyway.

"We're going to go out, get shit-faced drunk, and find you a man."

"*No,*" I say forcefully. "I'll let you take me out, I might even have a drink or two, but I'm not taking anyone home."

She sighs. "Whatever, as long as you go out, I'll be happy and cut you some slack."

She won't, but I don't feel like arguing with her.

It doesn't take us long to get to her place. She shoves me in her bathroom and orders me to shower, claiming I smell like donkey ass.

When I come out, she's already changed into a skimpy red dress and has one equally as skimpy waiting for me. It's white, not as tight as hers, but sexy nonetheless.

"Get dressed," she orders. "Then I'll do your hair and makeup."

I do as she says, forgoing a bra since with the low back there's no way I can wear one. She ties it in the back for me then forces me down in her desk chair. She dries my hair and then curls it in loose voluminous waves. When my hair is done, she moves on to makeup. She does a soft smoky eye and a light pink lip.

"Innocent, but sexy," she says, stepping back and admiring her handiwork.

"Are you done?"

"Nope, not yet." She grabs a bottle of perfume and I cough as she spritzes me. "*Now*, you're ready."

She grabs my hands and hauls me out of the chair. "Put this on and we're going—oh and these too." She hands me a long dress coat and a pair of heels.

By the time we leave her place it's after eight, and I know she won't be satisfied unless we stay out until at least one—which I'm *not* doing.

The drive to the club takes forever, literally, since we have to go into the city. By the time she parks I'm already counting down the hours in my head until it'll be acceptable to leave.

"Give me your keys," I tell her.

"Why?" she asks, but hands them over.

"Because, I'm not getting shit-faced but knowing you, you will. I'll drive us home."

She frowns. "But tonight is about you."

I shake my head. "No, Kira, it's about you. I told you I didn't want to go."

She frowns. "I'm a shitty friend, aren't I?"

"No, you're not. You ... this is how *you'd* want to be cheered up, but not me."

She bites her lip. "Do you want to go home then? I feel bad now."

I shake my head. "We're already here, we might as well try to have some fun."

I follow her inside, we check our coats, and then she heads straight for the bar. She orders us shots and I take one to be a good sport but have no intentions of having any more.

I hop up on an empty stool and before Kira can sit down a guy is already asking her to dance.

She gives me a look.

"Go," I encourage. "Have fun."

She flashes a smile and let's herself be pulled into the crowd.

"Pining over someone?" I turn at the sound of the voice to find a guy a little older than me sitting on the stool to my left nursing a beer.

"Uh..."

He smiles. "Don't worry, I'm not trying to hit on you. I am too—pining that is," he sighs.

"It's not fun."

"No, it isn't. I'm Jake, by the way."

"Mia," I reply.

"Nice to meet you, Mia."

"Likewise."

The bartender comes over and asks if we need anything.

"A water please."

"Designated driver?" Jake asks me when the bartender moves away to get my glass of water.

"Self-imposed designated driver," I laugh. "I'm not much of a drinker. Or a partier. Or ... honestly, I'd rather be home sleeping right now."

He chuckles. "You and me both. That was my friend who dragged yours away. Apparently, they both thought to get us out and distract us from our broken hearts—only it's them who is having fun."

The bartender hands me water and I drink down half of it, hoping to get rid of the liquid fire taste of the shot.

I've probably been sitting there an hour, maybe longer, chatting with Jake when he says, "Do you want to dance?" I make a face. "Just dance," he adds. "That's not code for anything else." He cracks a grin. "What do you say?"

I mull it over and nod. "Yeah."

He stands and I take his hand letting him pull me into the crowd.

It's a fast song, but I do my best to keep up with the beat, and honestly ... it feels pretty damn good to let loose, to not think about Hollis, or how much I hurt, to just *be*.

"IN YOU GO." I PRACTICALLY SHOVE A DRUNK KIRA INTO THE passenger seat of her own car. I swear when she's drunk she weighs three times her normal weight.

Across the lot Jake is doing the same with his friend. He waves and I raise my hand.

He offered me his number.

I declined.

The last thing I need right now is a rebound. I need to focus on myself.

When I slide in the driver's seat Kira is already passed out snoring. I turn the radio up and crack the window so cold air blows in to keep me awake during the drive.

There's little to no traffic so it doesn't take nearly as long as usual to get from the city to home. I drop her off at her apartment, basically dragging her up the stairs.

I leave a note, letting her know I'm driving her car to my place since I don't feel comfortable walking the streets this late and that I'll bring it back.

Parking in front of my apartment building I turn the car off but sit there for a few minutes, looking at the snow covering the ground, now dirty and gross, and the streetlights which normally look magical to me now seem to be just something in the way.

I hate being so mopey. It's not me. I always bounced back quickly from my previous relationships because I didn't love them—yeah those relationships made me weary of pursuing others, but I didn't feel this deep yearning ache in the center of my chest like I do now.

Feeling like this ... it sucks. I want to rant and rage, but

I know it'll do no good. No matter how much I cry or scream it won't bring Hollis back.

I chose him.

I chose him over my father, over my family, but in the end, he didn't choose *me*.

The car grows icy since I turned the engine off, no heat blowing in my face. With reluctance I get out and head inside.

I open the door and startle at the golden light flickering inside.

Puzzled, I stare at all the candles lit throughout the space—on the counters, on the floor, on shelves, the coffee table, and even the windowsill. They're everywhere.

Without turning around, I close the door behind me. I don't lock it, though I don't imagine many robbers break in and light candles.

"Hello?" I call out.

"I've been waiting for you."

I gasp as Hollis steps out of the shadows. He looks exactly as I remember, why I expect him to have changed in a week is beyond me—maybe it's because I *feel* so different.

"You're ... you're *here*. In Winchester. In my apartment. I thought you were in L.A.?"

The golden light of the hundreds of candles flickers over his face. "I didn't go back to L.A. I went to see my mom. I ... I needed to see her. I suppose I needed to talk to someone who was my family, who felt like home ... like you do to me. She reminded me of things, and an old friend too. You know, I've struggled with thinking I don't deserve you, that because of the way I've acted in the past I'm not worthy of you, but I also know no one will ever love you the way I love you. Wholly. Completely. You're it for me Mia. I'm sorry I let what happened with your dad drive me away. I guess I ... No, I *know* I was terrified one day you'd either regret me or you'd choose him over me, and I couldn't live with either option, so I removed myself from the equation."

I close the distance between us and shove his shoulders, tears clouding my vision. "Why?" I raise my voice. "Why couldn't you talk to me? To listen?"

"I don't know." He shakes his head. "Fear. Weakness, I guess."

"I needed you, and you *left*."

"I know." His eyes close and when they open, I see pain there. Pain I'm sure he can see reflecting in my eyes as well. "I'll never forgive myself for it either. I'll regret it for the rest of my life. I was an idiot."

"Yeah, you *are* an idiot," I tell him.

"Are you angry with me?" he asks softly.

"I wish I was," I confess. "But I love you too much."

He reaches out and cups my cheek. I swallow past the lump in my throat and lean into his touch.

"You're real," I breathe.

He chuckles. "Yes, baby I'm real."

"I kind of thought maybe I was dreaming."

He laughs. "I'm better than any dream."

I shake my head. "Always so cocky. I found your present for my birthday, you know," I confess.

"That so?" He raises a brow.

"I already knew you lied when you left, but then I *really* knew you lied, and I also could see how much you love me."

"And how much is that, Mia?"

"A lot," I whisper, leaning even closer to him.

"I'm so sorry." He brushes my hair away from my eyes. "You have no idea how much I wish I hadn't left."

"But you did," I remind him.

"But I did," he agrees.

"Can you forgive me?" he asks, looking pained.

"Are you ever going to do something stupid like that ever again?"

"No," he answers emphatically.

"Then I forgive you."

He grabs my cheeks and kisses me. It's a kiss I feel all the way to my toes. It's the kind of kiss where all the oxygen seems sucked from the room—it's the kind, where in movies fireworks would begin to go off. His lips move against mine and mine seem to know exactly what to do.

I was made for kissing him, for loving him, for ... just *him*.

He pulls away and looks down at me. "I'm never leaving you ever again, Mia Hayes."

I place a hand over his. "Even if my dad doesn't approve?"

He grins. "I talked to your dad before coming here."

"You did?" I ask, shocked.

He nods. "I told him everything, about how much I love you, how much you mean to me. I told him I plan on marrying you one day and even if he hates me, I'm never leaving you. Not again."

"And?"

"He understands, I think ... I think he might even like me now," he chuckles. "I mean, I got our contract back and I didn't even ask for it so that's got to be good, right? The guys will be flying back as soon as they can."

"You mean...?"

"We're going to be here for a while, baby—and when the time comes to head back to L.A. we'll figure things out. You okay with that?" He rubs his thumb against my cheek. I'm not sure he even knows he's doing it.

"More than okay," I breathe. "I'm so happy for you guys. I couldn't believe he broke off your contract."

"I can, but I'm glad it's all worked out now. I think we understand each other."

"Oh, really?"

"Yep—he loves you and wants you to be happy. I love you and want you to be happy, so really, we want the same things."

I smile up at him. "I don't want to talk about my dad right now."

He grins back. "And what do you want to do?"

I don't answer him with words. Instead, I kiss him. Which leads to him turning me around and slipping his fingers under the sides of the open back dress. He then kisses the back of my neck, and my head rolls back against his shoulder.

"I hope to God you weren't wearing this dress for another man."

I can't help it when I giggle. "And if I was?" I challenge.

Before I know it, he's undoing the tie around my neck and the dress is falling from my body into a puddle on the floor.

"I guess," his voice is a throaty growl, "I'll just have to show you what I can do to you that no other man will be able to."

He spins me around and I'm facing him once more. He pulls me down to the floor, and makes love to me surrounded by all those candles and all the love we have for each other.

EPILOGUE

Hollis
New Year's Eve

"This place is fancy," Fox says, taking in the ballroom of the Wentworth mansion where an annual New Year's Eve party is held. Apparently Trace Wentworth is Hayes's cousin or something, so we're all here. Me, the guys, Mia, her family, and all the other guys from Willow Creek and their families. Not to mention a million other people I don't know.

"It is," Rush says, equally in awe, with Kira on his lap.

I watch Mia across the room talking to her dad. They made up, but it's still a little tense and awkward.

I glance beside me at Cannon. "I forgot to give this to you." I pull out the envelope his sister gave me for him from the inside pocket of my tux's jacket—yeah, we're all in fucking tuxes. It was required. I'd complain more about the penguin suit if it weren't for how fucking sexy Mia looks in her formal gown—*and* how her eyes devoured me in it when she saw me, promising all kinds of wicked delights in the near future. I watch her in her dark green gown, fitted to her breasts and hips before flaring out. She looks stunning, but then again, she always does.

Cannon takes the envelope and I discreetly start to record him with my phone as Mia joins us once more. She opens her mouth, probably to ask why I'm recording, and I quickly shake my head so she doesn't say anything to ruin the moment. The truth is I have no clue what we're about to witness.

Cannon opens the envelope and glitter goes everywhere. No, not glitter...

"What the fuck? Why am I covered in multi-colored dicks?" he asks, staring around at the confetti now sprayed all around us.

None of us can stop laughing to give him an answer.

"Calista did this, didn't she?" he asks me, and I nod.

"Oh, this is war," he growls. "I don't know what I'm going to do, but it's something. She's going to regret this."

I stop recording and send the video to Callie in a text before I can forget. It isn't long before she replies.

Callie: I knew it would be epic.

"Come on," Mia tugs on my hand, "the fireworks are starting soon. I want to get a good spot."

I let her drag me away, the guys and Kira following, and we end up on a large balcony. I slide my tux jacket off and drape it around her shoulders.

Inside the countdown begins.

"Ten! Nine! Eight! Seven! Six! Five! Four! Three! Two! One!"

Fireworks explode into the sky, and I kiss Mia to shouts of, "Happy New Year!"

I don't know what this New Year has in store for us, but something tells me it can only get better.

ACKNOWLEDGEMENTS

I always wanted to come back to this series. To write the final two books, to make this one better, and to see my growth.

Wild (it was Wild Collision at the time) was my first book I wrote post transplant. It felt so good to WANT to write again. To not feel tired and exhausted. This book was the start of me getting back on my feet. That makes me even happier to revisit it and spruce it up.

A big thank you is owed to Emily Wittig. It's been a wild (haha) decade of friendship with a lot of craziness in both our lives and an incredible amount of growth. I'm so proud of us and can't wait to see where the next ten years brings us. We're truly so lucky to have found each other and to have a friendship like ours. A lot of people never find that in their entire lives. You're stuck with me for good. Thank you for just being you and ya know for the incredible covers as well.

Kellen, you're another friend I'm so lucky to have. You were one of the first sets of eyes on this book back in 2018. I can't believe how far we've come. Thank you for your endless support and help. And for loving 5SOS as much as I do. Can't wait for the next concert.

Melanie, I can't thank you enough for your help with getting this book in shape. You helped sharpen it and make it a much stronger book than it once was. Your insight was invaluable.

Janiece, for who this book is dedicated, not a day goes by where I don't thank you for your selfless sacrifice to give me a kidney. I don't believe I'd be here today if it weren't for you. You gave me a second chance at life. Everything I do, every accomplishment I have, is because you chose to save me. I know you think it was a simple thing, something anyone would do, but you're wrong. You're the most special human being I know and I'm so lucky to have you as my aunt and my donor. You're my angel on earth.

And to you, dear reader, as always there aren't enough words to encompass what it means to me to have you read my books. Not everyone gets to live their dream and because of you, I do. I hope you continue on this journey with me. I have lots more planned.

ALSO BY MICALEA SMELTZER

The Wildflower Duet

The Confidence of Wildflowers

The Resurrection of Wildflowers

The Boys Series

Bad Boys Break Hearts

Nice Guys Don't Win

Real Players Never Lose

Good Guys Don't Lie

Broken Boys Can't Love

Trace + Olivia Series

Finding Olivia

Chasing Olivia

Tempting Rowan

Saving Tatum

Willow Creek Series

Last To Know

Never Too Late

In Your Heart

Take A Chance

Willow Creek Box Set

Always Too Late Short Story

Willow Creek Bonus Content

Home For Christmas

Light in the Dark Series

Rae of Sunshine

When Stars Collide

Dark Hearts

When Constellations Form

Broken Hearts

Standalones

Beauty in the Ashes

Bring Me Back

The Other Side of Tomorrow

Desperately Seeking Roommate

Desperately Seeking Landlord

Whatever Happens

Sweet Dandelion

Say When

The Road That Leads To Us

The Game Plan

www.ingramcontent.com/pod-product-compliance
Lightning Source LLC
LaVergne TN
LVHW030332070526
838199LV00067B/6252